A True Story

Dakota William Szaniszlo

A True Story
Dakota William Szaniszlo
ISBN 979-8-9929729-4-8
Copyright © 2024

Anna Graham Publishing

To Donna

Chapter One

I would like to tell you a story.

I apologize for beginning that way; I know literary critics will cringe and spit on the page, closing the book shut with a scathing review about how I have broken the cardinal rule of storytelling in beginning with a direct address to you, the reader. Oh, I know many prospective readers may have been turned away already by such an opening line, more still before even beginning, possibly swayed by others' vicious rumours and slander—people on the streets crying out filth and lies.

So again, to all the literary critics; to all those turned away; to all the students who have been taught that a line like that is unacceptable; to the family and loved ones; to the gods of literature, weighing out swift judgment, gavel in hand; I offer my deepest, humblest, most sincere apologies. But you, my dear reader, you did not listen to the lies; you covered your ears and pushed forward, maybe even enjoyed the opening line for its fresh change of pace from the drab, droll, grey, listless heap of trash we have come to know as proper—so to you, I know I need not apologize. But should you have the least bit of doubt, any slight uneasiness at all—well, I just could not live with myself for letting such a terrible thing like that happen, my dear, sweet reader, so allow me to explain myself, for, of course, there is no way I would ever start a story in such a way without specific intention.

As I started, I would like to tell you a story—but before I

can do so, I feel there are certain things that must first be done. Before we can even begin to delve into the story I have yet to unravel for you, all barriers must be broken down; all pre-conceived notions and misconceptions must be eradicated, eliminated from the furthest reaches of the mind. I need, yes desperately need, to put myself at the forefront, to remind you, yes you, my dear beloved reader, that I am indeed speaking to you from the depths of the soul, directly, without pretence, without affectation. I need, yes again need, to ever remind you, my dear forgetful reader, that I am a person, living and breathing, with blood coursing through my veins, wholly separate from the story I tell—completely even and unbiased, completely free from restraint—and that I, your humble narrator, am here for you always, taking it upon myself as holy duty to be your guardian angel, the light to your darkness, etc., etc. and that I, put in such a position as the sole link between you and the story, understand the gravity of my words, and promise—fully and utterly promise, heart crossed, on the lives of my children—that I will tell you nothing but the absolute unbridled truth—or may god strike me down where I stand.

So, now that the air is cleared and all's out in the open and we have acknowledged each other, first by a glance, then a warm smile and a handshake, we can finally move on. We can move past the typical false pretences and shallow obsequies and together immerse ourselves solely in the story—pure and true.

Ah yes, my eager, excited reader, we are about to start on the story, so prepare your fresh, new, open mind for the journey before you, for just around the corner, congealed in endless possibility, everything will unfold, and I, yes I, your loyal narrator, am quivering with excitement for you.

****

This is where I had planned on beginning the story, and I swear it is not my intention to drag it out and keep you hanging in suspense, and if it were up to me, you would already be slowly unwrapping, like a beribboned gift, the rich web of intrigue and drama that I so very much desire to share—however, upon re-reading everything I have written so far, I cannot help but feel I have come up horribly short of the elusive point which I felt so constantly near making. Just as I feel I have reached the cusp of grasping it, I find my hands empty and see the thought dashing merrily away into the unreachable planes of abstraction. Through all my attempts at hitting the target, I hope you at least can see the general direction of my throws and forgive me if you find my tactics pompous or heavy-handed.

Actually though, I am quite hurt you would even think such a thing of me. If my words have in any way come off a bit airy—please understand, it is only because of the earnestness with which I wish to express our connection. In fact, my respect for you is so great, I have elected to leave every page completely unedited; every word I have written is there for you—so you can see for yourself that I have been perfectly innocent—and every word I will write shall be here for you as well, each letter serving as a soul-binding contract between you and I of absolute trust and equanimity.

So onward we shall trek, through the wilderness of materializing story-lines, taking the twisting, turning pathways left by ink-droplet letters that spill onto the page, flitting between plot-points and penumbrae. Just follow the trail and you will not be led astray. Ignore the rustling in the leaves, the howling in the wind; there is no need to be scared, for I am with you, and there are no wolves here.

****

The scene opens on a large white townhouse. Nicely kempt front yard. Recently trimmed cyprus trees lining the driveway. Landscaping rocks still tinged green from recent weed spray. Front door—wide open.

Mr. E. pulls his plum, powderless rubber gloves on, each with a snap, as he crosses the yawning threshold, dustcoat trailing behind him. One hand shoots backwards and fingers the doorjamb—No signs of forced entry.

In the foyer sits a quite ruffled hardwood desk, rummaged papers lying strewn across the floor, the rest just peeking out from within the relative safety of the haphazard drawers, checking to see if the coast is clear to make their great escape —Clearly rifled through.

Opening up from the foyer, the (barely) living room lies in hopeless disarray, gasping its last breaths. From the gaping entertainment centre, the black wire entrails of various devices spill out its gutted front side, reaching helplessly for their severed connections. Curio cabinets stand torn open, thoroughly pilfered; scattered in front of them, the shattered remains of their contents. All of the pictures on the wall (most of which consist of a decorative frame housing a smiling, dark-haired family—some together in various groupings, some individual) are all crooked or coming unhinged, and the way the light hits the glass causes a glimmering, transparent reflection of the room's disorder to be transposed on top of their striking features. One frame lies broken on the ground, shattered glass around it—Picture missing.

Further back, the sliding glass door is visible through a small den connecting the living room to the dining room—Cracked open like a safe.

Following the trail, E. walks determinedly to the back of the house. The furniture in the den appears wholly intact, if only mildly disturbed; this relative calm gives the impression of walking through the eye of some savage storm, as E. crosses from the chaos of the living room into the chaos of the dining room, which stretches out to the left and blends into the kitchen.

The entire area is a battleground of wanton destruction. Shards of porcelain and glass cover the ground, accompanied by cutlery and silverware. Foods of a vast spectrum of texture and colour streak the walls and countertops, collecting in little globs here and there across the mad topography. Further in, a layer of white flour coats the room in a perimeter of about thirteen feet. Through it, a pair of bootprints round the corner. Mr. E. follows.

To the right, through an open door, there is a garage—with a broken-down beamer and a beat-up sedan, some spilled boxes of miscellaneous holiday decorations, and a variety of carelessly strewn tools; directly ahead awaits a lightly curled staircase with a white, boot-shaped smudge on the dark wood of the first step—The trail leads higher.

Tiptoeing the stairs, his gloved hand glides along the smooth metal banister, elegantly curving upwards; his foot stutters at the top step a brief moment, unable to cross without a slight sense of trepidation.

The doors that branch off from the claustrophobic hallway are all pushed wide open—all but one.

Mr. E. hones in on the closed door like a tracking basset hound, drawn closer and closer by some unshakable force, some unconscious intuition compelling him forward.

He glances left and right at the chaos in each room as he passes by: here an overturned mattress, there a dismantled dresser, from all angles clothing and wall décor and various kitsch lie in disarray like some chaotic mass oozing out of the doorways—Noted for further inspection.

For now, Mr. E. is on a fixed path, creeping forward slowly in apprehension of what lies concealed behind that closed door.

He reaches out to grip the cold round knob and, with baited breath, hesitantly twists his hand. The door creaks ominously, inching backward just a crack. Through that crack E. is washed over by a wave of thick foreboding air.

He stops for a moment to collect himself. His palms are warm, his neck cold, and his palate uncomfortably dry.

Deep from within his chest, a tightness is beginning to spread out, all the way through to his face and extremities.

He closes his eyes to focus, letting the dread fade a little, and presses his palm flat against the white-washed door.

Eyes still closed, he pushes the door fully open and lets out a steady breath, centring himself as he prepares to step through the gaping maw of this portentous beast.

One more slow breath and, finally, he opens his eyes, seeing there on the ground before him…

No, I'm sorry… it's just not right.

The angle doesn't work; the lighting is off—it is all wrong. I apologize again, I apologize a million times, but it just will not work. I see now, only just too late, that I am going about this the wrong way, that I need to attack it from a completely different angle. I know, my sweet naïve reader, I know—just when we were starting to get somewhere, just when we were getting going and the drama was rich and tense, everything is derailed, deconstructed and dismantled. I beg of you only patience dear reader, patience. It just would not do for you to have the wrong perception, which was bound to happen cont-inuing our prior trajectory, so forgive me again, sweet reader, but when change needs to occur, there is nothing to be done but let it take its course. You need to understand, and in order to do so you need the whole story; you need to get to the bottom of things. If this story existed solely for my sake... or just for yours even, then maybe... but no, this is a story that exists of itself, a story that was crafted by Fate with I serving as a humble conduit to You.

Truth be told, I was enjoying myself; I did not want to stop the story. In fact, it would have been far easier to let it continue unfolding the way it was, but for a story like this—a true story—you must have the whole picture, and so I could not go on; some pruning is required for it to grow to full bloom. I am realizing just now the task I set before me is far more difficult than I initially anticipated. I promise you though, loyal reader, things will change. Yes, things will surely change. That rushed opening will do nothing but confuse and distort your perception, and I really couldn't live with myself like that, so please—and I will ask this only once—disregard everything you have read so far. I have sworn an oath to you to leave my pen strokes unaltered, but trust me when I say this: it is all unnecessary, superfluous. In fact, you would be smart to just tear all of these pages out. No seriously—rip 'em out, shred 'em, burn 'em—completely efface them, this page as well if you like. Rid yourself of their foul taste and forget. Forget and forgive. Around the corner, a fresh start awaits; a new beginning is already forming on the other side of the horizon. What I need now is rest, just a night's rest, then we shall continue together to that horizon, set on a new path.

Yes, a brief rest—then, a new chapter begins.

Chapter One

John Smith awoke at precisely 4:56 am, as he had the morning before and the morning before that, and so on and so forth, backwards into the temporal horizon. He would continue to lie there, the numbness along his left side, caused by the fetal position of his curled slumber, slowly beginning to transform from an ineffectual hum into a vibrant, fully-awakened, buzzing tumult—coupled with the panicked thoughts that perhaps the alarm clock was not properly set and the act of sleeping had been drawn out longer than allotted or, perhaps, Mary had turned it off out of ineptitude, or malice. Just as this mental and physical roar was nearing its fevered pitch, in chimed the alleged alarm with a blaring harmonious crescendo —solidifying his hazy surroundings into a firm waking reality. First to sharpen into clarity were the blinking, bright-orange, block-numbers of the alarm clock, piercing through the haze, which at first appeared as nothing more than a jumble of twenty-one intermingled lines. Slowly they transformed into the structure of 5:00, as each bright red or dark-negative line of otherwise-would-be 8's appeared in their fixed and proper place. Before the last set of lines had time to rearrange themselves into a new number, an arm shot across his line of vision. A momentary lurch of his heart warned him that somebody had intruded on his private sanctuary, but as the fingers hit snooze, John felt the hard plastic of the button click down and he leaned back, sighing in relief, having verified that it was, in fact, his own arm.

Next to resolve into clarity was the swirled mess of satiny chocolate-coloured sheets and matching down comforter, which took a moment for the mind to unmeld into two separate entities, as if they had fused throughout the night into some strange creature whose sole objective in life it was to entangle John's lower extremities into its confused mass. Slowly he shook them off and swung his legs sidewards, sitting himself up along the bed's hard wooden frame.

Elbows on knees, his head dropped into his hands and John began to rub his half-wakened face, pressing with his palms firmly against the soft sockets of his eyes. Swirling chequerboards started to appear in blotches along with little phosphene stars that erupted in the corners of his vision. The harder he pressed, the more clearly he saw the flashing lights and variegated patterns dancing here and there on the inner screen of his eyelids. Just as his vision was reaching a completely swarmed cacophony of complex dazzling intricacy and he felt he could look upon it no longer, John pulled back his hands, stretching his face along with them sideways toward his temples, making his vision glow, first from a rich magenta to a burning orange then a warm cadmium, like a private sunrise playing just for his shuttered eyes. He then let his hands fall, clasping them behind his neck, only to lift straight up over his head and fall down again—this time to his sides in transverse little arcs, stretching out his torso into the pose of a crucified Jesus, with an open-mouthed yawn appearing in imitation of his holy, anguished face.

As his eyes opened and looked around, he could still see

the negatives of little phosphene blotches swirling to and fro, superimposed and flashing in renewed but diminishing vigour with each blink of his eyes, taunting him with their lingering presence as if they held some hidden meaning he was unable to discern, some sort of mockery pointed directly at the reality that was pushing its way back through from behind.

Through that lingering haze, he could see the long white threads of carpet fibre growing up from between his curling toes. It spread like a vast lawn, halted at the edges by dark cherry floorboards, which lined the entire length of the smooth eggshell walls. To his left, a sleepy-looking hardwood end table was pushed up against the wall and the edge of the bed. He mechanically reached for the lamp on top of it and pulled the chain, bathing the room in a yellowish glow. Beneath the lamp, his large silver wristwatch gleamed. He grabbed the watch and latched it onto his wrist, making sure as he did so to verify that both the watch and the alarm clock had their stories straight—the times matched up.

He continued his investigation of the room. Nothing was out of place, at least nothing noticeable. For all he could tell, it was, in fact, the same room within which he had gone to sleep. His closet yawned slightly, the sleeve of a starched tuxedo jacket just peeking through the cracked door. In the corner, a full-bodied mirror was leaning back at a lazy tilt. Within it, John could see the bulk of the room; everything was in place, though symmetrically reversed. His thirty-inch flat-screen TV was there, hanging on the wall, just as it should be. His favourite Monet hung to the right (or the left, according to the mirror) and was juxtaposed by his favourite Van Gogh, which hung to the left (or the right if the mirror proved to show an other-worldly reality that held greater truth than our own). He let himself swirl around in their ambiguity, entranced. Although they were two very different paintings, John couldn't help but think the true subject of both paintings was, in fact, one in the same—that is, a certain blending of subject and object, a deafening or blurring of perspective. He saw in them a representation of the reality that is seen differently by everyone—a portrait of the undefinable and ever-changing, that only gets its meaning when observed, as if they did not even exist until his eyes had gazed upon them.

John's townhouse had been recently refurnished and redecorated, and so he could not help but let his mind wander, separating from his body to flit from room to room, admiring the décor that had really come at quite a steal.

As he wanders like a spectral curator, let us follow him; let us take his mental tour, shall we?

Just outside the door, a hallway lies with several recently acquired paintings hanging in linear fashion down the length of it—all of them abstract impressionist (or post-impressionist, or abstract expressionist, or lyrical abstraction) and although they are admittedly reproductions, they are practically indistinguishable from the originals—one of which John has firm reason to believe is in fact not a reproduction at all, but had unwittingly been sold as such.

Truth be told, John could never quite distinguish which were which, but he knew that among them are pieces by

Pousette-Dart, Riopelle, Satie, Boon, and Kline. There is a Gorky or two, possibly a Cohen and, without a doubt, an improvisation by Kandinsky. The only one John could distinguish with reliable certainty, however, would be Jackson Pollock's *Number 23*, which you can see hanging at the end of the hall and is by far John's favourite of the bunch. Whenever walking down the hallway, his gaze would always fixate, the four edges of the frame seeming to hold infinity within its borders; the swirling mass of black and white so viscerally striking, so visually stunning, that John would walk like in a trance, like some strange somnambulist, staring straight ahead and stumbling forward, fixated on that painting, picturing the neurons in his brain twisting and firing, the atoms swirling and pulsing, all of it replicated infinitely from micro to macro, the same things occurring within his cells occurring in the cosmos —that is what he saw within that painting.

Separating these paintings into what John considered to be general themes or tones are three interspersed doors (four counting the one we just passed through from his bedroom). Although the doors are almost always shut, perhaps we shall take advantage of this spectral state and peer through them; we must be quick, however, so as not to get separated from our hypnotized tour guide as his mind wanders in its trance onward.

Through the first, there is a bathroom—gleaming white porcelain; glimmering brass; frosted-glass shower door and marble (or faux-marble) wall lining the luxurious spa-bathtub; the sink counter-top a matching stone; clear mirror hanging above. Fixed to the opposite wall, an even row of large brass hooks hold onto clean, white towels, all of which proudly display a stylized monogram. Stretching along the top of each wall, there is an ornate fresco: beatific cherubs floating gaily; small girls running naked, hand in hand, through filigree forest with flora and fauna abounding around them; satyrs and sprites dancing in fairy-tale splendour to merrie lyre and pan-flute melodies; and somewhere in the darkest corner, a knight-in-shining-armour pushing forward towards the light. All of it intricately connects at the ceiling into a decorative border, like the rich threads of a tapestry being woven together as one, wrapping beautifully around a gorgeous reproduction of *The Creation of Adam*.

The next door, diagonally across the hall from the prior, houses a small closet with folded linens and boxes of long-forgotten objects. There, hidden away, are some outlandish Dali's—great masturbatory circuses of morphing amalgamated sexuality and repulsion, of the divine and the disgusting, the pristine and the profane, the hidden madness of the ordinary blending into the secret sanctity of perversion. These had been deemed inappropriate for wall adornment, so John obligingly took them down and tucked them away, hidden in the closet along with one of Ernst's monsters and a massive poster vers-ion of Bosch's *Garden of Earthly Delights* which had been likewise deemed unworthy of display and instead was folded up into thirds and moved to the shadows.

The final door, again a diagonal movement across the hall, leads into John's office—very minimalist. An expansive, meticulously clean hardwood desk presses against the rear wall, upon which stands his crisp computer monitor, like an icon on display. Behind the monitor can be seen the blue glow of his top-of-the-line state-of-the-art computer that would have cost a fortune were it not completely, one-hundred-percent tax deductible. A luxurious leather chair is nestled into the nook of the desk, graciously tilting back in apprehension of a sitting body to comfort. Hanging above the whole display, the only decoration in the room—one of the original screen printings of *Andy's Soup*, which John could not help but recognize as the perfect marriage of art and industry, reminding him that even the mindless-heartless labour of work can still be a form of art, and also which always reminded him of childhood, and his mother.

And there he goes…

Quick, let's chase him around the corner before we lose him…

We mustn't let him get away…

John's mind is paused for a moment in the living room, which spaciously opens up before us as we turn from the hallway. A dazzling chandelier hangs from above, sending crystalline sprays of light across the room—bathing in its warm glow: the luxurious red-suede couch-set and leather recliner; the expansive oriental rug; the vast entertainment centre (replete with massive plasma screen TV, stereo surround-sound system, and all the accoutréments); the vaulted ceilings; and the dark grey walls, which upon each of the three not taken up by said entertainment centre, hangs a single painting.

For this room, John had actually consulted an interior decorator, who at first seemed ditzy, inept, and utterly incapable of providing any helpful insight to John's keen eye for aesthetics, but had actually by the end provided a tremendous aide in the whole affair—all of her suggestions proved to be so terrible, so completely asinine and incomprehensible, so utterly lacking in taste that Mary eventually caved and gave John complete creative control; once he had shown her how wrong she was, she had no choice but to surrender that he was right. John settled on an Ode to Venus—a choice which caused an understandable sense of self-conscious jealousy in Mary which, to her credit, she bore with an admirable (if not, at times, slightly annoying) taciturnity. The three Venuses adorning the walls (clockwise) are Rokeby, Dresden, and Urbino—with the whole affair completed by a full-sized reproduction of the De Milo standing armless in the corner. Incidentally, were you to stand right up against her body, and align your gaze with that of her perked nipples, most probably you will notice that directly from her breast, there is an invisible line connecting her symmetry to that of a portrait hanging in the foyer, of which, from that angle, you should just be able to make out a pair of dark, sultry eyes and a ravishingly coy smile, all lit up as if across that connection some silent secret were being shared—some not-altogether-unpleasant secret by the looks of it. The portrait is of his dark Madonna. Well, not *his* dark Madonna, but one none-the-less: *The Mona Lisa*. Stationed near the entrance to greet all incoming guests, his beacon on the shore, Libertas, signalling safe haven from the stormy seas of the world.

Further off is the kitchen and dining area—not quite as extensively decorated, but with sleek, modern amenities and a tastefully simple charm. The quiet hum of the fully-stocked refrigerator should just barely be audible as we cross the threshold of the hard tile. Instead, however, as John's mind creeps closer to the pantry, you can hear only his stomach growling from back in the bedroom.

And with that I think our spectral tour has come to an end.

With a snap, John's mind is reunited with his body—reminded of his flesh by the locution of its hunger.

As he let out one final yawn, he rose from the edge of his slumbering bed and, stretching with each step, walked towards the doorway; first to make his morning dew, then to sate his growing appetite.

Just as he was nearly through to the hall, he paused and turned around. His mind still wrapped up in the inventory of his various possessions, he wanted to verify just once more that everything was indeed exactly as it should be. His eyes moved slowly, searching about the room and finding nothing at fault, rested gently down onto the bed. There, nestled in the corner, curled up like a little mouse, the almost forgotten Mary lay sleeping in her peaceful little dreamland.

As John walked out the door, he contemplated the subtle impression she gave, with the partial morning light cast upon her wispy blonde hair and bone-white skin, of vague translucence—as if the morning haze had not quite yet cleared from around her; as if, in her slumber, she had begun to fade away and, now in John's waking morning, she had not yet entirely arrived. He was enthralled by this impression but momentarily, and with each successive step towards the welcoming call of the bathroom, the fragile, hazy image of Mary in her angelic repose faded further and further from the forefront of his mind.

Chapter Two

"I am in perfect shape," thought John to himself midway through his four-mile morning run. "I am a pinnacle of organic machinery." He could feel the perfect symmetry with which his entire body flew from each stride. His posture was straight, his weight balanced; his movement flowed from every twitch of his muscular fibres—he could feel his thighs tense and release, his calves spring, his back ripple, every muscle in his body working together, playing off of each other like the interconnected notes of some anatomic symphony.

A bead of sweat began to trail from the peak of his bristled salt-and-pepper hair, forming at his temple a gentle stream that rolled along the contours of his sinewy neck, catching up and reuniting with some other droplets into a saltwater river that flowed through the valley between his powerful shoulder-blades, spilling down the hillocks and curves of his muscular back and spine, rounding hip and buttock and, finally joined by other tributaries at the crux of his inner knee, dropped with a splat past his chiselled calves onto the dusty, dirty cement path just behind his heels—there it disappeared, evaporating into nothingness, leaving John's sun-tanned skin to glisten in the morning light.

His even footfalls reverberated around him, each step falling into perfect rhythm with his steady breathing. The air that rushed past was cool and liberating. His mind was focused, letting his body act in accordance with its natural splendour, unstifled and unrestrained, surging with atavistic glee. The sporadic whooshing of the traffic from the street beside him (along with the squealing tires, screeching brakes, and blaring horns that typically accompany said traffic) was, at first, a distraction to his focus, but now, as he was closing in on Zen, it had all fallen away into the background of white-noise, helping to lull John into an almost trance-like cadence.

He could feel his movements falling into a rhythm that was smoother and more graceful than anything he could have consciously attempted—a lion on the savanna (sinewy flesh rippling over tensed muscles) chasing down its prey, flying across a burning grassland. He could feel himself becoming more natural, more pure. He snorted his breath out through his nose, his open palms slicing through the air. His animal instincts surged.

Then, like an apex predator, John turned on a dime, without breaking his even gait, and stepped from the cemented sidewalk onto a less-tread dirt path. To either side, sparse mesquites and palo verdes were dotted here and there, interspersed with beautifully bloomed, but painfully foreboding cacti of varying genus. Across his path, a spry lizard scurried with its zebra-striped tail curled over its back, stopping here and there on its way to the shade of a nearby ocotillo in order to uncurl said tail and do a few push-ups. Further up, a prairie-dog kept watch, with its head just peeking out from the earth; above its attentively peaked ears, about a dozen craneflies were flitting playfully amongst the dry, stringy blades of buffelgrass scattered along the curving pathway. As John rounded the bend, a sudden, panicked burst erupted from above his head and—as he turned towards the flurried commotion—he could see four light-brown doves scatter from the spindly limbs of a gangling mesquite tree, beating a hasty retreat—back to headquarters for debriefing. Upon turning his attention back to the path before him, John came to the realization that a rock he had noticed in the middle of the pathway was, in fact, not a rock at all, but an almost perfectly camouflaged bunny, frozen in place with fear. "Why won't it move?" thought John. "Poor stupid thing. Maybe, is it dead?" Just as he could picture himself inevitably trampling the rabbit's little corpse, it suddenly jolted to life, scratching and scrambling at the ground beneath it, spraying dust and dirt as it struggled to get traction. It tripped over itself in a frenzied rush, falling backwards onto its cottony tail before finally getting its feet firmly beneath it and frantically darting away. A little way further, a soft-white cabbage moth languidly fluttered to-and-fro, dancing with the breeze in delicate semicircles around the broad fan-leaves and brutally spiked seed-pods of a blooming datura plant, before alighting on the labellum of its white trumpet flower. For a brief moment, it gave the impression of becoming a part of the flower, like both the flower and the butterfly were two separate, incomplete pieces now united as a whole. Just as quickly as it came, however, that feeling went as well, taking with it some ungraspable universal truth, fluttering off into the horizon, to be lost amongst the dull roar of the city that still permeated from the distance.

John revelled in the beauty of nature as he ran along his

lightly trodden path. The freedom and purity of the wilderness spoke to him. The artful way in which all of the limbs and leaves of the nearby trees grew—spiralling heliocentrically up towards the heavens—always seemed to him like some sort of secret message he was just on the verge of decoding. He too lifted his limbs to the sun, sucking in a breath of fresh air.

John began to imagine to himself what it would have been like not to have been born into this modern world of madness, but instead to find himself in this very same place in a much earlier time—like some primal, spear-wielding hohokom native, having to hunt down his next meal. The years began to wick away, flashing rapidly from centuries into millennia. The first notable change was auditory—that infernal, inescapable whooshing of the nearby road disappeared completely. Next, tactile—the parched sand beneath his feet ceased its dry crepitation as it slowly became more and more suffused in rich moisture. As the water tables hundreds of feet deep were refilled, the flora began to split and multiply, exploding upwards and fanning out into dense thickets, a rainfall of leaves covering the ground. The air was thicker, the insects more plentiful. A cloud of gnats crossed his path, intermingling with the twirling helicopter seed-pods and xanthous pollen fluff floating on the breeze. John's awareness and intent became hyper-focused; he could hear, all around him, the multitude of scurrying creatures that fled in every direction—knowing their place in the food chain. On the crisp air, cleared of carbon-emissions, he could smell one thing: Fear.

With predatory grace, he lunged forwards, his muscles

rippling beneath his glistening skin. Then, suddenly, a twig snapped. John peaked his ear to the left—there, a roadrunner streaked across his path, dashing into the presumed safety of some adjacent brush. Succumbing to his animal instincts, John gave chase to this quite worthy prey.

Springing forth from his bulging calves, he vaulted over the brier blockade. The instant his feet alighted once again onto the densely shrub-littered ground, they pushed off into a fevered sprint, spraying leaf and twig into the air behind him. From all angles, the sounds of scrambling creatures resounded: birds flapping frantically from every treetop; lizards rustling in all directions through the underbrush and fallen leaves; the rapid scampering and squeaking of a family of field mice criss-crossing in front of him. To his left, a prowling bobcat stood frozen, hunched close to the ground, a single paw extended. To his right, a little further off, a stray javelina, separated from the rest of its pack, tore itself away from its plump, prickly-pear snack and fled into the distance, snorting and snuffling the entire way. All of these things, however, went by unnoticed as John tensely focused, like a stallion wearing blinders, on the tips of the roadrunner's tailfeathers, which flashed with blue-tinged phosphorescence as his elusive prey flitted, evanescent spectre that it was, from cover to cover. All else faded away, melding into the slowly oscillating drone of the cicada choir, punctuated only by the sharp, rapid thumping in his powerful chest.

Ahhhh! Nature! Pure. Unrefined. Uncut. If it could be boiled down to its essence, it would be the number one selling elixir on the market. In nature, all is one. Everything, from the helical growth of each plant, to the random, yet precise movements of the animals, even down to the lightly eddying swirls of the morning breeze—all becomes the soft machinery that pulses together, the vast organism called Nature. Prey and predator dance together as one, joined by their instinctual relationship, by a tense bond that pulls them to each other, linking them inseparably. Sadly, however, modern man has separated himself from this pulse, isolated in a different rhythm. From time immemorial, Man has dominated this rock; save for a few hiccups with pesky Neanderthal, Homo sapiens has proved himself apex predator, clawing his way to the top of the food chain from the moment he wrested himself from the primordial ooze. Now, lazing away at the top, modern man seems to have lost something, something natural, integral. Modern man thinks himself so clever with his complex tricks and traps, but what he fails to realize is that what he is looking for, what he is trying so hard to capture, can only ever be found during the chase. Modern man has atrophied, letting waste away that predator connection with his prey. Man's senses, his animal instincts, are all repressed, filtered darkly through the hazy glass of our limited consciousness. Gone are the days of purity, of instinct. Gone are the days of Nature. Society has pervaded (or perverted) our lives to the point where now we live in our own artificial bubble of a world, broken away and shut off from real life. Put away are our spears, and with them our dwindling hearts. Animal blood no longer courses through our veins, but a mere hemoglobin-oil that just greases the creaky joints of our hollow, mechanical shells—empty of all our natural essence. Not knowing where we stand, modern man bounces around aimlessly, from one moment to the next, with no set place in life, no real purpose, and yet… moments arise, when the dying embers of animality are briefly stirred, and all that is needed is a little stoking for that fire to rise up and envelope one fully and completely once again. For most, these moments pass by unnoticed, cast aside into the hidden pile of missed opportunity—but for some, these same moments are pounced upon like rare, chance gemstones rising at sharp, jagged, crystalline angles through the mundane dirt and crags of everyday life. To be filled. To be purified. In these moments, Man can feel his animal nature; Man can once again sense the unified pulse that he has long been cut off from. In his chest and all around him, all beats as one.

John ran with all the fervour and earnestness of a wild animal. Branches flew past his head as he zeroed in on his dappled prey, drawing nearer still, so that the roadrunner's body was now fully in frame. Its sleek, dark tail-feathers were nearly half the length of its entire figure, angling sharply upwards from its lean body. Slender yet powerful, it was pointed straight, from its black-and-white speckled body to its light-brown beak, which almost looked like a dart shooting through the air, pulling its body along behind it, the powerful raptor-like legs having to rapidly pedal beneath it to keep up. Its soft, furry-looking underside of light-tan down blended almost perfectly with the dust it was kicking up. Standing out in sharp contrast to the rest of its features, there lay, beneath the black waving feather-crest, two blue-and-red streaks, which looked strikingly reminiscent of the brightly painted eyeshadow of a young geisha.

For John, in that moment, nothing existed save for that roadrunner and himself, and the invisible tether that was pulling them closer and closer—but then a loud rustle tore his attention to the left. There, on a raised rock dais, a regal mountain lion was lazing in the warm sun. It raised a single paw to its powerful mouth and licked between its outspread claws, giving John the leonine equivalent of the gentleman's wink and nod.

Reinvigorated, John turned his attention back to the roadrunner, but, during his brief lapse of focus, it had gotten much farther off than he had expected. It was now standing just at the horizon of his view, completely immobile, ostensibly frozen with fear. John dug deep, pulling out all of his reserves, and let out a sudden burst of speed—sprinting straight towards his dominated prey. Furiously, he charged, only to find out too late that what had appeared as the perfect silhouette of a fear-frozen roadrunner set against the rising sun, was, in fact, a façade—the deceptive roadrunner most likely having dashed to one side or the other while John's attention was diverted. As he drew near enough for the perspective to shift, transforming the bird into a bird-shaped chaparral bush, he also realized that the horizon it was resting at was actually the precipice of a steep little hill. As he frantically tried screeching to a halt, skidding rocks and snaring brush grabbed hold of his foot, sending him tumbling down that hill in a cloud of dust.

At the bottom, John lay collecting himself. He could feel his heart threatening to burst from his chest, and each breath had to be grasped at and pulled into his lungs—yet, lying there on the ground, looking up at the clear blue sky, he could not help but chuckle at the absurdity of his position.

Looming just above him, John could see the cross-hatching patterns made by the cut-off fronds of a tall, stretched-out-looking palm tree that, contrasted by the bright sun, looked like a dark firework explosion stuck onto a long stick. This palm tree helped serve John as a sort of anachronistic anchor, rooting him back into the modern age, transplanted from else-where, from a different time and place.

"Well, I'd better get up before the vultures come pick my bones," John said to himself. He sat up slowly, resting his arms on his knees a moment, then puffed out his breath. "Up we go."

Pushing off the ground with one hand, he rose—instantly, a sharp, burning pain shot up from his right ankle; before his knee had straightened and his leg was at full extension, he could feel it starting to buckle, forcing him to shift his weight to compensate. He wiped away the gravel embedded in his palms and poured some water over his dirty, skinned knee. Then, tentatively, he reached out with a limp foot, pawing at the ground—but before his foot could be firmly planted, his other leg came lunging forward to catch his hobbled gait. Just behind him, the lush desert oasis began to diminish, receding back into the forgotten past as John stepped—with a slight wince—onto the smooth, even sidewalk before him.

This particular sidewalk led him past the well-manicured lawns of a charmingly gauche country club down to a white cement bench moulded in imitation marble, which coincidentally, languished in direct view of the community swimming pool. And there she was.

"She was here yesterday, and the day before," John thought as he reached into his pocket, jostling around to find his lighter and his ornate silver cigarette case. "It's almost as if she were waiting for me." He lit a cigarette and raised it to his pursed lips, sucking in deeply, lustily. Upon exhale, he could feel himself begin to relax. He leaned back, both hands outstretched behind him for support, smoke curling past his curved index finger in a long, fluid trail, only to dissolve slowly, softly into the clear blue air.

Across the way, a young girl stood on the high dive, lightly bouncing, testing the springboard's pliability as she readied for her plunge. I say young girl, but really, with the amount of hormones in the food these days, it would be difficult to ascertain her exact age. She easily could have been seventeen or eighteen, or even as young as twelve. She had light-brown hair—like straw coated in honey—and golden-tanned skin that looked just as sweet. Arms that seemed just a touch too long were held outstretched on either side like a circus tightrope walker; skinny, girlish legs bent at knobby knees. A bare, little midriff peeked out from between her bright red, two-piece bikini. Beneath her top, her breasts had undoubtedly already budded, but they did not quite look fully bloomed—and if they were, the poor girl probably had to stuff her brassière with wadded tissues at school. All of these features screamed youth and innocence, yet... something about her portrayed a striking maturity, a maturity not come across often in life, even amongst those two to three times her age.

Her thin, spread-eagled arms; her dainty toes that curled around the diving-board edge; her cute little chest, rising and falling in even rhythm with each of her light bounces; her slender belly and sun-tanned legs, with their light aureate down; and, above the loosely-freckled bridge of her button nose, her dark, piercing-blue eyes that were staring directly at John, linked cornea to cornea—it all made a delightful shudder run through John's body. He matched the gaze, sprawled out like a Greek statue, golden thighs bared, and could not help but notice a slight blush rising on her rounded cheeks.

It is only natural for a young girl to be slightly abashed at her own arousal, uncertain of these yet unexplored emotions. As she stood up there—not just looking at John, but trying to pierce him, to peer into the depths of his soul—she was washed over with a panicked desire to please this man in some way, to impress him, to make him see her as something special. Still blushing, she let out the most coquettish little smile and waved. John stiffened, as if struck directly through the chest by that flagrant arrow flung from her cherubic little lips. He reached into his pocket to fish out another cigarette, his first one still burning languidly on the bench beside him.

Suddenly, her gaze turned away. John watched as she focused forward, giving a couple more light bounces before her arms shot out in front of her and she leapt, springing herself high into the air. Right at her zenith—just before her descent began—she kicked her legs straight up and dove head-first with a resounding splash into the clear-blue, crystalline water. "Well, I'm all wet now," thought our Adonis, our Odysseus. "Perhaps it is time to conclude this journey and head home. Yes, yes, homeward now, there is work to be done."

And so he went—limping slightly and thinking to himself that this must be how the lion appeared to the mouse in that old parable.

Chapter Three

Work, work, work.

Always a struggle, a real Sisyphean push, a long boring grind that can just drag on and on and on with no purpose, save to prove in the least, if anything at all, the objective relativity of time by the plain fact—observed by every Tom, Dick and Larry with any presence of mind, any powers of obs- ervation at all—that the mundane moments of life spent doing the draining, ennui-ridden activities such as work, always take far longer than the rest of life, even if less time is spent on them. Besides having that sole consolation, and economic sec- urity of course, most work (that is, job work, i.e. work for other people) provides nothing of real value, no means of per- sonal development or, at the least, very limited means— nothing more than a dull listlessness of bland time wasted, with only the night to look forward to. Only then, when all the businesses have closed, are possibility and excitement truly alive. Only then do people drop their façades. John Smith wor- ked from home as a "Customer Outreach Consultant" or "C.O.C." as his C.O.E. (Company of Employment) called it, which was basically cold-call telemarketing. The job was not what you might call fulfilling, but it was, however, not without positive aspects: working from home, John was king of his own castle, his own boss with no one to report to, save once a month with that pock-marked, gap-toothed Brenton that dared call himself John's superior; he was free to lounge around in his underwear, kicked back with his feet up on the desk, sipping a stiff Martini if he felt so inclined; additionally, the job was quite suited for his skills—that is, his cunning silver tongue and uncanny mastery over the art of pathos.

His work day would begin, when deemed the right time, by logging into a company account on his home computer. Amongst a slew of tabs with no real indication of purpose or meaning aside from small, seemingly random icons, John would click on what would appear to be a minimalist rendition of a small telephone. A number would then populate in a phone pad on the computer screen. John would hit dial. Work would begin.

Donning his headset, his first target answers. John usually skips the standard script and, saying this and that, charming them from the start with amiable chatter, he completely wraps them up. He shows interest in what they like, soothes them until they trust him, then pulls tight and reels them in—thus is the method.

John is a master of reading a person from the moment they pick up the phone; the subtle variations in cadence and inflection would sing to him of the possible paths he could lead them down. He was regularly top of his department. He had been employee-of-the-month for an entire year and a month consecutively, all without ever really trying or caring.

Most of the calls would be to former clients of the company he was representing, in an attempt to get them to reinstate coverage. The rest—numbers gathered by the marketing and web advertising department. Regardless, every single one of them, no matter who they were, they always had something to say, some story, some tale to tell; all you need do is listen and you would be able to hear everything, the entirety of their lives, the very moment they answered the phone.

The broadest sweep is to start with an apology; it does not really matter what for, just make them feel a little bit superior—we know this is a false sense, but they'll cling to it like a drowning man would a life raft. If you choose this route, however, you will have to make sure from then on out to let them think they have the upper hand; everything has to be their idea. Again, this is a good general sweep, but it can make things rather difficult, for even the smallest power is corruptive and that sense of superiority fills some heads rather quickly.

No, a much better hook is instead to thank them. Instead of begging for their forgiveness—express a deep gratitude (sometimes you can even do both); this will have the effect of shifting the power dynamic, bringing things to an (almost) equal footing. There on that level plane you can meet eye to eye. You can make them feel like they have done you a good turn, and so now you simply have come to return the favour. What is most important in the end is to establish some sort of bond, some connection, and from there you simply work your magic.

Normally, John was exceptional at gaining people's trust; he always knew what routes to take, what words to say, what tones to use. On this day, however, he was a bit distracted. His mind kept wandering insubordinately and, in a roundabout motion, revolved always back to the night—the illustrious exhilarating night—when the stars begin to twinkle, spread out in their dazzling diaspora, constellation dancing with constellation—when the city lights glow with the pale moon, everything suffused in spectral hues—when the real fun begins.

John could hardly focus on pomp and circumstance while his mind was frolicking in the nightlife—one foot in the past and one in the future, bridged only by the boring events of the soporific present.

Recently, John had rekindled a friendship, a friendship he had thought long dead and gone, yet had returned like Lazarus, and through this friendship gained access to the secret thrills of the night. It was tiring, sure, but the rush made it all worth the while—that indescribable electric rush. For the past several weeks, John and Bruce had been going out nearly every night to party, and under the cover of darkness… well, maybe I had better rewind.

Allow me to explain a little more.

About a month and a half ago, John had hired an exterminator. His house had been victim to a group of pack rats and their insidious plot to burglarize his home of its insulation and anything else they could get their grubby little paws on. John put out traps and poison pellets and even managed to get three of them—one caught in a steel cage, the other two lying on their sides, bodies bloated from the poison. Alas, the scratching and clawing each night continued as before. Worse still, were Mary's incessant complaints, which annoyed John more than the rats. Finally, completely vexed, he called an exterminator.

When the exterminator arrived, John was already in a poor mood and was fully prepared to share this mood with the poor unsuspecting man, yet as he stepped from his work van, John noticed that this man looked strikingly similar to his old friend Bruce. The resemblance was uncanny. John had to rub his eyes, making rapid mental calculations while approaching this person who looked so similar to his long-forgotten friend. As the distance closed, the resemblance grew no less striking, the magic that was morphing this stranger in accordance with memory grew no weaker. In fact, as details came into greater focus, it was as if the raw clay of life were being refined before his eyes—as the facsimile, if you were to wick away the signs of age, slowly melted into the original.

The thick head of now-greying curls, the bright green eyes, the slightly drooping corners of his mouth, and the long, slightly hooked nose—all of these were like little hints laid by nature to some riddle that John was pretty sure he already knew the answer to—but none was as clear, as blaringly obvious, as the name patch on his shirt, displaying that answer in cursive stitching: "Bruce".

Even in the face of such confirmation, John still could not shake that lingering doubt, even as he stretched his hand out to greet him.

"Bruce? That really you?"

A look of confusion jumbled the doppelgänger's features.

"Perhaps not," thought John.

Then a twinkle of recognition.

"Oh. John? How… how are you?"

"How am I? Oh, fantastic, just great—How long has it been? Really, it's just great to see you. Brings memories flooding back, you know what I mean?"

"Yeah, so…"

"So this is what you're doing now? How long you been killing for?"

"What?"

"The job." John chuckled, whilst poking Bruce's iron-on name tag with a deft thrust of his index finger.

Bruce retreated a step. "Oh, well, yeah, few years now I suppose."

John advanced a step and a half, wrapping his arm around Bruce's shoulders with a jocular slap, and led him into the house.

Bruce made quick work of the job—he laid out traps, planted poisons, he sealed up a hole in the wall. He did nothing John did not do, yet the difference a few years experience makes is remarkable. There was none of the fumbling, none of the hesitation; every action was calculated, every movement was smooth and calm and deliberate—the work of a real professional. Or just a very skilled con man. Bruce gave John some paperwork to sign and told him he would be back in a couple of days to pick up the traps. Then, he left as suddenly as he had arrived. As John stood there, holding the yellow customer copy of his receipt, he could not help but feel he had somehow been swindled.

The next day, however, four rats were found in the traps.

The day after that, two more were killed by poisoning. Then, the fateful night finally came when there was no more scraping and scratching. That night, the walls were silent.

The next few days were spent in a similar fashion to his current position in our story—that is, sitting at his computer, dawdling around at work, and imagining to himself what his next encounter with Bruce might hold. Until, the day finally came.

****

John Smith sat there in his computer chair, a chance lynchpin between two distinct points in time, yet unawares that the call he was about to make would join these two points in his life inseparably. Through some cycle of physics, some pattern of energy, some great alignment of forces beyond our control, John found himself sitting in the exact same place, experiencing the exact same thing, with several weeks spanning the distance between.

He held the receiver pinched between shoulder and ear as he clicked dial—a local number. He rubbed his temples and cleared his throat, the phone ringing approximately four times before a soft, exceedingly feeble hello cut off the noise.

"Ah yes, hello," John said with a smooth lilt of the voice.

On his computer screen, a customer profile had already populated.

"Mrs. Black, is it? How have you been?"

"Oh, quite well, thank you dear."

The first time all of this occurred it had seemed commonplace. The second gave a scent of hopeful déjà vu. John pursued the track, trying his best to mimic word for word the conversation of the past.

"Wonderful, just wonderful, Barbara. May I call you Barbara?"

"Oh please, call me Barb."

"Barb—how beautiful."

The old lady seemed to be playing along in this bizarre duplication that was unfolding; she unwittingly fell right into pattern. When John mentioned his name, she reminisced on her dearly departed husband of the same namesake, then briefly doted on her granddaughter. Finally after all that, she asked, "What did I call you for again?"

"Ah, yes, Barb. This is a courtesy call in regards to your insurance plan."

"My insurance plan?"

"Yes, well you see, it has come to our understanding that your plan was recently downgraded."

"Oh, yes, well, Annie thinks..."

"I just worry that if something were to happen –"

"Oh, dear."

"I just want to find the right plan for your needs, Barb."

Up to that point, the two calls matched up beat-for-beat but then began to diverge. The first time—John continued to dance around with her, to chit-chat about life and its potential risks: she told him a lot about her beautiful, smart, and talented granddaughter and mentioned her poor mother, alluding to some sort of illness. She chatted about her new low-calorie diet and the surgery her workout buddy Marjorie had recently under-gone. Then the topic changed to break-ins; John made up a quick story about how his house had been broken into last September:

He had taken the family out to the movies—a quaint little art film in black-and-white, during which the two boys, and himself to be honest, fell asleep at least three separate times. Between the entire family recounting the film on the drive home, they found that nothing seemed to line up, and they had somehow all seen something wildly different. Mary's version was probably closest to the truth. Although, truth be told, she never really had an eye for art, so the ultimate reality still lies obscured. All in all, however, they'd had a wonderful evening. Until they arrived home.

Pulling into the driveway, they noticed almost immediately that the front door had been broken in. All of their valuables were stolen—their furniture and belongings damaged and defaced. The worst part however, was the invasion of privacy, the complete obliteration of any sense of security they'd had. Every nook and cranny was suspect. There was no telling if the perpetrator had left or was hiding still, tucked away in the shadows like some dark predator in the night, waiting for the opportunity to pounce. Even as the fear began to ease away and you thought the whole mess was cleaned up, you would start to notice little things here and there that just would not let you forget. One of the intruders, a practical joker it seems, had switched the bags of cereal, so that none of the boxes matched; throw pillows were hidden; every lamp was turned a quarter turn; all the shows were cleared from the TiVo; every nook and cranny was looked over. It was as if every aspect of their sanctity had been perverted and defiled. Luckily they had top-notch insurance.

The entire house was refurnished and redecorated, and the insurance company took care of everything.

After that, it was easy to sign her up. She herself basically asked for the highest possible coverage with virtually no prompting. While processing the details, she dropped a bombshell, which almost passed by unnoticed, but just happened to get caught unconsciously by John's peaked ears.

She said, "Good thing too, I never lock my doors."

Now that John found himself talking to her again, he did not care why her plan had been downgraded, he did not care about shmoozing or selling; when the conversation diverged, he instead set himself down a fixed path. The moment he heard her voice, felt the déjà vu, his gears began turning, working his way towards his goal.

"Tell you what Barb, I actually don't want to change a single thing about your plan today."

She paused for a moment, not knowing how to respond.

"Annie will sure be happy. She got rather upset the last time I changed my plan."

"Annie... is that the name of your granddaughter?"

"Granddaughter? No... my daughter... my granddaughter, she..." Her voice trailed off. John did not care to ask her to repeat, putting it down to Alzheimer's or dementia.

"Well she sounds like a smart young lady. You know what I'm going to do? I've got some pamphlets here with me. Mind you, these aren't your everyday mass-mailed sales packets. These are typically meant for representative eyes only—they really break down all of the cost/payment ratios and fully detail each plan. Now, I want to send these to you—for you and Annie to look over together."

"Oh my," her weak voice broke with genuine surprise, "that is so kind of you…. well… I wouldn't want to get you in trouble…"

"Trouble? Nonsense. No trouble could prevent me from wanting to help a friend like you, Barb."

"You sweetheart…"

"Yes, so if I could just get your address…"

****

By the time Bruce had finally come around to pick up the traps, John was able to work out a battle plan. For the most part, he was able to script his entire argument. He had everything figured out—his points were concise, supporting evidence was in place, counterpoints were covered. It was all ironclad. Bruce, however, took no convincing at all. The moment John suggested they get together sometime for lunch or a drink or whatever, Bruce's face practically lit up; that initial stand-offishness must have been nothing but nerves—I mean, how could he not have at least a little social anxiety, re-encountering a long lost friend like that?

"Yeah, well, I'm actually off today," Bruce said through a half-crooked smile, "I just kinda happened to be in the area, thought I'd swing by, pick up the traps."

"Beautiful. I know the perfect café. They serve the worst

coffee and have the most nourishing little waitresses. And they have a liquor license."

"Oh, okay," Bruce said, as he threw the empty traps into the back of his van and slammed the door shut, "I'll follow you there."

"Here's the thing Bruce."

"Yeah?"

"Well my baby's in the shop. 1969 Corvette Stingray, 350 horsepower. Canary-yellow with black racing stripes. A sleek, artistic piece of machinery as I'm sure you can imagine. And she's in the shop until… sometime."

"Oh, alright. Well, I got the work van. It's a bit dirty, but if you don't mind, you can hop in."

He opened up the passenger door and a mostly empty beer can came rolling out, clattering against the cement. Bruce swept the wrappers and cups from the seat onto the floor and then scooped it all up and threw it into the back.

"There you go."

The conversation between the two long-lost friends steadily cruised the entire way from John's house to the café, broken only by the interspersed ejaculations of John's last-minute directions and Bruce's uncharacteristic road-rage barking. Throughout all that time however, it never managed to break the surface level, not really: they talked about sports—neither knew much, but they could both bluff it; they talked about politics—neither cared enough to really pay attention, but could not help being pessimistic about it all; they chitted and they chatted, but by the time they were pulling up to the promised café and the conversation was momentarily halted, John had still failed to learn anything of real value. He learned a few things, to be sure. He learned of Bruce's predilection for starting his sentences with some idiotic mumbled "oh" or "um" or "so anyway" which always gave the impression that he was picking up on some left-off conversation that, if having ever occurred at all, had only ever occurred within Bruce's scattered brain and nowhere else. He learned of Bruce's propensity for scratching or rubbing the antecubital fossa of his left arm when nervous. He learned that Bruce was just as gullible as he had always been. He learned that he was the owner of his own one-man pest company and that things were going pretty well, which only came off as half-convincing. Who he truly was and how he felt, and what he thought of John, himself, and the universe—these things he could not know for certain, and despite his best attempts to penetrate deeper, the conversation remained puddle deep. When they had seated themselves at the café and settled down, however, was when things started to thicken, and that puddle revealed itself to be more than just a puddle, as first impressions suggested, but rather the shoreline to some vast lake or ocean of deep dark waters, filled with the mysterious unknown.

First of all, he walked right past the radiant hostess with nothing more than a slight nod, as if he did not even see her, as if she barely even registered, which is madness considering her extreme beauty—to the point that any red-blooded male would typically be salivating at her feet the moment he rested eyes on her. But rather than wolf eyes and whistles, Bruce just kept walking past her straight to the restroom. He was in there for a good fifteen minutes, leaving John to secure a table on his own, which John thought odd, but did not mind too terribly, for it gave him time to chat up the cute waitresses. As always, they were sweet and smiling—that sparkle in their eye, the sign that either they were exceptional in their customer service roles, or they were genuinely pleased to see John. He could not help but think it was the latter; he certainly was pleased to see them, and the pleasure showed. Also, he was able to pick a table from which he could admire the view of the hostess podium.

Her dark red lips stood out like a starlet on the silver screen, practically luminous against the intense paleness of her stunning icy complexion, which was broken only by the slight, soft effusion of warmth powdered at the peaks of her breathtakingly high cheekbones. Her coal-black eye makeup made her already brilliant eyes shine like the long-awaited light at the end of the tunnel. Those light-filled eyes were a dazzling mixture of mahogany and gold, both intimidating and inviting in their intense warmth and brightness; they reminded John of a fine leather-bound book waiting to be read, or a hidden chest of mysterious treasure, of vast secret possibility, the depth of which was made to seem ever vaster and more enticing by the striking blackness of her small, pinprick pupils and the thick, sharply delineated limbic ring framing each iris. Her enticingly thin neck looked almost poised to snap under the tension of the black ribbon choker she wore wrapped around her pale, delicate throat, beneath which dangled a small moonstone pendant (matching the stone in her small septum piercing). She wore a sleeveless black dress with lacy fringe and a large frilly white collar or lapel of sorts which, by some sequence of events, either intentional or otherwise, had become unfastened at the top two buttons so that anytime she would lean forward, you could see the intoxicating milky white cleavage of her relatively small but firm young breasts, squeezing themselves into view ever so suddenly and without warning, only to disappear again before the initial elation had even had a chance to wane. A pair of dainty flats, which looked vaguely like ballet slippers, adorned her petite little feet, and travelling up from there—over those girlish ankles, over those silk-soft calves, over those knobby little knees that pointed ever so slightly inward, and nearly halfway up the length of those unbearably smooth and dulcet thighs—a pair of black fishnet stockings lustily hugged onto her legs, connected tightly by a lucky strap which disappeared beneath the lacy fringe of her dress' skirt, to attach hidden away somewhere in sensuous secrecy. Her long and lustrous hair was the rich near-blackness of dark-roasted coffee and, on that day, was pinned up in a pristine 1940s victory swirl, with a decoratively frilled miniature hat resting at a sideward tilt near the apex of her perfect Rita Hayworth hairdo. She wasn't always dressed like a gothic Elvgren girl—it just happened to be one of the most bewitching of her many looks. She did, admittedly, have a slight bend toward the sinister path (dark clothes, dark makeup, etc.) but just as often she would wear light floral sundresses or colourful jumpers, sometimes flashy technicolour spandex, with bright neon lipstick and new-wave makeup all across her face (which could be downright excessive to be honest, yet still never failed to elicit an alluring intoxication); sometimes still, though less frequently, she would wear no makeup at all, her luscious dark hair wild and messy or pulled back, her clothing drab and ordinary (usually a much-too-large grey sweatshirt with "LUMBERJACK" on the front in bold font and a pair of weathered yoga pants.) Even on those days, when she must have been sick or menstruating, she still radiated absolute beauty, pure and unadulterated. How many nights had John dreamt of those skinny, girlish limbs, as bone pale as the rest of her supple body? How many ecstatic nights did he embrace her young body in carnal bliss? Or even incidentally encountered her as she filled various different roles in the mental production of his nocturnal cinema? Let us just say she was a recurring subject of focus.

John always made sure he sat somewhere with a view. He particularly loved to watch her the moment a customer would walk through the door: the set of bells attached to the top of the door would jingle and the bored expression on her beautiful face would be interrupted by a quick, involuntary closed-eye sigh before transforming into a bright, welcoming smile. That smile would begin first when she opened her gilded eyes, which with a brilliant spark lit the rest; next to catch would be the bright pearlescent teeth peeking out from behind her plump, full lips, shining out like stars as the red curtain parts; finally, it was the appearance of a small round dimple in the centre of each cheek, which gently tugged the corners of her cute mouth even further towards them, that would finish setting the entire expression ablaze. The resulting inferno was a smile so intensely radiant that it would immediately penetrate anyone who gazed upon it and infect their hearts with a giddy effervescent fluttering. From somewhere within this rehearsed Welcome-In smile, the shadow of a glimmer (or glimmer of a shadow) would dance; it was a slight glimmer that flashed, but one that John recognized as that of someone who owns the world and is well aware of it, frighteningly so even —the same godlike look of serene pleasure can be seen in a child admiring his toys, or in a dominatrix as she breaks hers.

While waiting for Bruce to get back from the restroom, John ordered some Irish coffees for the two of them, rearranged and reorganized the objects on the table, and indulged in his favourite unconscious habit of eavesdropping on any conversation within earshot:

> Because! Life's not that simple...That's cause you always focus on the negative... you can't just believe everything you're told... He's not my President... Are you fucking serious?!? You're the one who just said the Earth is flat!...It doesn't take focus. If you can't see what is right in front of your face, then your eyes must be closed...Well, he kinda is...No. I said that I've never personally seen otherwise, so for all I know it's just as likely...No! I refuse to acknow-

ledge him as my President. He's...as it is round. Maybe even more so. Think about it; the horizon is not curved, is it? ... The entire oval office into a goddamned circus tent... And it's always the same distance away. I don't know, it seems possible that it's flat. All I'm talking about is using your own perception and a little Cartesian doubt here...But there is good in the world...Well, you're not wrong, but that doesn't change the fact that he's still in that office...I'm talking about using some goddamned common sense! What about pictures from space? What about all the scientific research saying otherwise...Yeah, as head goddamned clown. He didn't even win the election...Did you do that research? Did you take those pictures? Do you know how easy it is to edit a picture, how many cover pages have had falsified photos?...And he's doing a great job misdirecting public attention. I mean, come on, it's not the first time the role of President has been bought for one of their actors to play...And it's being blotted out by the bad...So, what? All of NASA is in on some vast conspiracy to convince the world population that the Earth is round?...know what I read today? There was this news story that said fifteen beagles were found all with life-threatening infections in their eyes and their respiratory systems...That probably wouldn't be their ultimate goal, but just a necessary falsification. They really locked themselves into that lie back on September Thirteenth, Nineteen-Fifty-nine...We just need to get his whole rotten party out of the Capitol...September...Christ, not more of your lunar landing bullshit; you're delusional. Alright, well what about when you are flying in an airplane?...you really think that will fix anything?...up there, you can see that the horizon is actually curved. I've seen that myself...apparently, the old lady that owned them was an obese shut-in, and so when she quietly died of a stroke one day, nobody noticed. By the time they found the body, it was ripped to pieces by the ravenous dogs... Hell yeah! Why wouldn't it?...Oh come on! Do you really think you get a clear view through six-inch curved impact glass with drastically different pressures on each side?...Both sides are just as corrupt as the other. I mean, historically speaking, no matter who has majority, the system has always been skewed towards corporate interests and away from the interests of the general population, pretty much from the very start. And, humanitarian progress, contrary to popular belief, hasn't been more greatly increased by one side over the other. Two sides of the same coin...Well... I don't know, I doubt it really makes a difference—what about the flight paths? They all have global GPS, don't they? They fly around the world every day. *Around* the world, key phrase. How do you explain that?...You can't be serious?! What humanitarian progress can be made by people like them? People lacking in any real values? What about this whole mess in the Middle East?...They said she had forty-three of them crammed into her cramped two-bedroom house, but as the faeces and rot built up, one by one they helplessly died or were killed by the rest of the pack and eaten...Well, for all we know, it could be a ruse. Those flight paths and the GPS too, they could all give the false impression of a round path by lightly curving a flat, indirect path over extreme distances. That way everyone thinks they're still going around the world, and they are right really...And what kind of progress can be made with what is obviously engineered bipartisan bickering? They make you focus on the issues that are

hardest to agree on, without really ever changing anything past the normal changes in
social zeitgeist... just *this* way and not *this*
way, and then in that way the planes never
will actually reach the edge...and while
you're fighting with each other over whether
you think the oval office looks better in blue
or in red, they are accepting bribes, letting
lobbyists write our laws, and slowly selling
us into corporate slavery. As long as we are
focused on the dancing monkey's side-show
speeches, we don't notice the havoc we all
wreak on the environment, the millions of
'third-world' lives destroyed by our daily
consumerism. It's all just a masquerade...
And what exactly is at that edge?...we can
just continue on like nothing's happening
and shift the blame of the symptoms onto
the politicians we don't like, instead of just
getting up out of our soft chairs and actually
doing something about it...Right now they
have those last fifteen locked up in quar-
antine. They don't think they'll ever come
back from it though...Do something like what?... They're probably going to have to put
them down...Well, the generally accepted
theory is that there's some sort of ice wall
with armed guards stationed around the peri-

meter to keep anyone from falling off, or probably from even discovering it in the first place...Like, unite together, as a people. An international nation of all mankind. Throw down our shackles and whatnot... But I've never seen it so I'm hesitant to subscribe to any theory on that. I just kind of picture nothing at the edge...Poor dogs didn't choose any of that shit...You know how ridiculous that sounds, right?...Jesus Christ ...Yeah, good luck with that...I guess at the end of the day, I don't know any more than you do...You need to change your news feed...I just try not to assume as much...Fuck you."

"I like that, it's got a certain Feng Shui about it now."

John's startled attention snapped to Bruce, who was pointing at the rearranged table. He noticed the peculiar slowness with which Bruce crept into his seat; he seemed to melt into the booth as he sank down—first the cushion gave a little, then his body seemed to give a little more, like a jellyfish in the sand. After that, Bruce just sat there slumped, staring into his silent coffee.

Just as John was about to end the silence, Bruce spoke, not breaking eye contact with his cup.

"It's strange. You know, you can't really trust your senses, can you? The whole time I was in there I could hear someone next to me... shufflin' their feet, clearin' their throat. Tried to talk to 'em even... but they wouldn't respond... thought they were just being a dick... but when I got out of the stall, there wasn't anyone there. If you can't trust your senses, what can you trust?"

"Isn't that the question?"

As Bruce was talking, his eyes kept drooping downward, and intermittently his head would bob closer and closer to his coffee cup before snapping with a jolt back to attention. "What can you trust..." He muttered, "Nothin'. Not really..."

"Exactly." John said, "Nothing. That's the only thing you can trust in. But instead all we can experience is our flawed perspective. But, even if it is flawed, those lies are our truth. Nothing else exists, nothing can exist, save for you, and what you create."

"Well, yeah... I suppose so... just, ummm... makes you feel kinda bad, y'know..."

"How so?"

"Well, like, what about all the other people?"

"I try not to concern myself with the other people. My thoughts are better focused on my own perspective. After all, it is all I can ever truly know. Nothing else is real. Nothing else matters, so I might as well appreciate the lies. Make the most of them."

"Nothin' is true... Everythin' is permitted."

"What is that?"

"Ummm, I don't know, just somethin'... somethin' I read once."

"I like it," John replied.

Bruce started to pour sugar into his now steamless coffee

and stirred a lemniscate pattern in slow motion into the melted whip cream, once again staring silently at his cup. This time John broke the silence.

"There's no limit, no bonds. Once you realize that, you are free. Nothing is actually real, nothing truly exists; you can do anything."

Bruce nodded slowly.

"Mmmhmm. So long as you can pay the consequences," he said with a sigh.

"Consequences, like anything else, are not absolute. They are just for those that get caught. Nothing is guaranteed. Ultimately, you have to take what you want from life and forget about the consequences—those that act are those that persevere. The sole purpose of life is to live, after all, anything else is an artificial constraint. Laws? Morals? Advertising and Economics? None of that really exists. It's all meaningless, signs without signifiers. In Nature, you have no rights, and your only duty is to live. And to live to the fullest."

"Yeah, well… easier said than done, huh?"

"Personally, I am tired of settling for mundanity. My life was meant for greater things. I've lately had this overwhelming urge. An urge to dismantle the structure of our everyday lives, to break through the distorted perspectives of society and make a mockery of all the constructs that bind us. It's like I'm filled with this electric energy that I know I am going to need for some grand undertaking—something that will prove completely the utter lack of intrinsic reality, to dissolve all illusions and once and for all settle everything.

Ultimately, to show that anything is possible, that you really can achieve anything if you set your mind to it. Eventually, I could raise humanity from its dark ages."

"So yeah, well, what is it you're gonna do about it?"

"I don't quite know yet. Something. Anything. Start a fire, rob a bank, break into people's houses. Maybe murder an old money lender with an axe, I don't know—would you stop looking at me like that, I'm not going to go all Columbine on you. I am not completely certain yet how—and besides, the exact details aren't important anyway—but what I want to do is completely cheat the system, break the laws in some way, shatter them really, just to show I can, just to prove that the truths we live by are not absolute, that reality is truly what you make it. Once you can see reality for what it is, once you know that truth is all lies, you can live those lies, you can work them to your benefit, or you can completely disregard them, if you so choose. That is the sort of freedom I seek. That is what I need to prove to myself that I can do."

Bruce looked shocked, but after a moment he leaned across the table and in a low voice said to John, "Well, if you're looking for a rush, I might know something." His lips pushed up and to the right in obvious contemplation. "In fact, lemme pick you up tonight. I've got a surprise I think you might like. Plus, I could use an extra hand."

Bruce stayed vague about the details of what he had planned and, despite John's best attempts at prying it out of him, he remained aloof, dancing a merry jig around all of John's questions and leaving his imagination to run wild with reveries of espionage and assassination. Whatever it was, it had Bruce excited, and that excitement was starting to spread, creeping over to John and pulling the corners of his mouth into a slight grin.

They finished their drinks and got up in near silence, having exhausted all of their necessary (or at least desired) dialogue. On their way out, John stopped by the hostess podium to slip her a hefty personal tip. Her bright eyes flashed as her trademark customer-service smile lit across her perfectly symmetrical face, almost knocking John down with its striking brilliance. Her lips pursed ever so slightly as a pink blush shown across her cheeks.

"Thanks, John," she said, biting the corner of her lip. "Have a good day."

"Sure thing, gorgeous," John replied with a dashing wink as he casually strolled out the door. "See ya later."

Chapter Four

"Did you know four is an unlucky number in Japan? It's the number of death," she said, popping out the 'd' sharply and letting her tongue unroll a slowly lilting 'th', "kinda like their thirteen."

"What a wonderfully useless piece of knowledge. What is it in reference to?"

"That's the number of times I… well, y'know…" she purred, nodding to the puddle in the centre of the bed.

Bella abruptly leaned across John's glistening torso and grabbed the smoking cigarette from his hand. She pursed her plump plink lips and pulled a long drag, coughing as she handed it back, her manicured fingers reflexively touching her chest just beneath the throat, the rest of her hand hovering lightly over her heaving breast.

"My God! That was amazing!" she said more to herself than to John, as she flopped back down and nestled up to him, wrapping her fat little thighs around his legs and resting her face on the side of his broad chest.

She looked up at him with her oversized, dark ebony eyes which (due to the shimmering magnification of a perpetual moistness, and to that intense darkness of her irises that seemed almost to blend together with the jet black of the pupils) had the same look of dolorous innocence as the Japanimation cartoons she was always watching. But why were her eyes perpetually moist, you might ask? Some people's eyes are just that way. As Bella looked up at John, stroking her fingers through the lightly curling tufts of rugged manly body hair spread across his gleaming torso and running her lacquered French tips along the furrows and grooves of his musculature, the soft glisten of light that danced on the pink-gloss of her lips started to tremble slightly.

"Oh, Su~mi~su~ san," she whispered, affirming that Japanime mental image in John's mind, "dai~suki~yo~." Immediately after saying it, she let out an involuntary little squeak and buried her ripening face somewhere between the tousled blankets and John's supine body.

With his arm wrapped around her soft, delicate curves, he gently pet her hair like a sweet house cat. His fingers traced the intricate overlapping pathways of each iron-curled strand as they ran from their umber roots, enlightening first to a bright tawny before drastically transforming into a brilliant, certified blonde, out to the well-produced, decidedly non-split ends.

"Mon chéri," he whispered.

She looked up at him once more.

"Mon petite belle," he said with a small kiss on the top of her head.

John brushed aside one of the honey curls that partially veiled her sweet face, tucking it behind her dulcet ear. Bella reached out and caressed his masculine jawline.

"Vous avez mon cœur, "John practically sang to her, "vous avez un gros cul et vous avez ma vraie âme."

He then kissed her deeply.

"I love when you speak French to me. Even if I don't

know what all of it means, it all just sounds so… beautiful, coming from your lips. Your sweet, sweet lips."

She kissed him again. Passionately.

"It seems you know a little French."

He tickled the soft down on the back of her neck.

She bubbled, "All I really know is 'Voo-lay-voo coo-shay ah-vick ~mwah."

"Et oui oui."

"Oh yeah, and 'wee-wee'. I know 'wee-wee'."

She burst into a miniature fit of effervescent giggling, then just as suddenly went silent.

"God, I've missed you," Bella cooed. "You know how lonely I get without you. I feel like I haven't heard from you in days. And then you just show up tonight out of the blue. And you were so… *mmmmm*… voracious!"

"I had a very invigorating night. In fact…"

John leaned over the side of the bed, reaching into the pocket of his black slacks, which had piled on the floor in an orgy together with Bella's lacy thong, his own boxer briefs, both of their shirts, and a solitary black dress shoe; the other shoe lay further off near the doorway, excluded from the fun, or simply indulging in voyeuristic pleasures.

"I've got something for you," he proclaimed as he sat back up, dangling a string of pearls with a hypnotists sway.

She gasped, "They're…" eyes wide, head shaking ever so slightly, "gorgeous!"

She practically squealed as John wrapped the pearls around her soft little neck, after which she draped herself over his lap, languidly staring up at him. The angle made the slight porcine upturn of her lightly freckled nose look drastically more pronounced than it actually was.

"Where…? Where did you…? They're not your wife's are they?"

John gave her his best dead-eyed stare. "I stole them."

"Wha… Oh, *O-kay!*" She rolled her eyes

"You don't believe me?"

"Of course not, don't be silly."

He silently pushed his mouth up towards his nose and raised an eyebrow, looking somewhere off-screen.

"You didn't really… did you?"

The way she implored him, reaching out for the truth with her enormous innocent doll eyes like a newborn kitten searching blindly for mother's milk, was practically irresistible to John. Sometimes, he could not help but tell her the absolute unbridled truth; sometimes he could not help but toy with her; sometimes those were one in the same. Whether he told her the truth or a lie, she always had an acute sense of whether or not she was meant to believe it. She accepted everything he said as law, but also always knew subconsciously how to separate and dismiss anything she needed to, anything she was not supposed to take seriously. It was because of this almost cleverly selective gullibility, or perhaps in spite of it (or a seemingly contradictory combination of the two) that John felt more comfortable, open, and honest with Bella than perhaps anyone else in his life, at least since his mother died.

John felt free to be himself (whatever that means), free to say what he wanted, and so he told her flatly, "I broke into someone's house tonight. It was exhilarating."

Her jaw dropped a noticeable degree.

"Shut. Up. No, you did not." Her mouth remained hung open.

"It was surprisingly simple to get in. All you had to do was lift the sliding glass door, maybe a half inch or so—that's all it took to slip the latch and slide in. It's a surreal experience, being in a stranger's house in the middle of the night. I'm certain you've experienced it once or twice in your youthful promiscuity."

She looked up at him with a defensively wounded glare but said nothing.

"That dissociation felt, being in the unfamiliar terrain of someone else's alien arrangements, it increases tenfold when coupled with the exhilaration of being in there secretly, without permission. So too does the painful frustration and anxiety of racking your leg on a wayward table corner. In fact, that is what nearly got us caught—that barking, no not of any dog, but of my poor defenceless shin."

He paused for half a second for dramatic effect.

"We were fairly certain there wasn't anyone home. But, as even absolute certainties aren't always absolutely certain, still we crept, quiet as killers, sneaking from room to room with the lights off. We grabbed anything and everything we could —jewellery, electronics, they even had a little cash squirrelled away in a drawer. We—"

"Wait, you keep saying we. Who are you doing this all with?"

"Oh just an old friend. No one you know."

"Is that who dropped you off? He was handsome—no, not nearly as handsome as you, you're the most handsomest."

"Anyways. He locked himself in the bathroom for a while, I'm assuming to raid the medicine cabinet, so I decided to have a little fun in the meantime. The idea just sort of popped into my head, like divine inspiration, and I had to run with it. The plan was beautifully simple—I would open up various cases of their movie collection and shuffle the discs all around. That's it. Do you understand where I'm going with this? Weeks, months later, when everything's all settled down, they go to watch a movie—it's in the wrong case. And then the chain reaction. They try to return the disc to its proper case, only to find a third mismatched movie title. Do they pursue the trail? Do they get to the bottom of things and restore the entire collection to its proper order, each movie safe in their own home? Or do they miss a few? And if so, how long until those mines, too, are finally uprooted, exploding back echoes of the event?"

Bella sat in astonished silence, shaking her head back and forth ever so slightly.

"So, I start making a beeline for the bookshelf of DVDs in the living room. However…"

Another (slightly longer) pause for dramatic effect.

"In my excitement, I failed to notice the coffee table, practically reaching out with a jagged corner to bludgeon the front of my leg. I end up running shin first right into its dormant trap. Though I tried to stifle it, that peerless fury, that seething rage peculiar to a stubbed toe, a hammered thumb, a barked shin—it boiled over and it forced its way out, even through my clenched teeth. It was in that moment that I became painfully aware that we were, in fact, not alone in this house."

Bella gasped.

"No—waking up from what I can only assume was a peaceful slumber, this woman wearing pearls and a cocktail dress suddenly rose with a start from the darkest corner of the most unassuming couch. Now, honestly, it was quite dark, but even then, I could tell she was about to scream or run or attack me."

"Oh my god, what did you do?"

"Naturally, I grabbed a pillow from the couch and I smothered her."

As John said this, he straddled Bella, pulling the pillow from beneath her, and recreated the act. He pressed the pillow firmly against her pretty little face and cackled hysterically. Bella shrieked and struggled, squirming her way out from under him.

"You asshole!" she yelled between gasps and giggles, thudding her tiny little fists against John's broad chest flirtatiously. "I thought you were serious! I can't believe I believed you!"

There was a hint of genuine anger in her tone, but it was completely undermined by her girlish laughter.

Now, I'd like to take a moment, just you and I, to discuss a few things, to fill you in a little bit about our Bella. Oh, do not worry about the two of them for now, we should allow them to do their thing in privacy. My, my, naughty reader—we do not need to know how John grabbed both of her little fists in his hands and pinned her down, remounting. We do not need to see Bella grinding her supple young body beneath his. The penetration, the secretions, the tactile and olfactory sensations —all of these details are better left between the two of them, behind the drawn curtain.

Bella Marie Schröeder was a small-town girl. She was a pageant queen at four or five, a little-miss-something-or-other, paraded around burlesque stages in garish dresses, buckled shoes, frilled socks, and Shirley Temple curls (a hairstyle she has kept to this day). She kept up with the beauty pageant circuit for a few years (or at least her mother kept her up with it) but quit after her first loss (she received honourable mention). She toyed around with the idea of re-entering in the young adults circuit when she turned thirteen, but ultimately decided against it; as she put it, "letting her reason overcome her misplaced nostalgia." The entire experience must have left quite the impression on the little girl; she did keep the trophy sashes, although she talked about it rather infrequently, almost as infrequently as she would speak of her family. Bella was head-over-heels, madly in love with John, yet even to him, rarely would she make as much as the slightest passing mention of them, and those mentions were never honourable.

Now, now—would you quit trying to peek? Ignore the sensuous sounds of their pleasure-making. Just as I, for the last hour and a half, have had to ignore the noises coming through this cheap motel room's curtain thin walls of some whore fucking her john—just a term, no relation. Anyways, as I was saying...

According to Bella, her family was white-trash; that peculiar breed of Americana that takes a particular pride in their trailers, guns, and lack of education. She got out, made sure to get out, as soon as she could, fleeing on the tab of scholarships and federal grants, and has not spoken to them since. Now, I doubt even her psychiatrist (not that she had one) would even know in full detail what happened, but this is what I was able to piece together of her mysterious familial past:

Her father was an absolute monster, a lecherous slime of a man. He was a card-carrying member of the southwestern chapter of the Ku-Klux-Klan, a fervent Nazi sympathizer, and had a nasty predilection for prepubescent girls. Now, you cannot really blame someone for preferring their own race, that is just a natural extension of self-confidence after all, but this was something deeper. I cannot help but imagine this man was filled with such loathing and hatred that it just oozed out of every pore, and so he relished any opportunity to direct that hatred onto someone, anyone really.

Like many men of his class, he believed, fervently believed, in the American dream and he soaked up the ultra-violent hyper-sexual media with almost as much gusto as he did his grain alcohol, all of which he used to fuel his depressive-aggressive debauchery. Alcoholics lack self-control. Take John for example, he could drink every single day if he wanted to, with little to no risk of ever becoming an alcoholic. Why? Because he has self-control. He is practised in restraint. Bella's father had none.

Her mother had long been beaten into submission. She had learned where and how to step so as not to invoke his wrath, and she had not learned the easy way. Even then, at times, it was unavoidable. When his focus shifted from her to the children, it must have been a relief that was too great for her to bear. She hid from reality, choosing instead to pretend nothing was wrong, turning a blind eye completely.

When she (Bella that is) was about four, five years old, he started coming into her curtained-off "room" of the trailer late at night after he had finished his bottle of cheap whiskey. Her brother, Sylvester, tried to protect her, to step between them, but that hulking brute would beat him mercilessly—he would break his toes with the heel of his boot, put out cigars on the kid's back and chest, pull him out of bed in the middle of the night and throw him into a cold shower, lashing him with his belt until the water turned red. On top of that, the man would, from time to time, force the two children to strip and simulate sexual acts while he videotaped or took pictures, which he would use to subsidize his government-supplied income.

Yes, yes I agree, prudent Reader, that incessant (and downright excessive) grunting and moaning is becoming a little hard to ignore, especially at a time like this, when we are discussing such grave delicate matters. I apologize on behalf of both our John and Bella for such gross misconduct. Please, let us do our best to just keep ignoring them and hopefully our tale will finish by the time they do.

The two siblings were exceedingly close throughout adolescence (he is the only member of the family she would ever mention by name) but a rift began to form between them when they were twelve and thirteen, coincidentally around the onset of puberty. It may have been simply due to the burden of the crucible they had to endure together, a fracture caused by the unbearable weight of the shame they shared, or maybe there was some incident; maybe something darker, something far sleazier, occurred between the two of them. Either way, the rift proved irreparable. Sylvester would not get so much as a phone call on the holidays.

College gave her the ability, and the means, to get out of that hell-hole. Out of the frying pan and into the fire, as they say. No, actually, that is not quite right; out of the frying pan and into the freezer, more like. College was cold for her to say the least. What she wanted, more than anything, was to fit in, to be popular even, but she could not afford to join a sorority and, though cute, she was too awkward and shy to make frie-nds on her own. She also drew quite an unlucky card with her dorm mate, who passionately hated her for no apparent reason. Plus, at the end of the day, she always felt like a nerdy little girl from a trailer trash town. Most nights (if she was not studying) she would get all dressed up, spending forever on her hair and makeup, and use her fake ID to sit alone at one of the nearby nightclubs. That is where John happened to meet her.

She was definitely not fat (though she thought she was)

but she was certainly curvy—a figure she worked hard to maintain. Her blonde ringlets, bright cheeks, and diminutive stature belied a childlike innocence. She had the faith of an optimist. She happily accepted drinks from a stranger. She readily believed in everything—ghosts and the afterlife, Astrology, angels and aliens, fortune telling, crystals and chakras, love, Atlantis and Agartha. She believed that all religions were really one. She probably believed in Nessie and Bigfoot. Maybe even in unicorns. What was she majoring in? Something practical like Medicine or Law? No, she went with Asian Religious Studies, with a minor in Japanese Language (although she would never speak it in public, for good reason). Her eyes were an abyss in which one could not gaze too long. She had a tendency to laugh when she was nervous. Her legs would often cross and uncross sensually. She also had an apparent interest in enigmatic John Smith, and did not think twice about taking him back to her dorm, though she giggled and snorted quite a bit along the way. She opened up to him almost immediately, revealing herself fully, or as fully as she was capable of.

Her, for lack of a better term, absolute cunt of a dorm mate threatened to get Bella expelled, amongst other more violent threats, any time she would bring John over. Jealousy can make you act irrationally. One time she even took pictures of them mid-coitus, pictures which had to be forcibly deleted from her camera. Eventually, John decided to save Bella from her wretched environment, and rented a studio apartment for her near campus—a little love nest for the two of them. This is, in fact, the same studio apartment which lies behind the curtain we have placed.

By the way, the sounds of their intense love-making seem to have gone quiet, perhaps we should check in on them?

Well, well, well, modest Reader, allow me. I shall take the first peek, we wouldn't want to disturb their climactic finale after all.

It would appear the coast is clear. They are, once again, in post-sex repose. See for yourself.

"Sumisu," Bella gasps, inhaling deeply and letting out a long sigh. "Su~mi~su."

"Alright, I'll bite. What is this sumisu?"

"Why, it's you, Sumisu-san!" she giggles, "Mr. Smith." She rubs her cheek against his and gives him a quick peck. "Do you know how many John Smiths there are in the phone book?"

"Bella, I thought we talked about this. Why are you looking me up in the phone book?"

"Somethin' around two hundred."

"Bella, my pet, we discussed this."

"Sometimes I just want to talk to you so badly. I just get scared, y'know? Like, what if your name isn't really John Smith? Or, or, what if you're not really married? Or like what if you don't really love me? Like, what if everything I know is just a lie?"

"Look me in the eyes, Bella dear. This is the truth. This feeling. This absolute, undeniable connection between us. Don't ever let yourself doubt this."

She practically melts.

"But… when are you gonna divorce her?"

"When the time is right little birdie. But I told you, if she finds out about us she will make sure to take everything, and then I certainly wouldn't be able to pay for your apartment. No, I'd lose it all."

"You would still have me"

"Listen my love, I am sorry. Perhaps I have neglected you. It quite pains me, to be honest. I promise though, one day it will be just you and I, Bella dear, and nothing will stand in our way. For now, I will do my best to see you as often as I can, and I will certainly miss you dearly until the next time I do so."

"Wait, you're not gonna stay?" Her eyes moisten an extra degree.

"I wish more than anything that I could."

"Sometimes I wish she would just die."

"Now now, Belle-chéri, those are quite the incriminating words. I would be careful of saying things like that—if I didn't know any better, I would say you were implying murder."

"Well… No, no, I just… I don't know, I mean… Sometimes… Sometimes I just feel so… horrible. Y'know?"

As John buttons his black dress shirt, Bella gives him a look slightly like an air mattress in the morning.

"I do know what you mean, little birdie, I really do. I just feel terrible, leaving you like this."

Now he is slipping on his slacks.

"One day, it'll just be me and you, I promise. One day. Until then, may the distance grow our hearts fonder. We must be sure to love each other all the more next we are together. It's like they say, 'What's bad is good.'"

Now he is searching for his missing socks.

"Who says that?" Bella asks, her face half buried in the comforting embrace of her pillow.

Now he is stooped over, pulling the socks from their hiding spot under the bed.

"Well it sounds downright Slavic if you ask me, but no, that was actually from the French."

"Well, it's… stupid!"

Now he is tying his shoes.

"Yeah, I suppose it is, isn't it? Perhaps it's better in the reverse? No, that's still not quite right… Oh well, either way. You get the gist, I'm sure."

Now he is fully dressed.

"Do you really have to go?"

Her hands grasp his shirt sleeves, her naked breasts heaving unevenly beneath the pearl necklace, just barely holding back sobs of dismay.

He embraces her in his strong, protecting arms, one hand firmly at her waist, the other softly at her cheek.

Before kissing her and leaving, he pulls her close, staring deeply, directly into her dark glassy eyes.

Bella's eyes truly were the window to her soul (for lack of a better term). Her soul, her eyes, always reminded John of a still pond in the night. First and foremost was his own reflection shining back at him. That reflection was distorted slightly by the physical curvature of her eye: the front line of his naturally thick salt-and-pepper hair seemed to recede just a little; his regal, Romanesque nose (which happened to point at the apex of the curve) was made to look disproportionately large; his masculine jawline had the illusion of becoming a bit slighter, with the hint of a soft double-chin beneath it. The soulful reflection she saw in her mind's eye, however, was a peerless refinement, a portrait of unmatched perfection. Even in that reflection, however, there was the occasional ripple running through as something bubbled up from the depths. Those dark depths are what interested John most, what drew him further in. Beneath the illusive reflections on the surface, something deeper lurked, like some cosmic truth revealed in a dream that you do not consciously know, yet somehow know that you know or knew at one time. John longed to get to the bottom of it, to conquer the unknown, but overwhelmed by those infinite depths of possibility, he would instead resign himself to gazing at his distorted reflection, peering into his own steel-grey eyes through hers.

"Bella, my dear. I will miss you."

Then, as promised, he kisses her and leaves.

"Farewell."

Chapter Five

Where do I go from here?

It would seem our trajectory has once again fallen off course; the trail is running dry, the leads more sparse. Part of me wishes I could just start over and begin anew. Some things cannot be undone. For now, we must run with it; even if we are not sure if we are the ones being chased, or if we are the ones chasing, we cannot stop running now. No, not with this momentum. After re-reading everything I have written so far (yes, I admit, I had to refresh my memory, as I have not had a chance to continue with our narrative over these last few extremely busy days running around chasing my own tail, and as such have had to sacrifice intellectual momentum for physical momentum) I now am left with a bit of a conundrum—a question of tastes, of style. Do I, in keeping with a scrupulous loyalty to Truth, remain with our hero, following him as he leaves Bella's apartment? Do we stay with him as he calls a cab and rides back to the banalities of home-life—small talk with his wife, eating, drinking, urinating, defecating, masturbating (perhaps), pacing around the house (definitely), or a million other trivial mundane actions that occur periodically in life, but are almost never included in the stories told about that life? Do we detail each night he went out and partied with Bruce, even if nothing eventful occurred? Or do I take the artistic shortcut—jump ahead to the next point of action? At this moment, I am more inclined toward shortcuts. Had you been to eight different motels in half as many days and seen the same car at every single one, you might just feel the same way.

Let's just dig right into the meat of things, shall we?

****

Bruce slid the slender pick into the keyhole, keeping tension on the lock with the other hand. It almost groaned, seemingly disgruntled by the unknown intruder poking around, but Bruce fought to win it over, nimbly manoeuvring the pick up and down, in and out, trying to coax the lock into turning over. It was dark, and this ornery lock was proving a defiantly clumsy dance partner in this illicit Hokey-Pokey, yet Bruce's hands moved with expert precision, manipulating his tools with deft little twitches of the finger.

"Yeah," he said without turning his head, "a lock doesn't really provide security. Anyone can get through a lock if they want to; it just provides the illusion of security. Y'know what I mean?"

John knew precisely what he meant.

Suddenly, Bruce yanked out the pick and twisted the doorknob. Still locked. Bruce shook his head and sighed, "This one's got some well hidden secrets. Sometimes you barely gotta dig. Sometimes you gotta dig deep." He unzipped his leather case and swapped out his pick for some sawtooth looking deal. "That's the thing about locks though, there's always some sort of semblance of truth, some answer hidden away somewhere in there, all you gotta do is find it, y'know?"

At this point, he began to rapidly thrust the keyhole with this new saw-pick. Some of the grace and finesse of his previous technique had deteriorated, but the confidence of his vain sawing was embolstering. Why was it vain? Well, I guess it in itself was not vain actually, more like 'in vain' in fact; the lock still refused to budge.

Bruce sighed again, deeper this time. He shrugged his shoulders as his head shook back and forth. "Fuck it."

He walked off to the van, muttering something to himself incoherently about the secret inner mechanisms of locks. When he came back, he had a can of aerosol dust-remover (any generic non-specific brand). Bruce pushed the sleeves of his black hoodie up above his elbows and inverted the can. He slipped the plastic straw into the lock and sprayed. A glaze of hoary frost instantly spread to the surface of the lock. Now, at this point, Bruce shoved what looked like some sort of equine dental tool or a leatherer's botkin into the frosted keyhole and smashed it in with the butt of his palm. There was an intensely satisfying pop as the handle finally turned and the door swung open for the two of them, a choir of angels singing harmonious exaltations.

They slipped in, two shadows in the night. Completely silent, they bypassed everything in the cluttered utility room and crept closer to the heart of the beast. They swept through the kitchen, the living room, the hallways. They peeked into the bedrooms—turning doorknobs with the silent focus of safe-crackers. No one was home. The two men glanced over at one another from across the hall, and broke into mirthful laughter for a moment. Almost in perfect synchronicity, they both wiped the corner of their eye with the ridge of their index finger and sighed a contented sigh, in near harmony.

Bruce broke away first, moving with a definite efficiency. He slid right into the bedroom he had just peeked into, which happened to be the master bedroom, and in one fell swoop, tossed the black pillows and the comforter from the bed; they were, in actuality, a matching dark, olive green, but in the lighting (or lack thereof) would have surely appeared more black, especially once they were all piled in a crumpled heap on the floor. He then grabbed the conveniently displayed jewellery box from its perch on the bedside table and spilled its possessions out onto the mauve bedsheet.

His attention then turned to the unsuspecting dresser resting against the wall. He disrupted its sleep for a rough cavity search. Like a petty criminal, the goods were found in its socks and underwear and it was left to watch in shame, vacuous and exposed, with its drawers either partially or completely removed, while Bruce tossed a wad of cash and a couple expensive looking watches on top of the pile of jewellery.

After that, he went to the closet. He pulled out a few high-end dresses and held them up to his black-clad body, making little kissy faces at the mirror before flinging them onto the bed. A tailored suit came out after to join the amorous pile. From the top shelf, he pulled out a small metal lock-box without even trying to open it, he pressed it down onto the rest of the loot. Then, he did a quick 360, dropped down to check under the bed and, finding nothing else of interest, bundled up the corners of the bed sheet, flung it over his shoulder like a satchel, and headed out into the living room.

This household was evidently very leisure-oriented, as seen by the fully stocked entertainment centre. As Bruce spread his picnic blanket out onto the floor, his mind had already begun to calculate which devices to take based on their relative trade-value and the amount of weight and bulk still able to fit within the bed sheet. He settled on a video game console and a tube-amp stereo, adding them to the imminent feast. He left the turntable, the VCR-DVD-combo player, and the flat-screen; the last of which was to be slated for the second voyage. Bruce wrapped the entire haul up, hefted it onto his back, and headed out to the van, chuckling to himself the entire way like a jolly Saint Nick.

John was on a slightly different mission. Primarily, he sought out secrets.

Now, secrets come in many forms. Some are certainly darker than others, but every one of us, every single person, has a hidden secret or two; perhaps it is human instinct to hide things, some remnant from our lizard brains that keeps us in fear of being seen. We hide the things we are ashamed of, almost like a cat covering its faeces in sand. We hide the parts of ourselves that we do not like or do not find beneficial. We hide the things we hate, certainly, but we also hide the things we love, the memento mori of time long lost or, in some cases, the cherished hopes of days yet to come. These are all the sort of treasures that are undoubtedly another man's trash: photos of departed family members, punched ticket stubs, flattened coins, latex and whips, medications, heirlooms and hairpieces, diaries and journals. These things were insights into people's lives, and John enjoyed trying to see them as their owners did. That is, he tried to see the conjured images, to sense the memories that stirred within. He sought to make these ordinary objects glow with the personal sentiment of someone else's nostalgia, and so he would sniff out clues, for without insight and perspective, none of these objects would be anything more than lumps of vibrating molecules.

In this particular room, there were a few clues to the identity of its lodger, besides the obvious pink and plush scattered all around. The first clue John found was a diary, which may seem like the jackpot when forming a biography, but which actually tends to reveal surprisingly less about a person than you might expect. She (at this point it has been assumed they are a she) wrote in feminine curves largely about concerns with academics—nerves with tests and choir recital. Now and then, she disparaged one of the crude and immature boys at school and then fantasized about being swept away by some knight in shining armour. From the little he read, John could deduce that 1.) She most certainly had daddy issues, and 2.) She was probably unattractive. The second deduction was corroborated by the next clue that his investigation uncovered —a school ID lying on a small white vanity desk. A chubby-cheeked brown girl with myopic eyes wearing braided hair and comically large glasses stared up at John flatly from the surface of the desk.

"Poor girl," thought John, as he tossed aside the card.

Her name was, probably still is, Sylvia Bojorquez. She went to some unmemorable K-12 that for all we know has closed down by now. The card did not mention the grade she was in when it passed along the other information, but the picture looked to John to be of a girl of about thirteen or fourteen or so; had the full body been portrayed he may have felt a little more confident in the accuracy of his estimations, or not. By all reports, she was a normal middle-class little girl.

Her treasures suggested that, like most of her class and age, she bore a fond nostalgia for the past and a hopeful, if not naïve, expectancy for the future. In the back of one of the vanity's drawers, a small decorative box was housed, which had been tasked with guarding a ticket for a school dance, a strip of photos from an eponymous booth, an incredibly smooth river rock, a blue ribbon for some unspecified event, an enamel pin from a theme park, a cherry stem tied in a knot, a wren feather, and a diamond encrusted brooch of the sort generally passed down from a dying grandmother to her only granddaughter. Under her pastel-pink sheeted mattress, there was hidden a stash of cash—about two-hundred dollars, wh-ich, I might add, is quite a hefty sum for an innocent schoolgirl in junior high. Perhaps it was an emergency escape fund, if ever her white knight should come a'riding, perhaps not. Ironically enough, her piggy bank (plump as it was) only held a few pieces of foreign currency (some colourful bills, a couple pesos, a one and a two dollar Canadian coin). It did, however, make an extremely satisfying spray of ceramic shards as it exploded against the wall.

John's secondary goal was a similar shattering, but one of a much more metaphysical nature. The shattering of reality, felt the moment you walk into your house and realize that someone has broken in and stolen your belongings—before that actually, before you are able to process or think of things like property or privacy—that initial split-second haywire before you are able to really make any sense of anything, that primal overload that occurs when suddenly and unexpectedly confronted by the complete loss of a security you had thought you had, a security you have unconsciously based your entire reality around. You are not even sure where you are. That instantaneous feeling, that short-circuit loss of reality, is what intrigued John about the entire affair most of all, in fact. He hoped that enough fractures could build up over time and eventually shatter their invisible prison. All that was needed was to engineer situations in which that same feeling would be relived—aftershocks, as it were, reoccurring organically as they continue on with their lives. Eventually, one would hope, these tremors may shake them awake, now content in their slumber to do nothing but sit and watch shadows on the wall. Of course, those feelings of defilement (the uncertainty of safety, the frustration at fate, that loss of privacy and possession, the anger and sadness and fear, the shame of being compromised, akin to having your naked flesh exposed to a stranger) would inevitably come rushing back as well—an unfortunate but necessary tax on far greater riches.

He pocketed all the treasures from the wooden box and placed it back in the vanity drawer exactly as it had been. On top of the desk, he noticed several small vials of nail polish lined up against the mirror. He pulled aside two of them—a bright blue and a bright red. He unscrewed the top of Blue and pulled the brush out, the glossy coating of polish glistening with its rich pure blueness. Then, with the brush of Blue gripped between thumb and index, the bottle of Red gripped between index and middle, John opened up Red with his other hand, the glistening redness on this brush equally pure.

"Hey Red, have you met Blue? Well, allow me to introduce you. Blue, meet Red. Red, Blue."

With ambidextrous precision, John simultaneously plunged the brush of each respective colour into the bottle of the other, which immediately engulfed the brush with its own vibrant colour and became, once the lids had been screwed back on and the bottles returned to their proper places, completely indistinguishable from the untampered vials they had once been in the past, only now they held the hidden truth that each of these opposing colours secretly contained the essence of the other. Some designer will probably make millions off the same idea.

He then grabbed the foreign currency and exchanged it for the cash hidden under the bed, stuffing it into his inner jacket pocket. Before letting the mattress down, he tossed the girl's diary under there as well, just so she would know that someone had read it. He thought about taking a piss in the corner but quickly decided that it would be far too vulgar and moved on to the next room.

As he walked to the door at the end of the hall, he could hear Bruce rummaging around in the living room. He took a moment to admire his diligence before opening the door. This next room housed a small office. The office was rather ordinary—a hardwood desk with computer on top; some file cabinets, locked; Little messes of papers and coloured pencils piled here and there, which gave the impression that it was a family workspace, or a least used by little Sylvia to work on homework from time to time. Usually it is the most ordinary things that house the greatest treasures. This time, that was not the case. After searching the shelves and drawers, and the tiny closet, even after finding the key to the twin file cabinets, John found nothing of substantial value, nothing of real sentimental value even. He did, however, learn a bit more about the Bojorquez family.

The man of the house was Jorge Bojorquez. His wife was Maria (interesting coincidence) and his daughter, as we already know, was Sylvia. According to his check stubs, he was employed by a local missile manufacturing company contracted by the government (which, for legal reasons, I am unable to disclose the name of) and pulled in about thirteen-hundred a week, though he regularly worked fifty-hour weeks. According to the calender, the family was on vacation. Where to, it did not say, but from a picture on the desk of a moustachioed man waterskiing whom John assumed was Jorge, the deduction could be made that it was somewhere with a lake, or ocean access. Interestingly enough, the speedboat said 'Gonzalez'—not 'Bojorquez'. This vacation was most probably in celebration of Maria's 40th birthday, which had just occurred the previous Wednesday—information gathered from the same source.

Other than that, there was not much else of interest; the computer probably held a few secrets, to be sure, but John wanted more tangible evidence than that, so he chose to leave his hacking skills untested. He took a few documents from the file cabinets at random, in the hopes that one or two of them would become important at some time. He then grabbed some of the coloured pencils that were within his immediate reach—seven in fact, a perfect rainbow—and started smacking them against the surface of the desk, making sure not to damage the outside, but to fracture the pencil's pigmented cores so that as they were sharpened further and further down, the tip would constantly keep breaking and falling out—like a gilded rose that has long since withered away, yet still appears just the same, until the outer facade is finally scraped away enough to reveal to the intelligent observer that, within the hollow rose-shaped husk of gold, there is nothing; there is no rose, at least, not any longer. There is, perhaps, the detritus of a former rose, the dust and debris of a memory, but nothing more. No, that golden rose-shaped imposter is no more a rose than words are thoughts or the picture of a loved one the real thing. John set the pencils back, hoping that with each shaving of cedar, so too would their preconceived misconceptions begin to be shaved away as well.

As John looked around, giving the office a final once over, an idea popped into his head, an idea so diabolically precise, so artistically elegant, and so frighteningly simple, that he marvelled at the fact that he had not thought of it sooner. He had already considered destroying the computer, smashing it to bits, or bytes, but decided that would be too barbaric, the effects far too evanescent. Now, his new idea provided a much more sophisticated sabotage. The idea was this:

He would open up the side panel of the computer tower, locate the processor chip, slap a fridge magnet onto it, and seal the case back up, providing a slow lobotomy to the computer's brain.

Feeling like a low-key trickster god, he excitedly beelined straight for the refrigerator and immediately found the perfect magnet for the job. It was a picture frame magnet of Sylvia in her (probably first) school photo—all pigtailed and googly-eyed—with a border of cartoon wildflowers against a what-used-to-be-white background, practically begging for hire. The magnetism was just barely strong enough to hold onto the stalwart fridge, which ironically is what pulled John towards it all the more.

He imagined to himself the process of the computer's decay, the slow decline of its mental health. The magnet certainly would not be strong enough to destroy the machine immediately. No, it would take weeks, months maybe, before any real symptoms would appear. First, there would be a gradual slowing of its faculties, small, seemingly random hiccups in its general processes. Then the occasional system crash, and at first only during start-up. Eventually, the poor thing would not be able to tell a one from a zero and would be constantly haunted by the blue screen of death. Finally, it would stop booting up completely. At any point, will they think to open up the computer like amateur surgeons, or will they just assume it is a software issue? Perhaps someone in the family will be suspected of watching pornography. As the disease progresses, will they chuck the machine in the trash and buy a newer model? Or, will they take it in for professional repair? And if they do take it in, what will the repairman think of the magnet stuck to the motherboard? And will the Bojorquez's make the connection that this small magnet that most likely had not even been noticed missing was placed there by the same person who had broken into their house while they were out on vacation? Or, god forbid, had he come back another time to do it? Maybe come back many times more?

These thoughts endlessly excited John as he hurried back towards the office. When he reached the hallway, however, he noticed that the entertainment centre had already been almost completely looted and there was neither sight nor sound of Bruce anywhere to be found. John's stomach lurched involuntarily when he realized this. "Perhaps," John thought, "Bruce has finally shown his true colours, turning tail and fleeing, stabbing me in the back and leaving me to take the heat while he makes off with the loot."

"That rat bastard!" John spat, punching a hole in the drywall with his black-gloved fist.

Luckily for John, Bruce did not hear this outburst as he came walking in through the doorway mere moments later.

"So yeah, I'd say we got a pretty good haul tonight. I just loaded a buncha good stuff into the van... what happened here?" Bruce pointed to the freshly wounded wall.

"Oh, nothing."

"Anyway, will you give me a hand carryin' out the TV?" Bruce nodded to the oversized flat screen sitting in the living room.

"Sure, I'll be right there, just give me a few seconds."

John walked down the hall and back into the office while Bruce headed for the living room to detach any cables still clinging to the television. After about thirteen-and-a-half seconds, the TV was unbound and John came sauntering into the room. As they carried the large TV to the van, which was waiting for them around the corner where they had left it, John told Bruce about his efforts, detailing the information he had gathered and explaining to him the artistic brilliance of his subtle subterfuge. Bruce was captivated by this explanation. So much so, in fact, that he agreed to, actually insisted on, going back in for some "last final touches".

The first of those final touches was a trick that had magically popped into John's head as he had been taking the magnet from the refrigerator, something that he remembered hearing about somewhere and which had occurred to him with a scintillating flash when his eyes swept across the wooden slats of the pantry door; now was his opportunity to materialize that concept. John pulled out various boxes of snacks (cookies, crackers, breakfast cereals, etc.) and started swapping around the different bags inside. Bruce loved it. He laughed a deep rich laugh as he thought about these people sitting down for a bowl of cereal and getting the wrong kind, or reaching for a chocolate chip cookie and pulling out a chicken-flavoured cracker. How many times would something like this have to occur before they grew distrustful of the entire pantry? How long until they checked every box, or chucked them all out?

Bruce had never thought to do anything like this. He had broken into people's houses before, stolen stuff, sure, but he had to admit, having a partner, particularly a partner like John, was a completely different story. He sincerely wanted to continue the lofty efforts of this family's mental emancipation, but his ideas tended to the base—mostly involving simple destruction in some capacity (bending silverware, breaking dishes, clogging drains); he was most likely influenced by the angry hole John had made in the wall, misinterpreting its meaning entirely. He did, however, have one idea that John found particularly interesting—he proposed they rearrange the furniture, or more specifically the furniture in the living room, which being directly in view of the front door, would in theory amplify that initial disorientation they were sure to feel, walking into their home which not only had been burglarized, but was also in a completely foreign arrangement. The effect would certainly be overwhelming.

No sooner had they lifted the couch and started walking it towards the opposite wall, however, did the two of them stop, suddenly and abruptly. They looked at each other, then the door, then back to each other, trying to affirm that the other had in fact heard the same thing. The sound they thought they had heard was that of a key sliding into a lock and the turning of a deadbolt. Turns out they were right, but the two of them did not plan to stick around long enough to find that out. They dropped the couch and bolted, sliding out the back as a volley of cries and curses fired off behind them.

Just who was this person barging in like they owned the place? According to the calender, the entire family was on vacation for another three days. They had no pets, not even fish, not even a house plant. Why was this random person strolling into this house in the middle of the night? And why did they have the key? For what purpose? These things will forever remain a mystery. Whoever they were, they were certainly upset and certainly called the cops.

If you have ever been pulled over, then you know that suffocating claustrophobic sensation when, reflected in the rear-view mirror, red-and-blue flashes completely fill the vehicle. Those horrible sirens certainly do nothing to help the disorientation. John and Bruce had the unfortunate privilege of experiencing that sensation while hopped up on adrenaline and hauling stolen cargo, amplifying it all for them exponentially. Bruce started to slowly pull off to the side.

"What are you doing? We can't just turn ourselves in!"

"Yeah, well, y'know, maybe we can talk our way out of it?"

John seemed annoyed, visibly so, at both the submissive obeisance of Bruce's decision to pull over and the obvious lack of confidence he displayed in doing so.

"We are dressed, both of us, head to toe in black. We have a goddamned movie theatre screen in the back! Along with every other missing item from that house by now reported stolen. Tell me, just what the hell do you plan to say!?!"

"Well, we sure as hell can't just gun it. We run, they're gonna chase."

"And if we stop they're going to catch us! You need to go, now!"

As the two of them continued to argue in this manner, Bruce still slowly pulling into the bike lane, John vehemently trying to coerce him to stop (or stop stopping, I should say), the wailing sirens and blaring lights grew nearer and nearer, the tension higher and higher. Finally, like out of some perversely banal comedy, the squad car sped by, blazing past them towards the horizon.

Perhaps Bruce's extemporaneous plan to "flip a 'U'" and head back towards the crime scene wasn't quite as stupid as it had first seemed. Perhaps it made no difference. Either way, that police officer was headed the same direction as them, which meant that soon he would arrive at the Bojorquez residence, and soon he would be on the lookout of two men dressed in all black driving a white van. If there were any actual eye-witnesses (which I was unable to uncover during my investigations) they certainly would not have been able to provide any other information than that; the very possibility of just that info being leaked, however, was enough to ensure that the two of them needed to get off the road and get rid of their cargo as quickly as they possibly could. Luckily, they both understood this and Bruce started heading directly for a guy he knew, someone who bought and sold stolen goods and had a structure they could use to hide the van until the heat had died a little—I believe the term is "fence".

Well, now that we know where they are headed, we can catch up with them later; right now, while we have a moment, I would like to fill you in a little on John and Bruce's past.

They met in high school. Bruce was a couple years older than John, but John made varsity football Freshman year, so the two were able to get to know each other through the bonding experience of team sports. This camaraderie eventually grew to a friendship that existed outside of practice hours, until the two were practically inseparable—John, the hotshot quarterback and Bruce, his reliable wide receiver. Bruce also held the record for most sacks. In fact, both of them had been scouted by multiple colleges. That is, until John blew out his knee during the State Championship—master of the trick play, he ended up running the ball straight through the scrimmage, sprinted sixty yards, and finally was tackled by the defensive linebacker just barely into the end-zone, scoring the winning touchdown and tearing both his ACL and meniscus in the process. Shortly after that, Bruce was kicked off the team when they found a bottle of prescription painkillers in his locker that were not prescribed to him and he was forced to submit to a urine screening.

The death of their football careers did not kill their friendship along with it, however. Truth be told, without the obligation of practice, the two had more time to hang out than ever before. They filled their idle time as many other kids their age did, with rash attempts at living life to the fullest, without really knowing what that meant—skipping class, smoking cigarettes, parties, sex and alcohol, defacement of government property, tasting oblivion and reaching for omniscience (or vice versa). But, all good things come to an end. As do all bad things. So, more accurately, all things come to an end; John and Bruce's friendship was no exception. Fate had many devices which she used to pull them apart—time, distance, impracticality, the most memorable being Jessica Finlay.

Jessica Finlay was the head cheerleader—smokin' hot with perky breasts and the tight supple body of a gymnast. She had long hair of aureate fleece and eyes of winter ice. To say the least, she was a gorgeous, well-developed young woman with sizeable intellect, a caring heart, and limitless potential. She was also Bruce's long-term girlfriend.

Once, after a night of partying, an overly inebriated Bruce had to be carried home by John and Jessica, one arm around each of them, stumbling and mumbling the entire way. When they finally got him into bed, which was no more than a twin-sized mattress on the floor, he passed out immediately. The other two, also fairly intoxicated, sat down on the floor beside him and talked, getting to know each other better. This was not the first time they had been alone—that is if this time counted as being alone—but it was the first time they were able to really get to know each other on a deeper level, to bare themselves a little. They both found the conversation naturally stimulating. Jessica bit her lip ever so slightly and tucked her golden-blonde hair behind her ear. John lightly touched her thigh with one hand, reaching with the other for the soft curve of her cheek. Jessica closed her eyes and tilted her head back as John kissed her full, loosely parted lips. When he pulled her towards him, she mounted him swiftly, the two still making out hard every beat of the way, now stripping off each other's clothes. When she climaxed, dangerously loud, she was lying on her back with her arms behind her head, her hands grasping tightly onto Bruce's unconscious hand. Perhaps it was done out of simple depravity, perhaps, in her confused child-like way, it was an honest show of true affection for Bruce; afterwards she cried. But that did not stop her from coming back for more.

Bruce started to grow suspicious. Eventually, he confronted John. He confided in him his suspicions of infidelity. He said that Jessica had been distant, evasive even, at cheer practice more and more, said he had no proof, just a gut feeling that was tearing him apart. John told him it was probably best not to overreact or confront her until he knew for certain. After school, when John told Jessica about this interaction, she was obviously racked with guilt. She immediately told John that they should stop seeing each other completely, that it just wasn't right, not to Bruce, not to themselves. If confronted by Bruce, she would have cracked; that fact was obvious to John. So, the next day, during his first period class, John casually mentioned to one of his fellow classmates, who just so happened to have notoriously loose lips, that he suspected Jessica was cheating on Bruce with Marcus Brown (one of the Negro boys on the football team).

The speed with which rumours light up in a high school is astounding, and this particular such rumour blazed particularly intensely. By the end of the day it had completely exploded across the entire campus. It turned out to be a case in which a lie is, in fact, not a lie. Apparently the two of them had, or had been having, sexual relations. Apparently someone had actually caught them in the act and was sworn to secrecy. Marcus' testimony was equivocal at best. Jessica refused to even testify. She did, however, transfer schools within the week, which pretty much confirmed it for the rest of the school.

Bruce was heartbroken, understandably so. He had just lost a girl that was several leagues out of his own and knew there was no replacing her without trading down. He had a lot of trouble getting over her, slowly growing more reclusive and self-destructive, his friendship with John more and more distant (John never found out for certain whether or not Jessica had told Bruce about them, but if you were to ask me, I think she probably did) eventually Bruce graduated and moved away to go to an automotive mechanics trade school, and the two of them just sort of drifted apart, lost touch.

That is pretty much the gist of their school-yard history. I highly doubt either one of them had so much as a passing thought of the other or of those childhood days forgotten through the years, and they certainly would never have thought they would see each other again. Yet, here they were, together again, brought back into each other's lives by the strange machinations of chance. Before we join up with them at the fence's house, I think it is about time for a break; it is late and my hand is tired—it is having a much harder time keeping up with my brain, and even that is running slower than normal.

Besides, John surely would have thought of this visit as a new chapter in his life. I say we honour this perception and let it be so.

Goodnight, dear Reader; I shall rise with you again in the morning.

Chapter Six

Good morning, loyal reader.

Now, before we get started on this next chapter, I would like to address the fact that you could have, and very well may have for that matter, kept reading through from the last chapter on, not having to pause like myself for a night's rest. It might not be morning for you. The reason I bring this up is not to chastise you, my dear mistrustful reader. No, nothing of the sort. I simply wish to acknowledge the disparity between the here and now for me as I write this and the here and now for you as you read it. Two completely different worlds, really. By the time we have reached your here and now, where you can read these very words I write, I will be long gone from this current here and now I occupy, watching it fade away in the rear-view mirror along with the rest of this crumby little town. Actually, by then, this town will no longer be in the rear-view; by then, it will be nothing more than a distant memory, a short stop on a long journey that I will have certainly moved on from. As you trace these words in sidelong sweeps of the eye, messages from the past shining through like long-dead stars, who knows where I will be? Furthermore, by the time these words reach you, they will have been processed by a publisher, and while I may have sworn an oath to preserve the Truth, there is no guarantee that they hold such scruples. Do not worry, fretful reader, I do, of course, plan to negotiate that not a single letter be changed. But, publishers are notoriously dist-rustful, and all it takes is one daffy editor with an overzealous hand to completely pervert a piece of writing. Sometimes things just get rearranged or lost with the shuffle. Oftentimes, it is not even an intentional crime. In searching out typos, perhaps a white rook on the ground gets changed to an ordinary white rock, or a brocade in the road into a blockade, or any other various mistranslations that occur when trimming typos or adjusting punctuation that could completely altar the meanings of certain homonyms (e.g., tire, slip, lie). As a little insurance against this, I intentionally placed a typo in the fourth chapter; clever readers should have no trouble finding it. If you cannot find it there, it does not necessarily mean you are not clever, but if it truly is not there, then that does mean you have proof, proof that those charlatans have altered the Truth in one way or another. To what degree, there is no way of yet knowing; we can only hope that the essence of it remains unchangeable. Best case scenario: the editor is a rarity amongst his breed and honours my wishes to respect the sanctity of Truth. Thus, my words appear to you pure and unedited; that little typo still is hidden there like a key to that truth, spared from the cold grasp of the editor's would-be grammatical genocide. Worst case: the publishing house is run like a looney bin and the editor tears madly through my work, leaving nothing but wreckage in his wake, turning deadlines into deadliness, and making swordplay of my wordplay and futility of all my utility—small adjustments here and there, rearrangements and subtle changes, flat-out falsifications. At that point, would it even be the same story? What would there possibly be to trust in? All I can say is that I will do my best not to let this scenario occur. I will do everything in my power to ensure these words do not fall into the hands of such nightmarish tyrants as would defile or otherwise pervert the purity of Truth; alas, anything beyond that I cannot promise. The rest is up to your interpretation.

I think I have digressed long enough; without any further ado, let us return to the story.

****

Last we left off; John and Bruce were headed to unload the stolen gear. We can assume they made it to their destination without any other notable occurrences. Right when they arrived, they quickly unloaded the van and hid it under a tarpaulin in a wooden shack-like garage just around the corner, aided by this mysterious fence Bruce was somehow acquainted with.

His name was Pepe. He was a relatively light-skinned Black man with a grill of silver teeth and a headfull of cliché dreadlocks. I say cliché only because of his vocation; he looked like a stereotypical drug dealer, which, it just so happens, he was. Turns out fencing was just a side gig; the real money is in drugs. Who knew? It was through this primary line of work that Bruce had first met him a few years back. Since then, he had made himself a repeat customer. In fact, after Pepe had finished appraising the goods and the three had settled on a price they could all agree on, Bruce opted to take his half of the payment in heroin, something which John had never seen in person before.

"Why does it look like that?" John queried to the open-air of the kitchen.

What it looked like were little cakes of hardened tar. Umber amber. Obsidian sludge pressed into flat bricks. Dark, but not fully opaque and certainly not translucent. It looked as if somebody had drained the inky sap of some black heart, mixing it with soot and shoe polish, boiling it all down, and then forced it with geothermal heat and pressure and possibly some dark, black magic to coalesce and crystallize. If Mr. Daniels and Tartini were right, this stuff looked like what the devil would use to rosin up his bow, right before he plays us out. Quite a trilling finale, I am sure; violins and chaos all the way to the end.

"Whatcha mean?" Bruce took up the query, but almost immediately turned his attention back to the freezer bag Pepe had just tossed onto the round yellow kitchen table at which he had sat himself down. "So, umm, that's all you can do?" Bruce asked as he picked the bag up.

It was a gallon-sized zip seal bag, filled almost a third of the way with what looked like various chunks of midnight formica and petrified encephalopod discharge. At least a half ounce or so.

"Whatcha mean?" retorted Pepe. "You still owe me from the last front, remember?"

"Yeah, well, I mean, c'mon man... You know I'm good for it."

"Alright, tell you what. I'ma give you a extra eighth from my personal stash. Just cause I like you."

"Well... thanks. Anyway, you got a clean rig? I'm startin' to get sick."

"Yeah, I got you, cuz." Pepe pushed himself off of the counter he was leaning up against and turned around to open a drawer. "Here, take a pack."

He pulled out a box of insulin syringes and tossed a plastic-sealed ten-pack over to Bruce.

"Thanks."

Bruce grabbed the saltshaker and used to it crush one of the asphalt black chunks in the bag, breaking it up into smaller pieces that shot across the inside of the bag in a spray of splinters and dust.

"Is that really heroin?" John piped in.

"Yeah, well umm, you wanna try some?"

"No thanks. I wouldn't mind a cup of coffee, though," John said, turning to Pepe, or more accurately, looking past Pepe at the pot of coffee sitting on the coffee maker in the back of the kitchen.

"Help yourself," Pepe nodded towards the cabinet on John's left. "Cups in there."

You can tell a lot about someone by the mugs they own. Or at least a little. For instance, in this particular cupboard, there was a set of owl-shaped mugs, a slender wine glass, an oversized teacup with a charming floral print, and an under-sized one in pastel green with a matching tea plate beneath it. These pieces attested to a feminine presence in the household. There were also some baby bottles, the meaning of which sh-ould be simple to deduce. There was also a decorative beer stein with a little Dutch boy and a porcelain dam, which was a tougher case to crack, though I'm sure it had its own story—

this knave of cups reversed—from its genesis on through its current revelation. Then there were the random mugs crowding the shelves, each with no clear relation to the next one. Altogether, the story the cupboard told, what it all really, truly revealed, if anything at all, John was not able to completely ascertain at such a quick glance. He snatched up an inconsequential white mug with anthropomorphic cartoon animals on it and brushed it off. Just as he had started towards the coffee maker he was stopped by Pepe's intimidatingly deep voice.

"Ey, get me one too, well."

Without responding, John turned back and pulled another white mug from the cupboard, this one with the M.I.T. logo printed on it, probably meant to be ironic. As he walked to the back of the kitchen nook, he could not help but notice the relatively high quality of all the appliances and kitchen accessories with a surprised twinge of jealous admiration. He had suspected drug dealers to be of a lower breed that would not value such luxuries; a sort trapped in a poor return-investment cycle; a sort that is forced to feed off of others to support their own lifestyles and addictions; a sort not drastically different from your average workman of today; a misrepresented class for sure, but one that is not completely faultless in its own struggles. The outside of the house had not done much to persuade him otherwise. The interior, however, was almost enough to overcome that first impression. It was very well decorated, both homey and cozy, but at once modern and fresh—like a good jazz café. Sure, there was a lot of clutter, a lot of random stuff in piles here and there, but it was generally clean and well-kept clutter, the kind of clutter that would feel less like unnecessary junk and more like furniture or décor, or a room-mate that had showed up one day and made itself at home, like it was just meant to be there. Nobody seemed able to argue against it.

As John was pouring the coffee (the steam whispering a soft curling promise—that promise of the fresh taste of a recent percolation), Bruce was getting up from his chair at the table, the perfect piece of fractured black tar clutched in his palm, the bag of syringes pinched between his thumb and the hairy knuckle of his index finger. He nodded to Pepe and jerked his head over his shoulder.

"S'alright if I use your chair?"

"Yeah man, go for it."

Bruce turned and walked through the small living room to an open door, peeked his head in quickly, and then walked into the room and out of sight of the other two.

"Ahhh, Broosie! So goot to see yoo! Yoo look handsome as ever!"

This last sentence was punctuated by the loud smack of a kiss. Exactly where that kiss had landed, there was no way for the other two to know. Pepe, however, seemed unconcerned, so John decided to let the mystery go unsolved.

You and I, however, are unrestrained by the same spatial and temporal constraints John and Pepe are currently bound to. We could simply step to a different angle, find the proper vantage point in time and space, and see for ourselves. What do you say? No need to be shy, it's just a kiss.

If we were making bets, where do you think it was? Sensuously on the lips? Amicably on the cheek? Maybe a motherly press of the lips to his forehead? Or, perhaps we have it all backwards and it was a chivalrous kiss from him on the centre knuckles of her dainty hand? Or a passionate smooch on the intimate crevice of her neck? Just on sound alone it would have certainly been difficult to tell if it was the sound of one or of two pair of lips smacking. Pepe was annoyed, but overall was left surprisingly unperturbed by this little mystery.

But, enough about them, bets are closed. Let us find out for ourselves, shall we?

Just a few steps over this way and… there we go.

The entire room is now in view. We can see that chair Bruce was talking about (a large, puffy, blue suede recliner) next to a rather imposing armoire that seems to puff its chest out at you at any angle you look at it. On the other side of the chair, a queen-sized bed with silk linen and microfibre plush rests between its dark wooden bedside companions, a white wooden crib lying just beyond that. Across from the bed, a rather heavy-set entertainment centre sits shrugging a large television up on its shoulders like Atlas. The open door to the master bathroom is just within view. You can even make out the floor-to-ceiling mirror doors of the closet, which double the entire room, but reveal nothing in their reflection that was not included in the original, though perhaps from a slightly different angle. From this vantage point, we will be certain to catch it. Now, let's just turn back time a little…

There is a beautiful raven-haired woman in a crimson

negligee set with a matching robe. She is sitting on the side of the bed. There is a baby in her arms, and she is gently rocking it back and forth, cooing softly. Her lips, although only slightly pursed, are so full they look as if they are about to pop. As do her breasts, which (only partially obstructed by the baby) are threatening to spill from her gown. Now she is standing up. It is worth noting the incredible roundness of her figure—not of a singular globe, but of an entire solar system arranged just so, in perfect balance and counterbalance: Her round, Russian nose and cheeks hold above them, caught in their gravitational pull, the twin moons of her circular, smokey silvery eyes. The planetary orbs of her supple breast are almost perfectly matched in size and strength of attraction as the orbs attached to her wide, child-bearing hips, while her slender waist and thin limbs provide just the right amount of empty space. Altogether, it gives the impression when gazing upon her that you have become the sun, the very centre around which her celestial body revolves. More likely, it is her orbit you have been ensnared in. If she were a prostitute, she could tack on an extra zero without her john being any the wiser—it would certainly get lost amongst all the other circles and curves. The baby is asleep, spittle leaks from its tiny somnolent mouth. Perhaps we went too far back... is that sunlight coming in through the window?

Yes, we certainly overshot the mark on this one. Not to worry, we will simply fast-forward from here and we will be sure to catch the kiss. Sped up, she quickly stands and scurries like an ant in a sugar bowl over to the crib. Now she is bustling to and fro, tidying up some clothes here, dusting a bit there. Now she is looking at the contents of a small oriental box. Now she is skittering about again, from the TV over to the mirror for a moment, then back to the box on the bedside table, then over to the doorway. Now she is saying something, calling out through the doorway, but it is not discernible at this speed. Now Pepe scuttles into view. Now a touch of affection. A kiss—this one most definitely on the lips. Now he is gone and she is jitterbugging back to the bed. Let's see if we can't speed this up a bit more. She zips over to the crib, then back to the box on the night-stand. Now she is in the recliner. No, at this speed, precise details are too difficult to make out... maybe slightly slower. Best not chance missing the entire reason for this whole detour in the first place. Now she is holding a torch up to a spoon. Now throwing in a piece of cotton. Filling up the syrette. Tying a tourniquet. Now she is shooting up.

After a short while of nodding off in depressive elation, she crawls into bed, falling asleep before her head even hits her special-order designer pillow. All the while, the soap opera on the television screen flashes rapidly between tragic clichés and comedic commercials (or vice versa). She tosses and turns a bit, yet sleeps soundly nevertheless. Her tousled hair, usually parted precisely down the centre like Lyudmila, is now swept wildly over her face, her limbs spread out across the large bed, the orbicular curves of her sultry flesh draped over with an amount of silk not quite cut for the job. She snores softly. She drools slightly. Her child wakes up and cries until its chubby caramel cheeks turn amber. Pepe rushes in and scoops the crying child out of its crib. He disappears with her. He returns a while later, his daughter now sleeping in his arms, and drops her off in her crib. He tidies up the paraphernalia then disappears again. The sun is now beginning to set. The heroine of the soap opera has already fallen in and out of a coma; still this one slumbers. Now it is dark. The room is illuminated by the light from the television screen. Her long eyelashes are fluttering apart. She yawns and stretches; the universe expands slightly. Now a man's face appears at the doorway, peeking in. She tilts her head like a cocker spaniel as she surveys the greasy black curls, the hooked nose, the long cheeks. A smile of recognition spreads across her face as Bruce steps into the room.

"Ahh Broosie!" she yells with a start. "So goot to see yoo!" Now she is skipping over to him. "Yoo look handsome as ever!"

During this last sentence, they are embracing each other. No kiss yet, just a light friendly hug. Now she is grabbing the sides of his skull, her last sentence about to be punctuated. All bets are in, where will the kiss fall? She pulls his face close to hers. Moment of truth—smack dab on the mouth, she hits Bruce with the full force of her completely puckered, collagen-filled lips, knocking him back a step or two. How'd you do, reader? The blood from both his brain and body rushes to his face and to his loins, leaving him stupid and clumsy. They make small talk while Bruce stumbles over to the armchair to perform a similar ritual as she had earlier.

Now Bruce is flipping over the top of the chairs left arm, revealing a flat wooden lap table and a deep compartment. Now she is sitting on the other arm, twirling her finger around one of Bruce's curls. Now he is preparing a shot, already feeling much better. Back in the kitchen, John and Pepe are continuing on as if they had never heard the kiss in the first place. I suppose if it were meant to be secret, she would not have vocalized it so loudly. John came to the same conclusion, chalking it down in his mind as unimportant and moving on.

John was just turning around with the hot cups of coffee when he was stopped once again by Pepe's baritone voice.

"Pour me some cream too, well."

He was more than a little annoyed at what seemed to him like a passive power-play, but John was doing his best not to visibly show it. Again, he silently acquiesced. Locating the cream in the fridge was simple enough, but deciding how much "some cream" was, that proved more difficult. After a modicum of mental deliberation, John poured three, maybe four drops, having decided to match as closely as possible Pepe's dulce de leche milk chocolate skin tone.

"Sugar?" John asked drily, handing over the freshly creamed cup of coffee.

"Awe, thanks, but you can call me Pepe."

Pepe winked and chuckled, his silver teeth sparkling beneath the halogen lights. John did not laugh.

"Did you make that?" John nodded over to the bag of heroin on the table as he took a long pleasurable draught from his mug.

Pepe chuckled again, "Nah, nah, it ain't really work like that. This not no biker meth; ain't the sorta thing your average person can just do at home, dig? Not easily at least."

"So… what? You get it wholesale?

"Yeah, pretty much. The beans make it. They got the farms and labs and shit."

"But why does it look like that?"

"What, like tar?"

"Well, yeah exactly. I mean…" John cleared his throat, "Anytime I've seen it, you know, portrayed in the media, or otherwise, it has always been a tan, or whiteish powder. Nothing like this."

"Uh huh, uh huh, yeah man. Good eye." Pepe's head nodded rapidly then shook a few times back and forth. "They ain't talking about B.T.H. in the media. It sorta a Mexican speciality—not as refined but cheaper and faster to produce."

"Sounds about right," John thought, laughing to himself. Then John said, "It looks like it's made out of shoe polish or something."

Pepe shrugged his shoulders, both palms up, head tilted, the corners of his Charlie Parker lips pulled back, and his eyes opened wide—the universal "Je ne sais pas" pose. "Ain't unheard of."

"Wait, what?"

Pepe's silver teeth flashed. "This stuff, probably not. But some people'll cut this shit with just bout anything. Shoe polish, brown sugar, synthetics, antidepressants and anxiolytics— hell, I even met a guy who'd cut his shit with just a little dose of rat poison. Said it gave him the best high he ever had. Problem was he had to sell to keep his habit up. Ended up killing four high-school kids. Doing a whole heap of time now.

"Jesus."

"Nah, I think he pronounce it 'Hey-Zeus!'" Another quick silvery chuckle. "The best way just with a little lactose powder. Always does the trick." He snorted sharply and then cleared his throat. "Oh, check this shit out. I just got it."

Pepe reached into the back of one of the cabinets and pulled out a massive cannon of a handgun. All of the metal, from the trigger and frame to the triangular slide and barrel, was a gleaming polished chrome that matched almost perfectly in lustre with Pepe's shining metal teeth. Action film buffs would recognize it from nearly every movie made after 1985. I will not mention the exact make and model, solely because I refuse to provide free advertisements and endorsements (please contact the publisher if you wish to inquire about future product placement opportunities; I am sure their address is somewhere on the title page).

It was a very intimidating gun, more so when it was lifted and for a split second the cyclops barrel was staring directly in line with John's ripe skull. It was only a brief moment, a flash, before the gaze was averted and Pepe was popping the magazine out, but it was enough to send a shockwave of panic coursing down John's spine. Pepe racked the gun and caught the bullet that came flying out, winking at John and then handing the gun over to him.

"Check it," Pepe commanded.

John, at this point, was completely on edge. He did not trust this degenerate from the very start and now he felt threatened. Still he reluctantly took the gun. "Better to keep it out of his hands for the time being," he thought, "at least I can use this thing as a club, while his bullets are not doing him any good without a firing pin."

The beast was much heavier than John had expected; despite its exorbitant size, the heft was still surprising—at least three or four pounds, and that is without the magazine. John had to admit, the weapon did bestow a certain sense of empowerment, even in its neutered state. He held the barrel up to his line of sight, his finger hovering over the trigger, and looked through one eye, pointing the gun at various things around him: The fancy coffee maker; The chequered cookie jar on the fridge; The cuckoo clock on the wall, with its hands displaying a semaphore 'E'; The base of Pepe's skull, who had turned his back and was rummaging through the bag of heroin Bruce had left on the table.

At this point, John's nose involuntarily scrunched up as it became aware of an acrid smell. It would have been difficult to determine whether the effluvia was coming in from Bruce's boiling spoon in the bedroom or from the open bag sitting on the table, but John was able to intuitively pinpoint the source as heroin in general; even without ever having smelled the stuff, he knew that this was what it smelled like. It could not be anything else. It had the pervasiveness of burnt plastic, though less abrasive, almost subtle like lilacs, but certainly not floral; it was more reminiscent of a sickly-sweet brown sugar mixed with astringent vinegar, with undertones of bile—and not the kind used in perfumes. The stench came wafting to John's nostrils and puckered his face. His olfactory senses worked in tandem to produce a phantom taste that made him want to spit. He tried to wash it out with arabica, but to no avail. In fact, as he took a sip, he could not help but notice the similarity in the colour of his dark roast to that of the heroin sitting on the table, which infected the flavour with that stench, the steam of his coffee fighting in vain to cover it up, only worsening things in the process and causing John's stomach to churn.

He set the gun and the coffee mug on the counter next to him and, leaning against the wall, concentrated on calming his stomach. Pepe, having turned to grab a saucepan from a hook on the wall, noticed this look of disgust on John's face and averted his eyes, rubbing the back of his neck.

"Look, I like him and all. He a nice guy, but be real here, Bruce just ain't a safe bet." He scratched his nappy goatee. "Bruce he… well he just never satisfied, dig? He always want more, just a little more, like it gonna fill that hole where whatever he think he lacking supposed to be. We both know it not gonna. He even know it probably. Still, he always insisting on getting fronted more. Every time. Now, purely statistically, that bet gotta eventually fall short. Just a matter of time. Now I don't know bout you, but I can't afford no handouts or failed investments. You know what I mean? I got a business to run."

As he was talking, Pepe filled the saucepan with water

from the sink and set the stove to boil. Then, he paused for a moment, as if waiting for a response. John did not quite know how to respond, or simply elected not to.

Pepe continued, "It not like he even gonna be able to tell anyway; he still get to think he getting extra outta me—shit, if anything I be giving him some extra placebo." Opening a pouch of lactose powder, "And I get to shore up some losses on a bet we both know ain't gonna hold up forever. That gotta be bout as win-win as you'll get. Simple utilitarian practicality." He mixed the lactose powder into a plastic baggie with the large chunk of heroin, twisting the bag and tying it off into a tight knot. "Ain't a dealer out there don't cut they shit. Probably more priests that don't touch little boys." At this, Pepe threw his head back and erupted into a barking hyena cackle.

John could not help but break a chuckle with him. "So what exactly are you doing there?" he asked as Pepe tossed the bag of lactose and heroin into the boiling water.

"Well, like I said, lactose powder do be the way to go. You could use up to like a third of straight lactose powder before it start getting noticeable. Might make your dope a little sweeter, but it still look the same. Lactose binds well to heroin, so the texture stay the same too. Color ain't change neither. Cause the sugars in the powder and all, they caramelize when you boil it. Ain't gonna be harmful if you smoke it, less of course you got the diabetes," another cackle, "and it just gonna get filtered out by your cotton if you shoot it. So all-in-all, not the worse thing you could be cutting with." At this point, Pepe scooped the baggie out of the boiling water with a slotted spoon and turned off the burner. Then, using the bottom of his coffee mug, he pressed the brown-black sludge flat and left it to cool in the bag. After that, he turned and reached over to the counter next to John and snatched his gun, popped the magazine in, and set it down next to him. "So there really ain't no need to tell him nothing now, is there?"

Even without the implied threat, John did not feel overly inclined to say anything. He shook his head slowly. "No, I don't suppose there is."

At that moment, the crimson robed beauty, the Red Admirable, came fluttering out of the bedroom, blowing another loud kiss through the doorway. "Buh bye Broosie," she sang in her sultry, smokey Slavic accent, her outstretched hand still twinkling towards Bruce as she began to turn and glide across the room to Pepe. In her other hand was a round mirror, upon which were laid out several lines of white powder.

"Why you always insist on flirting with him like that?" Pepe asked sternly, still smiling.

"I like him. He remind me of little bunny. Cute, and tvitchy."

Pepe rolled his eyes, "Yeah, cause you make him nervous."

She pouted her protruding lips.

"Cause you just so damn hot!" Pepe held out his arms to embrace her.

As she flit over to him, her hips swayed lasciviously, her barely contained breasts bouncing in their sanguine silk.

Everything about her reeked of artificiality, from her false lashes to her extended hair; her sirin-esque acrylic claws; her collagen-enhanced lips; her heaving, saline-filled bust; her professionally-padded posterior—all of it so utterly fake, so completely artificial, and yet so real, like the ultimate art-form, more than real, an idealized perfection of nature, more unachievably real than anything nature could possibly conceive. Both beautiful and perverse, the kind of artwork that was just begging to be defiled.

Her curves reminded John of St. Basil's Cathedral. Her hair was reminiscent of Anna Karenina, her eyes of Sonya Semyonova. Her bearing and her demeanour were that of Catherine the Great. As she lifted her arms up around Pepe's neck to kiss him, her robe blew slightly aside and her négligée lifted itself ever so much. There, while the two of them shared a deep kiss, John was revealed a heavenly glimpse of the twin creases where her firm, bulbous buttocks met her soft, smooth thighs. John could feel himself becoming aroused, imagining himself riding her like a troika. When the two of them separated labially, they both immediately turned and locked eyes with John, an act which gave off a hint of implied meaning, but not one that was immediately discernible, or verifiable. He —with a self-assured grin; she—with a look of inquisitive distrust.

"Oh, Mashenka, this Bruce's friend John. John, this my mail-order Russian bride, Masha."

"Blyat!" she spat with the noisy ferocity of a balalaika being smashed. "Ya ne z Roshka! Vsi vony Moskali svyni!"

Pepe laughed. "She hate it when I call her that."

Masha shot him a look sharp enough to deflate the largest parade float, but Pepe apologized with his eyes and her features softened a slight degree. Then, turning to John, she offered him the cocaine covered mirror. "Coke?"

John held his hands up in front of him defensively. "Ah, no... No thank you. I don't... I don't do drugs. Well, not any more at least."

She scoffed and rolled her eyes, then proceeded to sniff a small bump from her curved cyrillic—sorry, slip of the pen—acrylic pinky nail before passing the silver disk to Pepe.

"Sorry?" John balked.

Pepe just put the straw to his nose and snorted away like a pig in a puddle, either hearing nothing or pretending as such.

"Vell, it just yoo haf coffee in hand," Masha retorted.

"I think there is a bit of a difference between—"

"Besides, yoo haf smell of cigarette. And between yoo and me..." she leaned in closer to John, sniffing for emphasis, "put like this, I can smell of cheap American votka on breath.

As she leaned over, her vast cleavage was exposed to John, who savoured the opportunity to soak in the view. She noticed his fixed gaze, yet said and did nothing about it; he noticed that she noticed, and also said nothing about it, but unconsciously bit his lip as he looked her up and down. Pepe also noticed all of this, and also said nothing.

"Well those aren't really drugs, now are they?" John replied coldly.

"Here I'm gonna hafta interject," Pepe interjected. "What

makes those things not drugs, huh?" I mean where're you differentiating tween them and say, this here coke on this platter, or the heroin on that table?" He nodded to each respectively.

"You can't even compare them really, they're worlds apart. First off, there is the legal distinction." As soon as he said it, John regretted it. Legality is a confines, a social construct, one of many other social constructs that keep humanity bound. John knew this was something he consciously wished to supersede, to free himself from. Yet, his first instinctual argument had been, disappointingly, legality.

"What, you a narc?" Pepe barked his hearty laugh. Masha shot him a worried glance, but was reassured by his confidence. "First of all, beside the fact legality ain't nothing more than a misused tool, that ain't even always been the case. Shit, heroin was made by the Bayer pharmaceutical corporation. Same guys who made aspirin." (one free advertisement— credit where credit is due) "And at one point in time cocaine was legal and alcohol wasn't. You ask me, I say legality pretty irrelevant.

"Then what of naturalness and artificiality?"

"What of it? Anything really natural? I mean how you define 'naturalness' really? It suggest some sorta freedom from any outside influence, or human influence—which raise its own philosophical debates—but such a thing ain't really exist. You know what I mean? You enter the world, you immediately affected by it. Naturally, you born pure, with nothing but your body and mind. Maybe a soul—I ain't bout to get into that. But if you gonna last at all in this life, you gotta take your first breath, you gotta eat, drink, interact with things around you, all that shit. Ain't those all foreign substances, unnatural stimuli?"

"Yes, well… no, not really. I'm sure it makes a difference, the relative proximity to naturalness to those foreign substances, that is. Air, water, food, those are all necessities for survival. While coffee and cigarettes may be less essential, they are at least naturally grown products. And alcohol is made via the natural process of fermentation."

"I don't know if I call factory plantations 'naturally grown'. And as far as alcohol, it gotta undergo a process of distillation fore you drink it, otherwise it still full of other by-products like vinegary acetic anhydride, which coincidentally is one of the key components in heroin production. Besides, not a one of those things get consumed in they natural state anyhow. Your coffee been roasted, altering some alkaloids, then steeped in boiling water to pull out the active ingredients and aromas. Your cigarette tobacco been grown with who-knows-what chemical pesticides, hung to dry in a warehouse, sprayed with preservatives and fuck all else, packaged in seignette salt ringed paper, which you then smoke through fiberglass laced filters. Sound pretty natural to me. Cocaine ain't no less the coca plant than sugar is sugarcane—don't gimme that look man, you know I ain't lying. Most 'drugs' is just plants, or the extracts of them. They just natural chemical processes that been demonized for the sake of oppression and control."

"I think the major differentiation is the social effect. I mean, alcohol aside, I don't see people destroying their lives and robbing the Stop Mart over nicotine and caffeine."

"Maybe not as much, but people do be stealing coffee and cigarettes all the time. But that really just gotta say more bout society than bout the drugs theyselves."

"Everything iz drug." Masha piped in.

"I agree with her," Pepe said. "Anything you take in, physically or mentally, it all gonna interact with your body chemistry. Neurochemicals release. Receptors be activating. Your body just react to the input, and naturally it create the effects. Just as it do for any other sensation."

Here, Pepe took a gulp of his coffee. The M.I.T. logo leered at John tauntingly, though now it seemed less ironically mocking and much more plausible. Despite his appearance, Pepe was quite intelligent, which was a bit of a surprise to John. In all fairness, Pepe did look and talk a bit like your average hood rat. He was wearing grey sweatpants and a stained wife-beater, which showed off his many tattoos (mostly skulls and devils and naked women, a few clown faces) and his equally intimidating muscles, both of which had been acquired in prison. The tattoos did not stop at the arms and chest either, they continued onto his neck and even onto his face. The ones on his face were small, but they were the definitively gang-related teardrop tattoos. I have heard that the left side is for the number of people they have killed and the right is for the years served, much like the notches on a soldiers gunstock, but I never learned if that was meant from the tattooer's perspective or the tattooed. Either way, Pepe had a total of four tears running permanently down his cheeks, three on one side and one on the other. His hair, as already mentioned, was long and dreadlocked. He was tall, intimidatingly so, at least 6'6" and lean, and he adorned himself with many large rings and chains which shone with the same lustre as his silver grill. His features were ethnically ambiguous, besides the obvious African descent (the thick lips and wide nares, the simian ears, the low, sloping superciliary arch and glabella) there was certainly something else mixed in, but that other something was harder to pin down. It seemed to change depending on the angle from which you looked at him, shifting ever so slightly from one race to the other. John's first impression was of Hispanic or Latino blood, but then he thought maybe Indian (either dot or feather). Then from the other angle, maybe Turkish. Then Arab, based on his Kareem coloured skin (just a joke). Then again, judging by that same feature and the relatively high cephalic capacity, some Caucasian genetics may have been mixed in. At any rate, his thuggish appearance did not lead John to expect much intelligence. Yet, here he was, expressing ideas that so nearly were in alignment with John's own that John was rendered speechless, unable for a moment to rectify the dichotomy between expectation and perception.

"The Phantom World" is what John had always called it: the grand illusion, created expressly for you by your own mind. Any and every sensation you ever experience occurring completely from within. Take pain, for instance, the most visceral of all sensations. Pain is nothing more than a trick of the brain, a reactive impulse, trauma stimulating a localized network of nerve endings, surging neurochemical signals to your cerebral cortex, which in turn creates an automatic warning system via perceived pain. It is nothing that willpower cannot overcome. Why, then, should man's consciousness not be able also to conquer our other senses? They, too, are nothing more than mirages masquerading as mirror images, created in the bowels of the mind in order to better comprehend (or more easily comprehend, I should say) the divine chaos of the universe. Nothing is real; it is all a phantom world projected by your mind, constructed from the raw stimuli of your sensory organs; vibrations translated by receivers into neurochemical messengers, translated by receivers into perceived experience. In one way, you are a constant part of the universe, one piece of the whole, affected always by outside forces; but in another way, in the only way you can ever truly perceive, that universe exists solely within your mind. Nothing else besides the mind can really exist. Physical matter consists of nothing more than vibrating particles and empty space. And inside those particles—vibrations and emptiness. And within those the same. And so on and so forth, on and on, ad infinitum, ad nauseam, turtles all the way down, as they say. At its core, all is emptiness, nothingness. Vibrations and nothingness. And should those vibrations cease? What then? John thought somehow Pepe might know the answer, but it was not a question he felt he could adequately phrase at that moment. I have to admit to feeling much like John right now in that respect; I only hope you are capable enough, my dear sweet reader, to at least catch the scent of my intended meaning and that you find it eventually, hidden away somewhere secret perhaps (though, more likely right out in the open) even should you have to forge your own trial to arrive there in the end—trail, sorry, slip of the pen, I told you I would edit nothing.

"Personally, I think of drugs as no different than, say, any other supplement," Pepe continued. "Like caffeine in the morning get you going. Little dope at night work better'n any sleeping pill what been invented yet. Feeling sick? Some vitamin C can help boost your immunities. Shit, so can grass for that matter. And if it bad enough, you take antibiotics or vaccines. You can get to the doctor and get pain killers, birth control, mood stabilizers, testosterone boosters. Have a lot to get done and absolutely have to stay up the next four days? Amphetamines gonna do the trick. You know what I'm saying? They all got they time and place and practical application." He punctuated this last statement with a juicy snort, followed by a clearing of the throat. "It just be about having the fortitude and wherewithal to recognize that time and place, dig?"

Here, Masha's and Pepe's eyes met for a second in some silent exchange, before turning back to John. It can be difficult for just about anyone to admit when they are wrong, and John would be no exception, but he was man enough to do it when the occasion arose, this occasion being no different.

"You know what? You're right. Honestly, I feel a little

foolish." John certainly did not want to anger his host and hostess. "You know, I have always figured myself as master of my own destiny. Perhaps not in control of the chaos of the universe, but certainly in charge of the most important thing, myself. And yet, I could be utilizing more means to my ends. As you said yourself, drugs, chemicals, outside stimuli, these are tools to be harnessed. My prior experiments with drugs admittedly yielded null results, never reaching the stage of practical application, but I think there is merit to what you say. Why limit myself? Based on what? On some preconceived societally-driven notion of what I should and should not ingest? Why, that's just not me. Mankind's power has led him to manipulate the world around him, bending it to his will, which has worked out thus far, but now is time to manipulate the world within him. Perhaps the next stage in evolution has to occur with an active role in our own advancement, focusing inward on ourselves, using our resources and intellect to change and adapt the very chemical makeup of our thought processes. Honestly, even with that end in mind, I still fail to see a practical application of many drugs for me, there is just no time and place for them amongst my goals. However, there is a certain application I can think of that is quite suited to the here and now, namely that of celebration—celebration for the night's bounty, and celebration for you having shaken me to my senses and reminding me that these confines of perception we were born into, which I had thought I had begun to supersede, or had completely shattered even, can and will return if you are not vigilant, stealthily rebuilt by habit and social conditioning while your back is turned. I slipped. And you helped catch me. So, in the name of celebration, may I?"

John gestured his hands toward Masha, who was still holding the round looking-glass tray in front of her.

"My, vat a long vay to ask for some coke," Masha giggled. "Yoo haf as much vind in yoo as Pepe!"

Pepe laughed sharply.

Masha sauntered over to John sensuously and extended the disc out to him with both hands like an offering to a priest. He reached out to grab the mirror, only to immediately realize she intended to hold it for him, either to be a gracious host, or from a lack of trust. Still, he maintained connection to the circular tray with his grip, just to keep some sort of tactile anchor with the floating disc of cocaine held before him, while with the other hand he reached for the tooter, which was made of polished ebony and tapered in at both ends (and had no conceivable purpose other than the consumption of cocaine). He could see the reflection of his fingertips rising up to meet themselves on either side of the tube. When his fingers met their reflections, would the mirror give, like liquid moonlight? Would his hand pass through the quicksilver mercury of the looking-glass, pulling him from this world into some new, wondrous land? No. Nothing of the sort would happen. The mirror remained solid. John grasped the straw and raised it to his nostril.

"Ah, left-handed are vee?"

"Actually, I'm ambidextrous." John smirked.

Masha raised her perfectly manicured and stencil accented

eyebrows enticingly.

As John bent to take his line, his own face came into view within the disc, but due to the angle and proximity, his reflection was grossly distorted so that his face was mostly nostril, with just the hint of the rest of a face receding into the background—a rather unbecoming portrait. To avoid looking at it, John averted his gaze upward, so his pupils remained parallel with the mirror's edge. There he was presented once again with the glorious view of Masha's heaving, bolshoi breasts. Again, she noticed his gaze, but this time leaned in closer to give him a better view, causing her luscious orbs to part a breathtakingly slight degree. He stared at this cleavage ferociously the entire time he was snorting the cocaine. The second he finished the line, he was hard. Surprisingly, despite his natural endowment, nobody else noticed.

Pepe continued talking, not having stopped the entire time John was doing the blow, saying something about drugs and apes and someone named Mackenna, most of which had been zoned out by John while he was soaking in the view. Masha swayed back over to Pepe, each cheek of her extended cab bouncing separately, first one then the other, in perfect diphthong. John had to fight the urge to reach out and squeeze her bulbous ass, to bury his face in the back of her deliciously smooth thighs. Pepe could watch for all he cared.

"… sure, it ain't as 'natural' (he did air quotes) as a shroom or some bud, but it still starts out a simple flower, you know what I mean? Papaver somniferum. Adormidera. The 'lotus' (again air quotes) of sleep encountered by fabled

Odysseus. Just a simple red flower."

Here Pepe took the baggie of heroin he had cut and pressed, having now had time to cool and harden, and he broke the chunk in half, tying one of the halves back in the baggie and throwing the other into Bruce's bag on the table, which was now indistinguishable from the chunk that had originally been removed. He threw the baggie next to the rest as a gift from "his own personal stash".

Masha looked at him disapprovingly. He returned with a self-confident air kiss. Her response was to strut off with a silent matriarchal huff to the connected living room and sit her sweet tush down on the arm of the couch, still within sight and earshot but decidedly removed from the action.

John started to let his imagination, and his lust, run wild, both of which seemed fuelled by the cocaine. He imagined Masha softly leaning back and spreading her knees slowly, delicately, to just barely expose the bright red crotch of her lacey underwear. He imagined she was licking her overfilled lips, groping her chest, rubbing her thighs, beckoning John with bended finger.

"...from there it be simple as harvesting the sap from the unblossomed bud. Only trick getting the timing right. Too soon and it ain't produced much of that milky opium sap. Too late it get flooded with other photosynthetic alkaloids, dig? What you wanna do, you wanna get it right before, just a night or two fore the fist petal starts poking its way outta the bulb."

Now John imagined her sucking on that same beckoning finger, wrapping her tongue around it, nibbling her acrylic tip, imploring with her desirous, Siberian husky eyes, begging John to take her.

"...that sap ain't no different than opium. Gets dried and collected. Nothing more, nothing less. Course opium ain't really all that potent. Plus, the shit stinks. Only 'drug' (this time no air quotes, but a definite inflection) more fragrant's gotta be pot, which do make it hard to transport as is. So outta economy, and I suppose inconspicuousness, most opium manufacturers gonna break it down into one of its active ingredients, dig? Usually codeine or morphine."

Now John pictured himself walking over to her, his jet-black blazer sliding off, his shirt unbuttoning. In his mind he was grabbing her, pressing his fingers into the ripe flesh of her inner thigh as she tossed her head back, moaning in delight. She wrapped her legs around his waist and kissed him hard.

"...both are used, y'know, pharmaceutically, but if you want heroin, you gonna need morphine. Which ain't all that complicated. You just gotta soak your opium in cold water and mix it till it get... what's the word? Mixed together and dissolved and shit... Homogenized. Once it get all homo-genized, then you can boil it with some lime..."

Now John was really letting himself go. His hands were gripping her hair tightly, pulling her head back, and his tongue was caressing the exposed area of her neck, just beneath her soft jawline, right along the pulsating jugular. Then he was completely naked, ripping her sanguine robe and sheer chemise to pieces and throwing the shreds into the air like confetti. He rammed his rock-hard cock into her wet and welcoming orifice. Masha let out a half-gasp-half-siren-shriek when the tip hit against her cervix.

"...at that point you just gotta stir it up real good and let it sit. Siphon all the morphine from the top in the morning. Now, you have morphine all right, but this shit ain't no good as is. This shit be dirty as a dip chewer's spit. So you gotta add in some ammonium chloride, heat it again and stir things up, let it sit overnight again..."

John was zealously thrusting, holding onto Masha by her hair and the back of her thigh (right at that magic crease), pulling her body onto his swollen shaft. With each thrust, she yowled like a Siberian she-tiger, her soft shaven vulva glowing nearly as red as her shredded nightgown, transparent secretions flowing like the Neva along the banks of her inner thighs. And what was Pepe doing during all of this? What was his reaction to all of it? Was he throwing himself into a jealous fit like his Moorish Shakespearean counterpart? Perhaps readying a glove to demand satisfaction (what a term)? No, he just watched like a cuckold as John ravaged his wife in front of him, all the while rambling on his incessant monologue, reading from the same script in this fantasy world as he had been given in the real.

"...everything dissolve in the ammonia but the morphine. So then you just filter out the precipitate and let it dry. Right there you got a morphine base you can use. Pharma'll use it just like that. Or they take a salt and crystallize it to make it more bioavailable. But we want the potent stuff—Heroin. Named for its heroic effects. Also known as diamorphine acetate, twice as strong as morphine, it be the golden goose of painkillers, the fine sand of sleep, the soft wave of bliss…"

Masha was up in John's arms, wrapped around his torso like a sable in a birch, her claws digging into his muscular back. Her massive tits bounced joyously. Her toes rapidly twitched back and forth between contraction and extension, bending and curling in quick succession. Then he had her pinned up against the wall, her legs still hoisted in his arms, just hammering her like a nail and knocking nearly all the picture frames off the wall in the process. "Da-Da!" she kept moaning (I believe it is Russian for 'yes' and has nothing to do with the daddy issues she may or may not have had) "Don't stop!" John had no intention of stopping.

"…to get that though, you got a bit of a process. First, you need acetic anhydride, which, I mean, good luck getting a large enough amount without the feds come knocking on your door. Though the beans own they own feds. Even then, sometimes they just make they own. Acetic acid pretty much just pure distilled vinegar—a basic acid (or simple acid, I should say) produced in fermentation. After you distil your vinegar fermentation into acetic acid, you gotta remove the water molecule. That what the anhydride part mean. You do that by heating the acetic acid to the perfect temperature, something like 814°, which ain't too far off the point where it might catch fire. More often than not they ain't bothering with that though, they just gonna throw in an acetic salt and call it a day. That salt'll pull out the water molecule and you got your acetic anhydride. Besides, that salt gonna get removed in the rest of the process anyhow..."

Now John had Masha bent over the couch, his hands gripping the meat around her hips, pounding away, her orgasmic juices frothing into a lather. He smacked her ass until the twin globes glowed fuchsia. His teeth clenched the back of her neck like a regal lion (minus the mutilating barbs, of course). Her makeup was a mess, her mascara running wildly from the tears of overwhelming bliss. Her snowy, husky eyes rolled back into her head as John doubled tempo.

"...so once you got your acetic anhydride, you mix it together with your morphine base and boil em. Then you take that solution and mix it together with a solution of umm... shit, what was it, not soda water... uh, sodium carbonate, which'll precipitate heroin from the rest of the mixture. Dirty heroin, but heroin still. Even the beans'll usually clean it up some. That involves dissolving it in hydrochloric acid and filtering it out through charcoal. Then good to go. Course, it could still use some refining. Which means ammonia, more hydrochloric acid, and acetone. That's how you get your tannish powder. Extra steps you just don't usually get round here. Less of course you know the right people. You know what I mean?"

Now Masha was shrieking, "Da-da! Fuck me harder! She was astride him on the couch, squatting onto his towering member, straddling him tightly. Her body would, without warning, spasmodically convulse every now and then in harmony with the contractions along her vaginal wall, sending sprays of sexual fluid with each thrust. She ecstatically slammed her body down from tip to hilt. Masha's syncopated grunts and moans began to increase in volume and tempo until they became blurred into a silent scream, her face red as borscht and all screwed up as he viciously fucked her senseless. John was painfully hard. He wanted nothing more than to bust his load, to fill her up until it all came gushing out of her. He grabbed onto her huge silicone tits and started squeezing. With all his strength he squeezed, digging in with his fingers, tighter and tighter until... POP! They burst like balloons, bursting along with them the entire delicate bubble of fantasy.

Masha was back on the arm of the couch, nightgown intact. Pepe was still babbling on. John was fully clothed, leaning against the wall where the kitchen connected to the dining area, still painfully hard. John could take it no longer. He decided to leave immediately and head to Bella's to relieve some of that fantasy with her.

"...anyway, it ain't much more processed than the junk most people eat. It just—"

"You know what," John ejaculated (poor choice of words, I apologize), "I have to get going." He looked towards the back room where Bruce was still nodding off, slipping in and out of somnolence. "I am just going to walk up to the closest gas station and call a cab. It was nice to meet you both. Tell Bruce I had to go, will you please?"

With that, John walked out the door and left.

Chapter Seven

John awoke the next morning in a room that was not his own, sweaty and panicked, unsure where he was.

What could have happened? Did he perhaps not make it home? Did Pepe quietly follow him and gun him down in the night? Was he just now waking up from a coma? Don't be absurd. Had he been snagged by the police and thrown in jail? No, no, nothing of the sort. Had he been hit in the head by a platitudinous plot device and fallen under an amnestic spell? Now now, no need for such melodrama. Why then, did he wake in such an obvious panic? Why did he not recognize his surroundings?

Sorry to disappoint, precocious reader, but this is not some major plot turn involving human trafficking or high-profile assassinations. This is not a cheap thriller. I am sure John was simply feeling a sensation similar to that felt by many upon awakening in a bed they had intended to leave in the middle of the night—a meaningless false impression of unfamiliarity, a strange neurological trick caused by the still-waking brain when seeing a room familiar only at dark for the first time in the morning light. It was, obviously, Bella's studio apartment, which we already know was his destination last we saw him. It only took a split second for the panic to subside and for John to recognize it as such. The memories of the previous night came rushing back, having been stored away in some sort of extra-dimensional pocket, kept safe through the night and returned to him in the waking morning. Rarely does reality live up to fantasy, or execution to theory, yet in this instance, Bella had been more than adequate in playing her role, as she and John reproduced (poor choice in words) John's vigorous sexual fantasies. Bella was just the right amount of submissive for John's aggressive assertiveness, never just lying there phlegmatically like a cheap whore, but actively seeking more, begging for more, passionate in her desire to please, and zealously pleasing herself in the process. In fact, it was hard to tell who had received greater satisfaction. At one point, Bella began to sob uncontrollably. But she did not stop screwing. When John finished, without missing a beat, she immediately got down and blew the embers back to flame. She shoved it back inside of her, shedding obvious tears of joy the entire time. They kept at it until their bodies turned to jelly and they had fallen asleep entangled together, both of them glazed over in one another's glistening, dried secretions.

As a rule, John never spent the night at Bella's; an exhausted body, however, rarely obeys the rules one attempts to place on it and so John found himself waking up next to cutesy plush dolls in a quaint studio apartment full of gem-stones and books on astrology.

A massive mandala tapestry covered the only wall with a window, which was just starting to glow with a faint square of morning light. This soft square on the tapestry (or more accurately, this soft square of light pushing its way through the tapestry's opacity) was not immediately discernible as the light coming from a hidden window. No, at that moment, it most likely would have appeared more like vague discolouration, either a production flaw in the ink or a washing machine mistake, perhaps even some intentionally idiosyncratic design —certainly not the natural aureole of morning light, as it turns out it was, silently implicating the window artifice hiding immobile behind the Mayan veil (No, not Mayan. Other side of the world, near the Himalayas. Tibet or Hindia). It was only as the square grew brighter and more vibrant (greys turning to aquamarine, browns to ruby and emerald, drab mustard and lead into pure radiant gold) that it would have become apparent as to the nature of the source.

On the bookshelf next to the bed there was an entertaining jumble of genres: a few books by Sartre and Camus and one by Derrida (all gifts from John) were mixed in with academic textbooks on Asian History, fantasy fairytales, New Age metaphysics, cheap romance novels and even cheaper true-crime magazines; the Bhagavad Gita was casually flung on top of, almost entangled with, the Kama Sutra; The Ching Brothers (I and Tao Te) were both there, sitting hand in hand next to a leather-bound copy of Confucian Teachings (side note: I have always loved how "Confucian" can be so easily mispronounced as "Confusion"—quite fitting for a man who espoused the virtue of obedience to the masses); the Kojiki was thrown in with an array of childish Japanese picture books about macrocephalic characters with names like Yuri and Nii-chan.

The apartment had a cozy sort of disarray. There were textbooks and papers strewn about here and there in anxious piles along various table and counter surfaces; clothing (more than just the articles they had removed that night) lay wantonly on the floor; candles and polished rocks cluttered every shelf, intermingled with bottles of nail polish, tubes of lipstick, mascara, and blush which overflowed from the bathroom counter and washed up in the various corners of the apartment; there was, however, no trash (unless you count some of the books on the tables and shelves), no grease or grime or grit, no dust even, really.

In the kitchen, or the kitchen area, more accurately, Bella stood, all 56 inches of her, completely naked, tending to a sizzling saucepan atop the stove. John rubbed his eyes and sat up, pulled nose first by the savoury scents. Bella, looking over her shoulder, beamed and rushed to John, bulling him over with kisses and mounting him on the bed. She nestled her body against his just like a kitten, purring ever so slightly.

"Oh, shit!" she said suddenly, as she jumped up and ran back to the stove, her wide, round little butt bouncing as she went. "I'm making breakfast. It's just about done."

Even without her turning from the saucepan, John could see the gleeful smile pasted across her cherubic face, or at least could hear it in her voice.

"I hate to break it to you, birdie, but I got's to get flyin'."

"No. No, please. Breakfast is almost ready. Please don't go."

"What are you making?"

"It's a tofu-egg scrambler."

"Tofu...egg...scrambler..."

Yes, a tofu-egg scrambler. It's got garlic and potatoes and

peppers and scrambled tofu-egg, y'know like with turmeric and... Will you please not give me that look? It tastes really good, and it's good for you too. Please don't go. At least have some toast. And some coffee. The coffee's just finished brewing."

"You know I hate it when you whine. Come now, stop the pouting. Awwh, come here. Come to me my little pet. That's right, sit down right here on my lap. That's a good girl. Now give me a kiss. Tell you what, my sweet turtle dove, why don't you pour me a cup of this famous coffee you've been raving about?"

Bella popped up with giddy effervescence, rushing to the cupboard. "Okay! Comin' right up! I'll get you a plate too. You just absolutely have to try this scrambler. It's so good, I'm telling you, you're gonna be surprised. You're going to love it, I just know it. Oh, do you want any cream and sugar? Like, just a little bit at least, y'know if you don't like it I can always make you something else... but I'm sure you'll like it. No? Is that a no to the cream and sugar or the scrambler? What do you mean 'both'? Oh, both the cream and sugar...so you'll try the scrambler? Pretty please? For me? Yay. Yay. Yay. You're not gonna be disappointed. Ooooh I am so excited!"

Over breakfast, the two had a small argument. Actually, argument is not the proper description. It was more of a discussion, one where they held differing opinions, but a disc-ussion nonetheless—not quite a debate and certainly not an argument, but a back-and-forth (innuendo unintended), an inn-ocent exchange of ideas.

"So? What do you think? Do you love it or do you love it?"

John had to admit, after adding some salt and pepper, the dish was actually pretty good. He could not help, however, being slightly bothered by the fact that Bella had referred to it as a tofu-egg scrambler. As he explained, the whole fad of calling foods something that they are not is a sly deception, a placebo-effect marketing ploy to trick people into thinking that they are eating anything more than a distant approximation of what it has been branded as. Vegan cheesecake. Bacon—in quotes. Chick'n and B'eef—as if throwing in an apostrophe or a misspelling could ease the deception. He had nothing against her vegan diet (which was not so strict as to not allow cheat days)—in fact, her argument that plants were higher lifeforms that got their energy directly from the sun, whereas the animal kingdom had to steal their pale fire, was one that John had difficulty combatting. But, ultimately, he felt that if you are going to choose to be vegan, or vegetarian, you should at least eat honest vegetables and not masquerade them as the flesh you have forsaken. Has anyone ever heard of tofu laying an egg? In all fairness, the average carnivore and omnivore does trick themselves in a similar fashion, changing names so as not to have to think of the meat they are eating as having ever been a living, feeling animal. According to Descartes, on the other hand, there is no way to verify that they truly are living and feeling, nothing more than simple automatons. Yet still, we have this strange social decorum, a promenade around the subject to help us mentally distance ourselves: pig meat is pork; cows give us beef, their babies give us veal; the Sea's creatures become (rather lazily) seafood; even wild deer get turned to venison; only the poultry retain their fowl names— nobody cares about the chickens, turkeys, ducks, and geese.

Bella rolled her eyes and changed the subject, surprisingly uninterested in pursuing the topic. "You know, it was amazing, being able to sleep with you last night."

John simply nodded.

"Maybe we can do it more… Oh! I wanted to tell you. I had the most wonderful dream last night."

"Oh yeah?" John did not even look up from his breakfast, which was basically country potatoes mixed with a vibrant yellow mush. I am sure it tasted better than it looked.

"Yeah, you were in it. And we lived together in this abso-lutely gorgeous little house with this perfect little garden that was like… well it was like… the whole thing like was on the back of this giant elephant, which is supposed to be a very auspicious sign, by the way. Have you ever seen that painting? Who am I talking to? Of course you have. You know, it's the one by… by, ummm… ummmm… ugh, it's on the tip of my tongue, I can't remember his name… you know, it's the moustache guy… the moustache guy… what's his name? You know the one don't you? Where the elephants have these long, long, stilty legs that look like they might just snap under their own weight? Well it looked kinda like that, only much more… I don't know.. regal? Well, anyway, it just sorta like travelled around the world, with us travelling along on top of it, and when it sprayed its trunk the sky was filled with gold and rainbows… it was absolutely beautiful. But John, the most beautiful, amazing part of all… John are you listening?

"Mmmhmmm," John lulled, wondering what Freud would have thought of her dream. "What was the most beautiful part, birdie?"

"Well… everything was like shimmering and gorgeous… and we were so happy together in our own little home… but the best part was that we had a child. A little baby girl. I saw her John. She was so beautiful… she had your eyes, and my hair, and she was such a happy little thing… her smile was like pure sunshine. John, when I looked at her, and she was just beaming back at me with such joy and purity… Well, you know, I… I felt that joy… you know, like… like, well, you know, like when I looked at her, I felt such a deep, loving connection, like nothing I've ever felt before. More real than anything else. I loved her so much, John. I can't even begin to explain how it made me feel… and when I woke up… Oh God! I missed her so much!"

Here a tear broke free from one of the watery pools that had been welling up in the canthus of her oversized glass doll eyes. This teardrop can be seen, if you so choose, as a sort of time marker, or a starting gun, if you will—for just as it broke against the laminate floor is when the argument began. No, not argument, discussion.

John stated that he never dreamed, and the few times he had, it was nothing more than nonsensical babble, an absurd exaggeration of the desires of waking life. To this, Bella took a slight personal offence. The timbre of her voice shot up a quarter tone in frequency as she argued that the experience of dreaming was a small piece of a bigger, grand picture, just as important to our consciousness, and to our very existence, as our waking lives. She also threw out the idea, based on string theory and multiverse theory (although I doubt she knew the difference), that while you are dreaming, perhaps you inhabit one of the infinite alter-realities in which you exist.

When John asked if she had gotten that idea from Edgar Cayce, her nostrils flared sharply. Again another rise in pitch. Bella cited several Taoist and Dharmic religions that revered dreams for their psychological and spiritual significance, in addition to their prophetic properties which, as she argued, was totally feasible if the past, present, and future all existed at once. In fact, she went on arguing, the basic tenet of Hinduism is that all of reality is an illusion occurring within the dream of a supreme godhead. John could agree that all of reality was nothing more than an illusion, but aside from that sentiment, and perhaps few others nitpicked selectively, John found the entirety of all religions to be fundamentally disagreeable. Even those that espoused that fundamental lack of reality, the pure nothingness that is the essence of everything, even those still build self-limiting and mind-controlling structures into that illusion, and immediately after addressing the true void of reality, they turn around and create some absurd fantasy world to fill it with, some spoon-fed mythology that is easier to choke down than the truth, the emptiness.

John argued (not argued, defended the idea) that dreams were just a simple sensory expression of your brain's information processing systems running while you are asleep. He stated that dreams could most probably be explained somewhere between the Jungian and the Freudian mindsets. Your brain, he asserted, is like a shark—if it stops moving it is dead. So, while you are dozing, your mind is still processing, active literally from stem to cortex, sifting through all the events of your day, and every single day before that as well, and at the same time, your sensory organs are still functioning normally, or semi-normally at least, and so phantom sensations slip their way in, or sometimes dictate the dream to a large degree: certain smells may evoke certain settings; characters can be created from all kinds of unconsciously heard sounds; indigestion from cheap highway food, poor circulation, fever or toothache, anything really, can affect your dream-self in various, exaggerated ways. Ultimately, John did not place too much value in dreams. He supposed they were not much more than an absurd amalgamation of random chaos, where your unconscious desires and anxieties meet the effects of exterior experience—all in all, not too drastically different from waking reality, if you think about it.

Bella looked as if she was going to jump another octave, this time breaking into a shrill major seventh. But, realizing she was outmatched, instead rolled her round eyes and huffed out a soft "whatever". Then she got up, set her plate next to the sink, and plopped her plump rump down on the small, overly puffed-up couch. As she shuffled through a pile of papers covering a good fourth of the coffee table, she sighed loudly. "Ugh, I've got so much homework to do."

"I'm going to take a shower," John said.

Partway through his shower, Bella came creeping into the bathroom. She slipped in behind John and wrapped her arms around his hips, grasping with both hands onto his natural handle, which swelled with delight at the company. John had not noticed her sneak in but was also not surprised nor startled in the least by her touch. He grasped her hand with his and slowly turned to face her.

"I'm sorry," Bella whispered, looking up at John like an injured puppy, her saucer eyes about to spill over.

John grabbed her trembling little chin, his thumb lightly caressing her lips, pulling the lower lip down slightly into a sultry little pout. Bella reached out with her tender pink tongue and pulled the tip of his thumb between her teeth, nibbling gently as her tongue danced across it. She leaned her head in and started to fellate the entire shaft, as she reached down with both hands to stroke his nearly vertical erection. In her small hands, John's natural endowment would have looked even more well.

John stood in front of the shower head, the water spray forming a soft halo around him, the suds dripping off the hard angles of his muscular body; Bella was soaking wet. She wrapped her arms around his neck and pulled his head down for a kiss. He scooped her up by her thick little thighs, his hands squeezing onto each cheek of her plump posterior. John slowly slid her down onto his pulsating shaft, her legs quivering every inch of the way. As soon as he hit the end, Bella convulsed with a full-body orgasm.

After that, John played a game with the shower head to see if it could wash away Bella's juices faster than he could produce them—it could not. He had her up against the wall, both legs in the air, than just the one; down on the tile floor, him on top of her, her on top of him; forwards, backwards, sideways; grinding away in the steam. They did it until the shower felt like it needed a shower.

Afterward, the two of them were refreshed; the shower had washed away the sweat and secretions of the previous night; the sex had washed away the foul mood left on the tongue from breakfast. Just as John was preparing himself for the protests at his departure, Bella saw the clock.

She scrunched up her nose like a little white rabbit. "Oh dear! Oh dear! I shall be late! For a very important test!" She giggled. "Shit. I might actually be late." No giggle. "But… Oh. My. God. MmmMmm. Worth it! I didn't even know it was possible to come for an hour straight. I don't know what's gotten into you lately; I mean, like, I know you're a Leo and all, and don't get me wrong, like the sex is always mind-blowing, but lately, you've just been so passionately fiery. It's just so… hot. So intense and so goddamn hot. Like honestly, you drive me so crazy, I just—Oooh, fuck! I'm getting turned on again just thinking about it… mmm! Fuck, okay! I have to get ready!" She started to hurriedly throw on a semi-coordinated outfit. "I'm not gonna have time to do my makeup."

John picked up the various parts of his midnight black four-piece suit and set them onto the bed, sitting down next to them to watch Bella's frantic rush.

"I'm sorry John, I have to head to the U like right now, but… I mean, if you want, you know… you're welcome to stay… like as long as you want, or whatever, but I'll probably only be like a couple hours or so..."

"Sadly, my dear, I too must be going, but you shan't leave my thoughts naught but for a moment."

"Hey," Bella inquisitioned as she walked over to John, climbing on top of him and straddling his lap.

"What is it, mon petit serin?" John punctuated his question with a quick peck on her perky lips.

Bella stared deeply into his cool, steel-grey eyes. "I. Love. You."

"Awe, I love you too, my sweet little pet." Another quick peck. "Good luck on your test today."

"Oh shit! That's right. I have to go! I'm late! I'm late! I love you! Mwah!" Bella rushed out the door, leaving John alone in the studio apartment.

John seized the opportunity to run a quick, cursory sweep for any incriminating evidence. He did not expect to find anything (he knew that Bella loved him too intensely to cheat, and if she did cheat, she would be smart enough not to leave any evidence at home), but he checked anyway, purely out of decorum and posterity. Just as he was about to give up, his labours fruitless, his efforts in vain, John suddenly came upon the realization that he did not really care enough for there to be anything to give up on in the first place. So, instead of giving up, he simply washed his hands of the whole affair in the metaphorical Euphrates and left the apartment, locking the door from the outside. Yes, forgetful reader, of course he had a key, he was paying for the apartment, if you recall.

He took a cab home. The cab driver smelled of boiled cabbage. His name was Mel Blanc, or so he said at least four times—although, if you ask me, it sounds like a fake name if I ever heard one. He said his favourite colour was beige. He said he had four children, but had not seen any of them in more than thrice as many years. Just as the cabbage—no, carriage—no, cab—was pulling into his neighbourhood, John saw a maroon minivan pulling out of his neighbourhood. This particular maroon minivan was under the ownership of a one Margaret Fleischer, who, it just so happens to turn out, was Mary's sister, had been since birth. Well, Mary's birth that is. Maggie was born seven years prior to becoming Mary's sister. She will always remember those years as some of the happiest of her life.

As John was approaching closer and closer in proximity to his house, he could feel his agitation increasing in equal measure. His blood was boiling, his mind seething, wondering why in the hell that woman had been over. To put things plainly, John and Margaret did not get along. She absolutely loathed him, which made it quite hard not to reciprocate. In fact, none of the Fleischer family were too keen on John Smith.

Allow me to elaborate—at this point I feel a little backstory on the Fleischer's and their familial drama is necessary. Naught but a few notes.

Karl Fleischer

- Patriarch.
- The "Butcher of Wall Street", so-called, besides the obvious etymological reasons, because of a delicatessen he owned, which actually was not technically on Wall Street, but was near there; and then also because of the killing (rim shot) that he made on the stock market.
- Later in life, he became a devout Catholic, donating a hefty sum to the Vatican, obviously from some sort of internalized guilt.
- Large, overly large, in stature—a great massive bull of a man, with beefy limbs and fat sausages for fingers, a pork belly gut, and a pair of thick mutton chops on his raw-red ruddy cheeks.
- Strict and severe.

Beatrice Fleischer née Brücher now Schulz

- Matriarch.
- Mary used to call her "Betty Boobs", on account of the massive breast implants she'd had done sometime in the early '80s—never to her face of course.
- The kind of shallow woman who valued appearances and pretenses over all else; adorned always in rich jewelry, sultry furs, and an effluvious air of vanity.
- Left her family and married a rival butcher

who, truth be told, was far more successful in the trade—this was, of course, before Karl hit it big on the lottery, I mean stock market.

- Greedy, manipulative, controlling. Especially in regard to her children.

Margaret Fleischer

- She preferred Marge or Madge. Disliked Margie. Hated Meg, Maggie, and Margo. Was confused by Peggy. But absolutely positively downright despised Margaret. That is just the way it was; she never felt inclined to tell anyone the reason why—and nobody bothered to ask.
- She took after her father, physically speaking, and knew how to throw around the weight she had inherited.
- Exceptionally butch, even for a butcher's daughter—as much so as she could possibly be without her uptight family suspecting she were not actually straight.
- Secretive and suspicious, almost to the point of paranoia.
- Petty and conniving.
- As mentioned, she held an inexplicable hatred for John.

David Fleischer

- The token black sheep of the family.
- Chronically plagued with bad luck and worse habits—far too fragile to take on his Goliath

alone, yet tossed out to the lion's den by his own family.

- Unfortunately for this David, there would be no kingdom, for when he came out as openly gay, he was completely forsaken by his father and no feats of bravery nor signs of faith could put him back in his good graces.

<u>Mary Smith née Fleischer</u>

- John's loving betrothed.

- Hypochondriacal and Agoraphobic.

- Born just over four weeks premature; she was frail and sickly and had to be kept inside an incubation chamber like a little white egg for the first thirteen days of her life—they say she never quite came out of her shell (no rim shot needed).

- Mousey and anxious, and as thin and pale as a ghost.

- John and Mary were introduced to each other at a small college party by a mutual friend whose name and face have almost been completely erased by the clumsy cerebral custodians in Mnemosyne's employ.

- Unbeknownst both to John and the person who had introduced him to her, John and Mary had history together—that is, though four years apart in age, they had, in fact, shared a history class together in high school. John had not noticed her then.

- She fell in love with John immediately, with a

passionate fervour so intense it drove her to the fathomless depths of despair to the breathless peaks of meretricious mania—until, on the brink of collapse, the precipice of suicide, she confessed her love, her adoration, her worshipful devotion to him.

- She was pretty enough, no doubt, and certainly was unobtrusive, and came from a respectfully wealthy family even—but what really won John Smith over was the intensity of her love for him. Never before had he seen anyone so enraptured, so completely devoted to another person—and for that person to be himself; it moved him. It could have moved mountains.

- He made her bear an unbearable thirty days and thirty nights without him, a torturous test of faith while he deliberated his resolution. On the thirty-first day, at dawn, he proposed to her and the two made love on the spot. She thanked god.

- Her parents did not approve—her mother made snide, passive-aggressive remarks; her father's aggression was less passive, even going so far as to threaten disownment should she go through with it. In his eyes, she had willingly forsaken him, her own father, who had provided a plate for her with veal from a golden calf, all for some dazzling magician with silver promises of fishes and loaves. Turns out his threats were not idle—her mother still attended the wedding, along with her gnomish new husband, but was incorrigibly mean the entire procession; her father never spoke to her again.

- Eventually, due to complications of cirrhosis and a progressive series of strokes, Karl Fleischer, sadly under par, finally lost something even St. Anthony could not return him. Even in his final days, he refused to let Mary so much as come to see him. David was no better off. Margaret inherited everything.

- Her mother would occasionally trade monetary help for condescending judgmental lunches and obligatory favors, which Mary quickly learned to politely decline. Margaret was more compassionate and felt Mary deserved her share of the inheritance, but she was irrationally convinced that John would steal the money and leave Mary, or worse, if he could only get his hands on it. As such she would only dole out what would have been Mary's share incrementally, instead of in one lump sum.

- To Mary, it was all worth it just to be close to the one she loved.

That should suffice for the backstory. Now, where were we? Ah yes, that is right—John Smith was reaching out to grip the cold round knob—or, no, that is not quite right, the door would have been locked—he was sliding the key into the lock.

Actually, let us step back a moment, for proper context; let us wind back the clocks to just a tad before John arrived on the scene. There are important details in Margaret's visit we might want to know, should know, if we are to fully understand the rest of it.

Allow me to set the stage:

DRAMATIS PERSONAE
JOHN SMITH
MARY SMITH, *wife to John*
MARGARET FLEISCHER, *sister to Mary*

ACT I
SCENE I
John's house. The kitchen.
[*Enter* MARY, MARGARET, *and a throng of* CITIZENS.]
[*My mistake, lose the throng of* CITIZENS.]

MARGARET
Do you remember Brenda? Brenda Pearlman? Well, I don't know if you heard, but she just got out of her night-marriage. Said her divorce lawyer was absolutely amazing. Got her the house, the car, the kids, and then some. You know Mare, I… I could get you in touch with her.

MARY (*setting the kettle to boil*)
Can we please just… not?

(Beat.)

MARY
Do you want any tea? I was going to make some anyway…

MARGARET
What kind you got?

MARY

Well, I only like Chamomile…
MARGARET
Oh yeah, that's right. That's fine. That's fine. You know Mare, I just really want to see you happy.
MARY
… I am happy.
MARGARET
You know what I mean. You don't look very good. Healthy, I mean. You're so… pale and thin. Almost like a ghost.
MARY (*avoiding eye contact*)
That's not very nice…

(*Beat.*)

MARGARET
Come on Mare, don't be like that. You know I only criticize because I care.
MARY (*rolling her eyes*)
You sound just like Mom right now.
MARGARET
I never could understand why you insist on calling her "Mom".
MARY
Because she is? I don't—
MARGARET
Barbara left us. She abandoned her role as our mother. She abandoned us. I can't believe you would ever compare me to her.
MARY
Madge…
MARGARET
No, it's fine. It's fine. It's just… nevermind, it's fine. I'm not wrong though. I mean, seriously, when was the last time you saw the sun, Mare? Does he ever even let you leave the house?

(*Beat.*)

MARY
I… I'm not a prisoner.

MARGARET
Might as well be.
MARY
Madge… please…
MARGARET
Okay, okay, I'm sorry, I know, it's just… I just can't help but think how much more you could have made of your life if it weren't for him.
MARY

…

(*Beat.*)

MARGARET
Do you remember Dad's bird?
MARY
Bird?
MARGARET
Yeah. You remember when he bought that Maltese falcon, don't you? What was his name? Something biblical… Oh well, it's not important. Do you remember after it tried to escape? Dad got its wings clipped so it couldn't fly away… I thought it was horrible… the way it just hopped around completely defeated, trying to stretch its wings. But it couldn't. It just couldn't do it. I remember you cried. And then Dad, in his own way, tried to make us feel better about it all. He told us he did it for its own protection, that, having been raised in captivity, not knowing how to fend for itself, it would have just died out in the wild. Maybe he was right, I don't know. I just remember afterward when its feathers started falling out. And then it just sort of stopped eating. And then one day, it was dead at the bottom of its cage, all stiff and gray…
MARY
Yeah, I remember Dad made us help him bury it underneath the cypress in the front yard. Why do you—
MARGARET
You really should eat something, Mare. Or else you might dis-

appear completely.

[*In tense silence and unnatural focus,* MARY *walks* U.S. *to the cabinet and prepares the porcelain teapot with a bag of chamomile.* MARGARET *sits down on one of the island barstools*]

MARY (*facing away*)

Look, Madge, I promise you… I—

    [*She is cut off by the whistle of the boiling kettle*]

MARY (Cont.)

Oh, the water's ready…

    [MARY *carefully pours boiling water into the teapot and places the cosy over it.* MARGARET *shuffles through her oversized, over-compensating purse and pulls out a folded envelope, placing it on the marble counter-top beside her*]

MARY (*setting the teapot down*)

Sugar?

MARGARET

Please.

    [MARY *takes another trip* U.S. *to grab the sugar from the pantry.* MARGARET *fingers the envelope.*]

MARY

Hey Madge. Whatever happened with that date you were going on? You… you never told me how it went?

MARGARET

Oh. Yeah. I cancelled. It was stupid.

                (*Beat.*)

MARY

Oh… I'm sorry, I…

MARGARET

It's just… It's not like I even have the time for dating. Besides, I'm sure it would have been a disappointment. In my experience, other people are rarely anything but.

MARY

What, ummm… What was his name?

(*Beat.*)

MARY (Cont.)

I'm sorry that was stupid.

(*Beat.*)

MARY(Cont.)

Here, let me pour your tea for you, it should be plenty steeped.

[*Pours tea.*]

MARY(Cont.)

Just strong enough to crawl out of the spout. Just like Oma liked.

MARGARET

Bobbi. That's what they went by, if you're that curious.

MARY

Bobby… Bobby and Madgey. Bob and Madge. Margaret and Robert? Maybe? I don't know Madge, it kinda has a ring to it.

(*Beat.*)

MARGARET

Yeah.

MARY

How'd you say you met him?

MARGARET (*continuously adding sugar to the cup*)

I didn't. It was a blind date, or a double-blind date, or whatever the hell they're called. They were just some friends of one of the ranchers that supplies us with carcasses. I don't know… it, it was stupid, and I didn't go. What else do you want to know?

MARY

Well, no good love story is ever simple.

MARGARET (*sighing*)

I suppose not.

(*Beat.*)

MARGARET (Cont.)

Listen, Mare, I can't stay forever, but, you know, we should really do this more often.

[*Takes a long sip from the teacup.*]

MARGARET (Cont.)

I have been extremely busy lately, but... maybe in the next week or two we can go out and do something.

MARY

Umm, yeah, I mean... That sounds nice.

MARGARET

Here, Mare, this is for you.

  [MARGARET *slides the envelope across the counter to* MARY]

MARGARET (Cont.)

It's... you know, just a little something to help keep things afloat.

MARY

Oh... thank you.

MARGARET

Honestly, I never agreed with Dad's decision. It's your money, too; you deserve it. But... I don't think he was wrong, not completely, at least.

MARY

...

MARGARET

I'm just saying I don't trust that man. I'm sure if he got his grubby little fingers on your inheritance money, he would steal it from under your nose, or kill you, or worse.

MARY

You know that's not true...

MARGARET

Do I? Do *you*? Do you really?

MARY

Madge... please stop... You don't know what you're talking about.

MARGARET

Look, I'm just saying, If you decide to leave him, you'd have enough in your account to live comfortably for the rest of your life. You don't need him.

MARY

I do need him. I love him. I… I don't want to talk about this anymore.

MARGARET

That's fine, just… just think about it, okay? Anywho, I should probably get going before the entire business falls apart.

MARY

Okay.

MARGARET

I love you Mare. You know that, right?

MARY

I know, Madge, I know. I love you, too.

[*Exit* MARGARET.]

[MARY *paces around aimlessly, washes the cups, sits at the counter, and buries her face in her arms. Then, stands and walks* D.S. *directly facing the audience.*]

[*The lights dim. Spotlight on* MARY]

MARY

What love could leave?
What love could ever fade away?
What darkened skies, what clouds tumultuous—
That threat to squeeze with blackened tendrils of
Pity and scorn and life's disdain,
The radiant glow of our consummate daylight—
Dare hopes accomplish such a foolish task?
Love is no flame, no fervid inferno—
Scorching earth cast shadows from its light
Consuming all the world, before it
Collapses malnourished in ashes,
Embers gasping with nothing left to burn.
No… God no… True love would never burn.
True love is gentle, warm, and absolute.
The very air of life itself
The soft glow of sunlight, reflected in the moon
Still there at night's darkest hours—

The atmosphere without which there would be
Nothing but dark, cold, suffocating emptiness.
To abandon love would aught profane it
Negating its existence—spitting
In the face of the one thing worth living for
And letting disintegrate the once held purity
And absolution of a grace divine.
Any life lived after the loss of one's true love
Is a hollow, empty fate worse than death
A blistering existence of numb nothingness
Of which there can be no escape.
Sans love's embrace—no joy exists at all,
Without this air of life to breathe.
Love, true love, would not, could not ever leave.
[MARY *cries silently. Then, she is startled by the sound of the
front door being opened and stares panic-stricken at the
entryway.*]
[*Enter* JOHN]

MARY
Oh, John, you're home!
[MARY *rushes over and embraces* JOHN]
MARY (Cont.)
I was so worried about you.
JOHN (*wiping a tear from* MARY'S *eye*)
Mary dear, there's no need to worry about me.
MARY
But—
JOHN
You know what I find amazing? Most people are so ugly when
they cry, their faces all screwed up and bulging, like some
revolting unnatural toad. You, however, my dear, somehow
become more beautiful. You wear your tears like some divine
adornment, like a diamond tiara. And as each one is falling
from your pretty face, it is as if I am falling in love with you
all over again.

MARY

Oh, John. I… I love you so much.

JOHN

And I you, my dear. More so than life itself.

[JOHN and MARY kiss.]

(*Beat.*)

MARY (*face buried in* JOHN'S *chest*)

John?

JOHN

Yes, dear?

MARY

Where, ummm… Where were you last night?

JOHN

Oh, you know, I got caught up with work.

MARY

Work?

JOHN

Yeah, work. Business relations sort of stuff, maintaining corporate contracts, yada-yada-yada. I don't want to bore you with the details, but basically, there is this textile company from Mexico, The Bojorquez Group, El Grupo Bojorquez, and they're considering purchasing a large insurance contract which requires a multi-layered escrow with several financial backers. Well, they were in town to discuss details, so naturally, I was asked to take them out, show them a good time, and close the contract. Which, I am sure you will be happy to know, I did. And I should be receiving a very generous bonus for doing so.

MARY

I… well, I mean, that's really amazing… but—

JOHN

I didn't expect to be out so late, that's for sure. Those Mexicans just don't stop. By the time I got home, you were completely out, and you just looked so peaceful, I didn't want to disturb you, so I just slept on the couch.

MARY
Your alarm woke me up in the morning, and you weren't here... I was so worried...
JOHN
Oh... I forgot about the alarm. I'm sorry, dear. I didn't get the best night's sleep on the couch, so I decided to get an early start on the day.
MARY
But it looks like you're still wearing yesterday's clothes...
JOHN
Ah, yes, well, I didn't want to disturb you. I was only running a few errands, I didn't think anyone would notice.
MARY
That's just not like you—
JOHN
I didn't want to disturb you. I was thinking only of you. By the way, I noticed that Margaret was over earlier.
MARY
...
JOHN (*nodding at the envelope on the counter*)
You want me to deposit that check for you?
MARY
Ummm... Yes, please.
> [MARY *hands* JOHN *the envelope*]

MARY (Cont.)
Tell me you love me.
JOHN (*leaning in for a kiss*)
I love you.
> [*Lights fade. Curtains drop.*]

END SCENE

Chapter Eight

The next burglary was a complete bungle—Bruce was late arriving, the van ran out of gas (luckily for them, right next to a station), and there was a closed road, which forced them to take a detour to get there. Plus, there were dark clouds in the sky.

John and Bruce arrived at their target destination under the cover of darkness, sneaking around to the back for their entry. Between them and the unsuspecting house lay a walled-off yard with an imposing wooden gate that was locked from the inside. The two opted to hop the wall, which in retrospect, was probably a poor decision on their parts—for reasons, which soon will be revealed.

Bruce went over first. Due to a combination of the intensely dark, moonless night and Bruce's undiagnosed myopia, he failed to notice the pair of aluminium trash cans waiting in the path of his fall. Unfortunately for John and Bruce, aluminium trash cans are the loudest of all garbage receptacles, and these two certainly would not keep quiet about having been so rudely and abruptly awoken by a careening body crashing into them in the dead of the night. Their clattering clamour of distress was immediately noticed by the guards stationed in the next yard over, who took up the cry in earnest. The more zealous of the two was a small, blonde terrier which had exploded into a frenzy of yapping as it blitzed the perimeter of the wall. Its partner (a fat grey bulldog in a red sweater) lay supine on the back porch, punctuating every third or fourth yap with a deep bow wow of its own.

John leapt to a clear spot in the yard, landing with cat-like grace, and the two men hid in the shadows. The dogs rattled on, joined by their compatriots throughout the neighbourhood in a canine call-and-response choir. Eventually, all of the dogs were brought in or tired themselves out, and the night once again fell to silent stillness.

What secrets are concealed in the stille night? What, in the dark pulsating mind of creation, lies aslumber? In the phantom chroma cast by the strain of cones and rods functioning without their necessary fuel of light—the verdigris and violet pinpricks fighting to overcome the oozing overtones of congealed maroon and ultramarine, condensing to an over-whelming darkness—the infinite sphere of possibility reigns...

But John and Bruce had no time for such thoughts; they strained their retinas to the limit, trying to make out the shadowy shapes that were almost visible at some indeterminate distance in the yard between them and the large black box of a house.

There was a small bit of fumbling. The two shuffled forward with their hands outstretched in front of them, groping around like a couple of blind beggars in a brothel. Suddenly, an unsuspected slope snuck up on them and they nearly lost their footing. Then Bruce accidentally pulled the old comic gag of stepping on a rake, which in accordance with the laws of nature and comedy, immediately and aggressively smacked him in his long, drooping face. Bruce let a profusion of insults fly at his metallic attacker and John had to sardonically shush him like a toddler. When they finally made it to the house is when things really started to go south.

There were no porch lights to aid in the affair, yet the two still managed to find the back door of the house with minimal effort. At that point Bruce realized he had forgotten the lock-picking set. I am sure you can imagine John's iration at this. Bruce tried to calm him, to provide assuagement. He argued that it really did not matter anyway, seeing as no one was home, and one could just as easily break the window on the door, reach in, and turn the deadbolt, as they could pick the lock anyway. Probably even easier, if you were to ask him. So, that is just what he did.

It was not until after the window was smashed, the dead-bolt turned, and the door opened that the alarm started going off. Bruce was dumbstruck. John was livid. He was about to explode with a litany of abuses when, just barely audible over the shrill sirens of the home defence system, the two heard the unmistakable sound of a gun slide being racked.

They had barely enough time to glance over at one another before the doorway erupted with a blinding flash of light and a deafening bang that roared and reverberated from the dark depths of the house. They turned tail and ran.

Another shot rang out.

Then another. And another.

Somehow, over all the noise—over the sound of the security alarm, their own pounding hearts and clumsy, fear-driven footsteps, even over the sharp, piercing whine of permanent hearing damage, they still managed to hear the chilling sound of the bullets whizzing past their heads.

They ran straight to the back gate faster than they had ever run before. It only took one push to realize the gate was padlocked shut, so the two immediately vaulted the wall, their adrenaline giving them a nitro boost of primal strength.

On a side note, in case anyone is interested in the shooter, this lone ranger—I have, through various interviews and newspaper articles, been able to acquire a great deal of information in regards our mysterious gunman. Regrettably, he wished to remain unnamed, and as he may or may not be in witness protection, we will have to abide by his wishes.

Without providing too much identifying information: He was (and at least to my knowledge at the time of writing still is) an older gentleman of diminutive stature who, according to his story, had recently been mugged when travelling through an underpass downtown. This event left him with a pervasive fear that slowly grew worse and worse. He refused to be out after sunset, and even then, he was always skittish and anxious, especially around any street corner or alleyway. Whole areas of town, particularly neighbourhoods of certain lower-class groups, became completely verboten, blacked out on the map of his mind, until his entire life consisted entirely of scrutinizing the myriad pathways in front of him and meticulously discerning the safest of all available steps. In the name of such a pursuit, he purchased a gun and, like most people deeply concerned with home security, he got the biggest, baddest hand cannon in the store. What he did not realize was that the biggest, baddest hand cannon in the store, when fired from a small hallway in the dark of the night, is like setting off a flash-bang right in front of your face. As such, he never actually caught full sight of the alleged trespasser.

Beyond that, there is not much I can tell you—exactly who he was and how he made his living, we will have to leave omitted along with any distinguishing features. I can, however, tell you what he was not. That is, he was not a money lender, he was not a pacifistic vegan, and he most certainly was not a middle-aged spinster with a dowagers hump and extremely fine, silvery blonde hair. I mention this only because his adjacent neighbour (not the one with the dogs, but the other one) just so happens to be all of those things. She also happens to have employed Bruce's pest control services in the past.

It was not immediately—certainly not as the gunfire was ripping through the night air around them, nor as they were scaling the rampart, but by the time they had fled to the van and were peeling out of the neighbourhood, Bruce realized his blunder. When casing the joint, the road had not been closed and as such, he always had approached from the other direction—and from the other direction, the third house from the intersection becomes the fourth, at least in this particular neighbourhood with seven-house rows, all neatly lined up like a freshly dealt hand. Bruce sat in silence, dumbfounded by his own stupidity. John seethed. They had both, as per tradition, shared a few drinks before they headed out, but Bruce was the only one who was wasted. John could have done better on his own.

****

They took a break for a week. Let things cool off. Then Bruce said he had cased a new spot. He said it was ripe for the picking. Ultimately, another bust. It turned out to have been nothing more than an old derelict house rented out by a couple of junkies who had already pawned everything worth a dime.

What Bruce failed to mention to John was that this particular couple of junkies had skipped out on a front he had lent them. Luckily for them, no one was home to get their brains bashed in. John got nothing out of it. I doubt Bruce was even able to recoup his losses.

****

John firmly insisted on picking the next mark.

After careful deliberation, he devised a brilliant plan: John Smith would rob his own house.

Step 1 – Remove Witnesses

- Spike the wife's sleeping pills with a little something extra brushed on that he would get from Bruce. He would have to spike them all to make sure she took the right ones.
- Turn off all of the outside lights on the house.

Step 2 – Secure Alibi

- Turn in to bed as soon as Mary swallows the last pill, feigning exhaustion, possibly pretend to down a sleeping pill as well. Mary would follow shortly after, falling asleep with her husband in bed.
- The two of them, as official statements would proclaim, would under the effects of their prescribed medication, sleep through the sounds of the robbery that occurred in the night.

Step 3 – Infiltration and Extraction

- Let Bruce in.
- Strip the place down, break a few worthless trinkets, tear some wallpaper, slice up some less desirable furniture, break a window.
- Bruce stores the goods until they can head to Pepe's together.
- Sneak back into bed and wait.
- Get up with the alarm at 5:00 and wake Mary with the panicked distress of a robbery victim.

Step 4 – Collection

- File a police report.
- File an insurance claim.
- Replace all of the stolen property with better, more valuable items using the inevitably massive insurance payout.

It was, as they say, the perfect crime, both in theory and in execution.

****

Then came a knock on the door, followed by a truncated burst of four more.

"What Mann is this a'knocking?" said John to himself, "Eh, Hugh, who are you? Some salesman of death? I'm coming, I'm coming. But none for me, thank you very much, you can take it back to Venice."

When John answered the door, he was greeted by a face he had never seen before. It was a sharp, angular face, with a slight rodent slant. This face had small, beady eyes and a searching nose, a twirled moustache and round spectacles. Over his tousled hair, he wore a purple bowler hat, which matched the suit and tie beneath his charcoal-grey dustcoat.

"Hello. Can I help you?" John asked in the most politely terse way he could.

The man spoke with a mild British accent: "Ethelbert E. Ethelbert, sir, I am pleased to make your acquaintance. I am here on behalf of Billings & Evermore to investigate your recent claim. You are, ehrm, Mr. Smith, I presume?"

"Investigate?"

"Why, yes sir, investigate."

"What about my insurance adjuster? Stacey? Isn't he supposed to come by tomorrow to assess damages?"

"Yes, well as an employee of the company, you would have intimate knowledge of its ins-and-outs, all of its various machinations, if you will—such as the normal assessment process and who your adjuster is, as you have just so elegantly demonstrated, Billings & Evermore simply wants to make sure that position is not being taken advantage of, so to speak."

"Am I to understand that I am being accused of fraud here?"

"No, no. Gracious no! Certainly nothing of the sort! No, this is just a simple, routine investigation, for the sake of posterity. I am sure you understand."

He was warm, jovial even, yet reeked of suspicion. John raised an eyebrow, but quickly let it drop.

"Of course, of course. I *am* familiar with the policies. I am just surprised you are here so quickly; it usually takes days to get an adjuster out to a site. I commend you on your diligence."

"Yes, well, Truth and Justice are two things I take quite seriously."

"As such you should. As such you should, Mr… Ethelbert, was it?"

"Yes, Ethelbert E. Ethelbert, pleased to make your acquaintance."

"John Smith. Pleasure's all mine."

"Is 'John Smith' your birth name?"

John chuckled and grinned.

"Listen, Ethelbert, don't blame me for my mother's lack of creativity. Besides, when it comes to interesting names, I think you've got me beat."

"Ethelbert? Why, it is a family name, passed down for generations. It is of noble etymology, meaning 'high-born'. I assume from your name, there was once a metallurgist in the family?"

John shook his head in defiance. "Actually, it comes from a bastardization of 'Kmet'—a Slavic name of similar meaning to your own. When my grandfather, mother's side that is, emigrated to the United States, his name was changed by a processor at Ellis Island—either out of a benevolent desire to assist in his assimilation, or from a simple mishearing in the pronunciation."

"Ah. I see." Ethelbert made a note on his clipboard.

"Anyways, not that this conversation about etymology and familial reminiscence isn't riveting, but as I am sure you are aware, I was burglarized just last night, so if there is anything

I can do to speed this process up a bit, I would appreciate that. There is still a lot of work that has to be done."

"Can you tell me what happened last night?" Ethelbert's amiable warmth was cooling.

"Certainly. But wouldn't that be a bit redundant, seeing as I put it all into my insurance claim, which you have right there on your clipboard?"

"Yes, ahem, well, that is all well and true, but just the same, if you don't mind, I would very much like to hear your perspective on the incident."

"Very well. I went to bed with my wife. When we woke up, we found our house had been burglarized and vandalized. I called the police right away and as I was waiting for them to show up, I filed my insurance claim. They came and left a few hours ago. Since then I've just been trying to clean up a bit. And calm the missus down as much I can, of course."

"I see. I see. And what did they take?"

"Pretty much everything that wasn't nailed down. Even worthless sentimental stuff. I supplied an itemized list in my claim."

"And do you have receipts for all of these items? Say, for example, the 'original Basquiat drawing' worth over $13,000. I assume you have a certified valuation?"

"I most certainly do."

Ethelbert rapidly scribbled a few more notes on his clipboard. "You managed to procure that list rather quickly."

"Is that a question?"

E shook his head. "Observation."

"I work a lot with spreadsheets. And I like to keep track of my expenditures."

"I see. Can you tell me how they got inside of the house?"

"Probably through the door with the broken window, if I were to venture a guess."

"Was the window broken prior to the incident?"

"No, they obviously broke it to get in."

"Obviously. May I see?"

"If you insist."

John led his amethyst interrogator around the back of the house to the door in question. E stuck his arm in through the broken window and turned the deadbolt. Then, he stooped down, picking up some shards of glass left by the broken window, turning them over, and setting them back down just as they were. Still stooping, he soaked in the view of the side yard with the look on his tilted face of someone who was measuring mentally a boot-print in the mud.

"Interesting," muttered Ethelbert to himself. Then, to John, "May we view the rest of the house?"

"Very well, but you must promise to be quiet, the wife is trying to sleep. Truth told, she is in a state of shock at the moment."

"On my honour."

John used the entirety of his self-control to not roll his eyes. Through the thin saccharine veneer of ingratiating cordiality, John was able to see this man for what he truly was: a self-inflated sort of charade, built from a pretentious façade of moral obligation and near pathological obsession; a meticulous and relentless Baskerville hound; some strange cryptid beast that transmutes his base animal instincts through a super-natural digestive organ into mythology and idealism; the kind of hyper-focused, detail-driven creature that would be a perfect fit for upper-management, or a holy crusade. Though John could see this strange man growing to become a potential adversary, he still obliged,

"Well then, follow me," said John as he unfurled his hand with the welcoming flair of a presentor.

As soon as they entered the house, Ethelbert began scrutinizing the entire household. No surface went unmolested by his gaze. John made certain to exhibit in full detail the damage caused by these intruding vandals.

"How do you sleep at night, Mr. Smith?"

"Excuse me?"

"I said, 'How do you sleep at night, Mr. Smith?'.

"I heard you; I'm just not sure I understood the question or what you are trying to imply by it."

"My apologies, Mr. Smith. My apologies. I meant no offence. What I mean is—how is your sleep? Do you and your wife often sleep restfully?"

"Oh, I see. Quite the opposite, actually. We both toss and turn and rest so fitfully, so lightly, that the sound of a neighbour's yapping dog, or even just nearby traffic, will continuously tear us awake the very moment we begin to doze."

"Is that so?"

"It is the absolute truth. That's why we both take sleeping pills. Strong ones; prescribed, of course. They certainly make sure you sleep through anything."

"I see."

Ethelbert took his time investigating, meticulously sniffing out any detail he could—fingering the slashes in the furniture; measuring the light squares on the walls of the missing frames; counting his steps from each room; taking photos on a small digital camera; scribbling notes; chronicling the destruction and calculating the damages. He was there longer than the police were.

When he finally left, he did so curtly, with a quick snap of his notebook, closing the case in his mind. "Thank you for your time, Mr. John Smith. I shall report my findings to a board for review, at which point they shall make a decision on your case. Have a good day."

As Ethelbert disappeared through the threshold, John had a sudden pang of clairvoyance—that is, from somewhere in the depths of his being, in some vague and indeterminate corner of his soul, he happened to stumble upon an augur of truth, a nugget of knowledge, accurate knowledge at that, as to what the future held, or at least a small portion of it. That is, John Smith knew, without a doubt, that this was not the last he would be seeing of Ethelbert, not by a long shot.

Chapter Nine

Ethelbert E. Ethelbert drives through town, mentally reviewing the evidence of the crime scene and recreating hypothetical scenarios to play out, not quite satisfied with the story given; John traces a lemniscate path through his home, lost in thought, still reeling from his encounter with Ethelbert—the introduction of this antagonist, the threat of his plan falling short, the possibility of having to stand and fight or flee, the possibility of being caught; Mary nods off in bed, having taken an extra dose of her medication; Margaret stares at two dozen cow carcasses just delivered by Bobbi, replaying their entire conversation in her mind; Bella is flirting her way through Economics; Pepe and Masha are intertwined, naked and strung out while their infant daughter crawls chaotically around the house like a Tasmanian devil; Donna Madeleine Ivey sits gracefully at her greeter's podium, a distant, ever-bored look in her sparkling eyes; a mangy coyote is trying to jump out of somebody's walled off backyard; Bruce sits in a jail cell waiting to make his phone call.

By the time Bruce was allowed his call, the coyote was limping off into the desert; Bella had already moved on to flirting with her Bio-Chem professor under the guise of discussing his insipid lecture on recessive gene transmission delivered in the previous class; Margaret had moved on to staring at the phone on her desk, having resolved to ask Bobbi out; Mary had turned over in bed more than a dozen times; Pepe and Masha had risen, done a bit of coke, and met with no less than three different people for various exchanges of goods; Donna had taken both of her fifteen minute smoke breaks back to back and had returned to her normal position of an ennuied empress in regal repose; John had shaken out a Martini, finally able to relax, having assuaged his own fears with Socratic logic and a strong confidence in his own abilities —when the phone began to ring.

When Bruce told John that he was in jail, John's blood boiled and his vision went red, he was unable at first to even unclench his jaw to respond.

"It's not a big deal, nothing to worry about really. Just a minor possession charge. So long as they don't try and go for intent to sell… It's just, well umm, you know… the van… it's —it's umm… You know, it's still got all the stuff… the umm, stuff that's wrong with it, y'know, that still needs fixing… and well, umm, you think you could pick it up and take it in to the Quicklube for me?"

John was barely able to bark out a cold, dry, "Okay."

"Thanks. I owe you one. Yeah, so anyway, it's back at my place. There's a spare stuck in the wheel well. I'll see you once they get around to processing me and letting me out."

John stood there a moment with the dial tone playing in his ear, feeling like his veins were about to burst. Bruce was starting to become a problem. John wondered what it would take for Bruce to consider a plea bargain and what information the police would be after or already be in possession of and how any such information might affect his own freedom and well-being. He did not enjoy such thoughts, but he had to consider the possibilities and to plan accordingly should said possibilities become a reality. For example: What if Bruce were to divulge information about his supplier? How would Pepe react? And would John not be considered suspect by Pepe (a known gang affiliate)? Or worse yet—what if Bruce had already squealed and there was a sting operation waiting for John to deliver the goods? What then? Would John be caught in the crossfire between the DEA and the drug cartels? Or what if Bruce let something slip about John? Would it be necessary to ensure Bruce's silence? And if so, how? For the time being at least, these thoughts were unable to reach fruition. They were cut off in a snap, along with the droning dial tone, as John hung the phone back onto the wall. John donned his spandex speed-suit and told Mary that he was going out for a long bike ride and not to wait up or worry in his absence. Mary barely registered his presence. As he walked out the foyer, Mona Lisa smiled just a little deeper.

****

Bruce's house was four lefts, three rights and a combined stretch of ten miles away. The entire route would take John exactly forty-four minutes and thirteen seconds.

As he was passing through the gates of his neighbourhood, the texture of the pavement changed sharply, as if John had crossed some barrier of social stratification which held the grungy effects of proletariat use at bay, as if within the fortified gates of his well-to-do community, time and decay did not share the same relationship as they did outside them. This was, of course, just an illusion—illustrious as it is—that gets created by only a small amount of wealth in a capitalist country; yet sometimes illusion can be more powerful than reality. And sometimes a lie is more real than the truth.

At that same exact moment, Pepe was walking out of his house, strapped with his silver hand cannon and twenty-five thousand dollars cash, wearing a two-piece tracksuit and the sober look (figuratively speaking) of a man about to make a potentially life-threatening decision.

Just when John was making his first right turn of the trip (not that he made any wrong turns) he saw in the bank off of the side of the road, a small frail bird that had obviously flown head first into a passing car now long gone. Its head was twisted a full 180 and caked with blood. Its beak opened and closed soundlessly as it pathetically attempted to crawl side-ways, dragging its mangled wings behind it. John considered stopping and finishing the job, wringing its neck or smashing its head in, to put a quick end to its suffering. But then, looking at it as he was passing, he thought to himself, "This thing has already lost everything else in life, the least we can do is let it keep its suffering." That, and he was already moving with both trajectory and momentum and it would have been quite inconvenient to stop.

At the same time, Bella was just getting out of Bio-Chem, with a small amount of time before Anthropology started. While shuffling through the crowded hallway, she overheard a small group of what you might call "the pretty girls" (marked by the Greek letters and a fortune's worth of beauty products) making derisive comments about her: "Ohmygod, did you see that fucking bitch?" "Who? Little miss piggy?" "Yes! Ohmygod, what a little slut! No wonder she's passing." "Ohmygod, I know right? It's like, hello? Go back to your trailer in tiny town, no one wants you. Thanks." Bella swore not to let it get to her and walked past with cool indifference, pretending not to have even heard what they said, which was difficult because what they had said was hurtful, especially the "little miss piggy" part—that was just rude, and downright inaccurate, as Bella literally worked her butt off at the gym everyday to maintain her figure. She kept her composure and passed by with her head held high, gracefully impervious to their cruelty. As she walked into the relative sanctuary of a nearby bathroom, she broke down and sobbed until her make-up ran, then spent the rest of her break fixing it so she did not look a mess in Anthro.

On the other side of town, Margaret was also in front of a mirror, wiping tears from her wide-set eyes, staring out in a way that she thought looked enigmatic, but in actuality just made it impossible to tell if she was happy or sad, like a dull emotionless cow trying to cut the line to slaughter.

By this time, John was rounding the final bend of what was his favourite road of the trip, a four-mile stretch of smooth asphalt flowing like a river, with sloping twists and turns that could transform even the most novice rider into quicksilver and windstreams. This particular bend in the road was the location of John's mental point-of no-return. That is, on an average venture, if he were to realize he had forgotten something like his water bottle or his cigarettes, or that he had forgotten to lock the door on the way out, or if he just wanted to turn back, he most likely would, up until he had reached the point-of-no-return—generally halfway to his destination. After crossing that threshold, however, nothing would bring him back until he had finished what he set out to do. Not even if Mary were to somehow telepathically call out to him, as she was desperately trying to do at that moment.

Just a few seconds prior, Mary had awoken drenched in cold sweat with blurred vision and an overwhelmingly nauseating anxiety coursing through her body in waves. The instant she opened her eyes, she was immediately in a state of full blown panic. She had not had an attack like this in years. Through hyperventilations, she desperately called out to John. When he did not respond, she hid under the blankets, trying to will her distress over to his immediate attention, wherever he may have gone gallivanting off to, leaving her all alone for god-knows-how-long in a just recently violated and vandalized homestead. She popped another sleeping pill to escape the lonesome dread. She thought it tasted funny, but had too many other things to worry about to even give it a second thought. She was out cold and snoring again before John had turned onto the next street in his route.

At the end of this serpentine, black river-road, he took a sharp right onto a street more endemic of the city's normal roadway maintenance. At times, many a cyclist will inevitably find themselves weaving through potholes like a slalom skier, and if they are not both highly skilled and hyper-focused like John, they may get their tire snared by one such pothole and then find themselves flying head first over their handlebars. John found the challenge fun, if not slightly irritating. The main benefit to taking this street, however, was that it had lain itself down directly in front of the little café where Donna worked. Even while passing, from across the street and through the occlusion of brick and mortar, John could see the majestic glow of her radiance, uncontainable and all enveloping. He blew her a kiss as he rode by.

The next stretch was mostly incline. The sun beat down hard, yet at the most strenuous point of one of the steepest hills, a cold chill ran through the length of John's body. He looked around him wildly, fully expecting someone to be hiding in the shadows, watching him through a pair of binoculars, possibly with a buck knife clenched between their teeth, all big and ugly and full of spite. Nothing of the such was to be found. Although, while it may have been nothing more than a trick of light, John was certain that he saw what could only be described as a "purple blur" which disappeared from his line of sight almost before he saw it. At the time, he did not realize the significance, but he was made to feel uncomfortable by the entire experience nonetheless. This uneasiness haunted him at least until the crest of the final incline of the trip, at which point it quickly fled his body, perhaps to find a host easier to control. John suspired with a long sigh. "Thank god," he thought. "It's all downhill from here."

****

"Okay, what's up, doc?" She crossed her arms, pouting ever so slightly.

"What size are you?" John eyed Donna up and down as he lit a cigarette.

"Excuse me?" She looked at him like he had just self-immolated and was reaching out for a hug.

"You look like a zero to me, same as my wife… ehrm, I mean ex-wife, soon-to-be…" John bit his lip and pushed out the most convincing tear you have ever seen.

Donna rolled her eyes, but deep down, she was touched.

John continued, "She's going to try to take everything in the divorce, I know it. She's just that sort of woman. And, well, I only just recently bought her all of these expensive designer clothes that she's not even worn yet, and I don't know why, but I thought of you and I—"

"Give me one of those, will you?" Donna broke in, pointing at John's smoking cigarette.

"Oh, yeah sure, here you go. Here, sweetheart, let me light it for you. A pretty girl never lights her own cigarette."

"What about an ugly girl?"

"You know full well that pretty people get better treatment. Anyway, as I was saying, I have all of these expensive clothes that I think you would just look great in, and besides—"

"Cool, I'm gonna stop you really quick. I'm not gonna fuck you. Just so you know."

John took a puff of his cigarette with a nonchalant James Dean smirk. He knew the fact that she had even mentioned sex meant she was considering it, and that while she may have said one thing, her true desires were otherwise revealed.

"Oh no, honey. You're beautiful, don't get me wrong, but

that's not what this is about. Like I said, I don't want these clothes wasted on my bitter ex-wife when they could be put to much better use adorning your exquisite structure. You know what I mean? I really do not want her going out on dates in clothes that I bought her. Look, at least come check them out. If you don't like them, fine, but I really think you will."

"Will that get you to leave sooner if I do?"

"If you so wish."

"Fine. Just hurry up. I took my lunch early because you insisted I meet you out here, but I really don't want to spend the whole thing with you. Y'know? Cool." Donna tossed her cigarette and plunged her hands into the pocket of her hoody— it was a sweatpants and hoody day, which may have accounted for the attitude. She stood off to the side, at a good safe distance while John opened up the back of the van.

"Woah," said Donna, stepping closer. "What's with all this stuff? It looks like you robbed someone."

"Don't be silly, all of that 'stuff' belongs to me. I'd just rather disseminate it to others than let my wife get it in the divorce. Which brings me back around to the topic of your size…" John plucked out a dress and held it up to Donna, closing one eye as he mentally undressed and redressed her. "Yeah, I thought so," he muttered, pulling out the various pieces of clothing. "These should fit perfectly." Altogether there were around twelve or thirteen of them, all with well known Italian designer names.

"Whatever," Donna huffed, perusing the clothes while feigning indifference. Every article was on it's best dog-at-the-pound-pick-me behaviour—she ended up taking them all home.

John helped load them into the trunk of her little grey sedan and made to leave, possibly to return when she was more amiable, after Mother Nature had run her course, after his freshly sown seeds of desire had a chance to sprout a bit. With just a small amount of tending, John predicted an inordinately bountiful harvest. Just as he had begun to turn back to the van, ready to give a cool, ride-off-into-the-sunset farewell, he was suddenly stopped in his tracks by an unexpected question from Donna.

"So what's up with Bruce?"

John said nothing. He simply scrutinized, trying to see exactly what Donna's true intentions looked like, trying to peer past all of her false pretences and façades, through her flesh and directly into the viscera of her soul. He was unable to get a perfectly clear picture, which must have shown on his face, for Donna quickly elaborated sans vocal prompting.

"Look, I know this is Bruce's van, isn't it? I've seen you two together here all the time, it's not like—look I just... I need to get in touch with Bruce. I've been trying to get a hold of him all day, do you know what's going on?"

"I could tell you, but then... well, you know." John winked and clicked his tongue.

"Groan."

"Just why do you want to get a hold of Bruce so bad? What, do you owe him money or something?" A wild guess— I don't know why he said it, John himself probably does not even know why he said it, but it just so happened to be accurate.

"How'd… Do you know when he'll be back?"

"I'm afraid he may be indisposed for some time."

"Ugh. Like how long?"

"Well, my dear, that is a bit hard to say, what with all the various factors involved, all of the moving parts. Let's just say he could be away for quite a while."

"And you don't have any way to get a hold of him?"

"Oh, I have lots of ways. What exactly do you think my relation is to Bruce anyway?"

"I don't know, something tells me you're not working for him. But, every time you guys are here, you're always whispering all secretively, and then now you're driving around in his van packed full of stolen goods while Bruce is up and disappeared… So, if I had to guess, I'd say something like either his partner or his boss."

"Something like that. Although, then, sweetheart, it would not be wise to talk about someone to whom you may be indebted, would it?

"Whatever, it doesn't really matter anyway. I'll just have to find another connect."

John was not sure what exactly that term meant in this specific context, but the slight hints of sexual connotation he was detecting made him feel both aggravated and slightly aroused.

"You, umm…" Donna bit her lip. "You wouldn't happen to be holding would you?"

John arched an eyebrow and gave her a sideways look.

"What? C'mon, please? You gotta have some…"

At this point, John began to realize she was talking about drugs.

"Sorry, sweetheart, I wouldn't have any on me."

"But you could get some, right?" Donna batted her butterfly lashes.

"Oh, I'm sure I could."

"I just need a little bit of dope. I've got twenty bucks, if you could just help me get like a half-gram. Or whatever you can get."

"Tell you what, hun. I'll do it, just cause I like you. Give me a couple hours, I'll be back."

"Word."

Quick aside, if you will pardon a slight digression; I personally have always disliked 'hun' as a pet name. I know that it is a diminutive for honey, and that is sweet and all, but to me it has always seemed somewhat barbaric, evoking images of Chinese Comanche-style horseback nomads, raping and pillaging their way across the Asian steppes. And yet, the way John used it was so smooth, so Casablanca casual, Donna could not help but melt a bit.

****

When John got to Pepe's, Pepe was not home. John was informed by Masha that he "vent out on biziness."

"Do you have any idea when he might be returning?" asked John.

"Soon, love. Yoo vait inside if yoo like."

John followed transfixed by her graceful steps. What do you call it when a man becomes mesmerized by the supple swaying of a woman's pelvis? 'Hip-nosis' (or 'Hip-Gnosis' if it reaches a religious pitch). A bad joke, I know, but it seemed fitting.

John sat stolidly and uncomfortably on the couch with Masha stretched out beside him in a languid alluring repose. Time seemed to stretch out longer than her soft milk-white legs. John felt uncomfortable for four separate reasons: First and foremost was due to the raging erection he was attempting to control with his crossed leg; the second reason was the simple craftsmanship of the couch, which was inadequately thin in cushioning at the spot where the structural crossbeam had been placed; the third being his concern as to what may occur should Pepe suddenly come home and chance upon the two of them in such a compromising position; lastly, and possibly most severely, John was uncomfortable because Masha, in some of her mannerisms and patterns of speech, reminded John of his mother.

John had a wonderfully close and loving relationship with his mother all throughout his adolescence. Around the onset of puberty, their relationship changed. She became convinced that he had been possessed by a demon, quite literally, and would make belligerent accusations that he was trying to poison her or make sexual advances, going so far as attempting a hunger strike and trying to perform an exorcism. It was not until it was too late and completely inoperable that it was discovered that Mrs. Smith had a brain tumour, slowly eating her personality away. Tragically, and slightly fortuitously, she died on John's 18th birthday, leaving her entire meagre life sum to her only child. As for his father, well… that is a story for another time. A story of adventure and exploration, heroic action and espionage… but another time, another time. As for now, back to the lumpy couch and smooth woman, both in near painful contact with John's body.

It was just then that the front door burst open and Pepe stumbled in, sweating profusely and splattered with blood.

"Ho-lee-fuck! I'm home, baby! I—oh, 'sup?"

John cleared his throat. "Well, I, umm… Is everything—I mean, are you…?"

"Nah, cuz, you know me, I was just taking care some business. Had a rodent problem, dig?"

"Those must have been some pretty big rats."

"Yeah, real nasty fuckers too."

"You don't mean… Are… are you talking about Bruce?"

"Da fuck?!? No. What the hell that supposed to mean?"

"Oh, did you not hear? Bruce got himself arrested, and—"

"And you thinking he mighta snitched on me."

"I mean, I suppose I had considered the possibility."

"Hmm. Alright, loc, listen, I'ma take a shower right quick, get this rat juice off me, then we can talk more bout this."

When Pepe returned, he handed Masha a small duffel bag, presumably filled with his blood-stained clothes, maybe his gun, and asked her to "take care of it". After she disappeared, Pepe and John got into the real meat of the subject. Eventually, they came to the unanimous decision that Bruce could not really be trusted further than they could swing a dead cat, or whatever the expression is. Despite this, Pepe insisted rather confidently that Bruce posed no real threat in the grand scheme of things—a position which John was starting to feel less confident about. Eventually the two did decide that Bruce's general unreliability should merit greater vigilance, at least given the particular circumstances. Over the course of the conversation, it seemed the two men were slowly retreating further and further into their poker faces, showing less and less of their hand, always making sure to keep a few cards hidden up their sleeve just in case.

After they had exhausted the topic, they got down to business—the unloading of the van, the appraisal of the goods, the barter, and the exchange. John even got a baggie of dope for Donna. Ostensibly, everything was good, and yet, as John was leaving Pepe's, he could not help but feel like he had somehow made an enemy. He was not completely wrong, but that enemy was not Pepe.

****

Back at the café, Donna was getting antsy. She had used the store phone to try calling Bruce thrice already and was contemplating a fourth when John Smith came strolling through the front door with a gallant look of heroism proudly worn across his handsome face. Donna practically gushed, running towards him from her podium.

"Hey Betsy, cover me a sec, will you? Please. I know, I know, c'mon don't be like that… I'll be right back… Thanks, doll, you're the best."

Out of the corner of his eye, as he was being dragged outside by the hurricane force of all 94 pounds of Donna Ivey, John saw something, or at least thought he saw something (for it would have been nothing more than a blur in such a span of time) that thoroughly sleeted his spine.

"You have it?" pleaded Donna.

John pulled out the small bag of heroin he had procured, glancing back at the café worriedly.

"Ohmygod, thanks, I owe y—" Donna bit her tongue, mentally kicking herself for saying exactly what she had wanted not to. "Anyway, here." She handed John a crumpled Jackson.

"I don't want that. How about a kiss instead, what do you say?"

"Fuck you."

John pulled the baggie back an inch just as Donna was tentatively reaching for it. "Oh, come on. Just a little kiss. What's it going to hurt, huh?" John winked. "I mean, after everything I've done for you…"

"Ugh, whatever, fine."

Donna stood on tip toes and John pulled her body close to his. He embraced her tightly, as he leaned in to place a kiss, firmly but gently, on her soft delicate mouth. He thought about how easily he could overpower her—push her to the ground and forcibly have his way with her; there is nothing she could do to stop him, no way she could fight him off. If he really wanted to—she was helpless in his arms. And yet—it was far more satisfying for him knowing that he had instead provoked it out of her own volition, that through the use of seductive reasoning, he had solved the mystery of her heart and now held the prize of his labours close to his chest, so close he could feel her warm, young body shudder with desire.

But there was something else on his mind as well, and that thing was proving so intrusively bothersome that it would require his immediate investigation, as much as he wanted to stay lip-locked with Donna in the parking lot for eternity.

Donna and John pulled away from each other simultaneously.

"I have to check something out. Here you go, sugar." John handed the baggie to Donna, glancing over his shoulder at the café once more.

What he was becoming more and more certain that he had seen in such a blur on the way out, was a man sitting alone at one of the tables in the back corner of the café, drinking a cup of tea, eating a scone, and reading the newspaper. What is so foreboding about that, you might ask? Well, this particular tea drinking, newspaper reading, scone munching man had a pair of small beady eyes, a hooked nose, and a twirly moustache, and to top it all off was clad in all purple, which, when calculated together, equals out to be none other than a one Mr. Ethelbert E. Ethelbert, whom at this point John was now convinced was following him. He decided to charge in and confront the pesky man.

John marched straight to the booth in the back corner, but there was no one seated there. The table was not empty, however. On the epoxied surface was an abandoned cup of

Earl Grey, still steaming with the steeping teabag yet unre-moved. Next to it was a newspaper, opened up to a partially completed crossword puzzle. On that open page, encircled bol-dly, was the hint for 13-Across: a 4-letter word for a Slovenian peasant. Ethelbert had undoubtedly been there just moments before, had seen that John had seen him, and left in a scrambled hurry—of this John was certain; exactly what it all meant, what he was trying to prove, what he hoped to gain, that was a little less certain.

John turned pale. He began to feel very ill. He decided to go home, parking the van somewhere nearby his neighbour-hood and riding back in on his bicycle—his profuse sweating did indeed make it look as if he had been out riding all day. As soon as he was inside, he threw himself head-first into bed, hoping to calm his worried stomach with sleep.

Chapter Ten

The fate of the moon and the sea is a tragic one: They are bound inextricably—a connection of love like no other pulls them together. The moon's radiant glow can be seen over and again reflected in each glimmering, multi-faceted wave of the sea, yet they are worlds apart; never can they be together. Forever, the sea must reach out with crashing waves, grasping for her ethereal light—eternally distant, yet eternally linked.

This tragic longing is felt most poignantly on those strange mystical nights when the sky is clear and the moon is full. The full moon, to those sensitively tuned, has an almost palpable tension in her beauty; she has a strange alluring midnight po-wer—Wiccan covens perform their pagan rites; sacrifices are made to Satan, Pan, and Bacchus; spirits are high; men turn to beasts and are hunted in the quicksilver moonlight, its soft sy-rupy glow thick enough for even teenage witches like Bella to bottle up.

Perhaps all of this tense energy was the reason why John was struggling so much to fall asleep. He kept tossing and turning like a shipwrecked sailor frantically swatting at the hu-ngry gulls that were dive-bombing his salt-soaked body. Every time he thought he was about to fall asleep, he would be jolted awake by one errant thought or another violently and obtrusively kicking in the door of his psyche and sending his parasympathetic nervous system into high alert. Heavy as his eyelids were, they refused to stay shut. His legs were restless and his pillow seemed depressed. Eventually, John found himself walking the moonlit streets, as he had usually done on the occasional sleepless night. The dark, expansive sky was a starless ultramarine. The air was still and the streets were empty, which gave his frenetic thoughts a little bit of room to breathe. John always found physical movement to be conducive to mental movement, and so he reasoned that if he walked around until his thoughts had worked themselves out, untangling from their Gordian knot, he could then return home clear-minded and able to finally rest in peace.

The streets around him were, quite literally, littered with trash, as if one of the city's garbage trucks had flown by at a hundred miles-per-hour with the back wide open. It was collecting in the corners and crevices of the gaunt twilight architecture, spilling into the street, filling the weedy gutters— fast food wrappers and empty bottles, spent lottos, broken needles and lost keys, partially disintegrating scraps of tabloid articles; plastic bags; soiled laundry; it all oozed like pus from the infected wounds of the city. Off in the distance, there was a lone coyote, once native to the area and displaced to the fringes, rooting through the garbage, trying to scrounge up a midnight snack. "Perhaps," thought John, "these are new renovations in accordance with city council's obviously intentional hidden agenda of making the city more comfortable for the homeless." At one point he was practically trudging through pile after pile of the stuff.

Suddenly, a plum 1968 Plymouth Road Runner went zooming past with a double beep of its horn, leaving John startled and in a cloud of dust. Then the car turned down a side street

John had never seen before. He had passed this way for years, sometimes multiple times a day, albeit typically while in transit, and yet somehow had never noticed it before. He considered the possibility that it had been only a trick of the light, that the car had not actually turned there, but instead somewhere much further off; still he continued forward, walking with the slow measured step of a skeptic. When he reached the place where the car had turned, there was indeed a path before him. There were no street signs. Nor were there street lamps for that matter, not that they were needed in the light of the full moon.

It was a relatively narrow pathway of Romanesque cobblestone (possibly a remnant of the civil war era) that sloped downwards and curved lightly off, tucking itself out of sight between the buildings towering around it. John's footsteps reverberated off of the uneven walls. Just around the bend, at the terminus of the alleyway, there lay nestled a quaint, rustic tavern with an inviting neon sign.

The place had a sort of 1940's post-WWII feel about it, back when Freedom still held meaning and The American Dream was alive and well. It also held a certain austere timelessness, giving one the impression that it could have been the clandestine meeting place of generation after generation of secretive stone masons. For some reason, as he was approaching the door of the tavern, John was filled with the distinct impression that there was someone waiting for him on the other side, and that whatever it was they wanted to tell him would irrevocably change his entire life. He opened the door the way Jesus Christ would have while on his way to the last supper—slow and trepidatious, yet with a steady, unwavering resolve.

The tavern was empty. The tables and chairs were empty. The bar was left untended. The only living thing inside was a spider busy spinning a web in the corner, and a few moths that, if all went according to the spider's plans, would not be living much longer. John decided to approach the bar and inspect the wares. He leaned over the counter, looking for the most expensive gin in the house, and noticed a light coming up through the floor. He knew immediately, without a vestige of doubt, that he had to investigate and find out more.

When he had gotten to the other side of the bar, he could see the glowing aureole of a trapdoor partially obstructed by a dishevelled floor mat that was haphazardly strewn onto the ground. It looked as if someone had spent a lot of time making it look as if the mat had been carelessly tossed in a way that would accidentally reveal the secret trapdoor beneath it. It almost seemed someone wanted him to find it, to dig deeper, to uncover the truth, whatever that may be. He proceeded to resolve, and resolved to proceed despite whatever foul beasts might be lying in wait for him on the other side.

Almost before he had pulled the latch, there came emanating from beneath a dull undulating roar, which John quickly recognized as the sound of a hundred or so separate conversations all coalescing into a single amorphous blob of intermingling polyrhythmic sound waves, all fighting to be heard over each other and over the muzak rendition of some

Cliff Friend tune (the title of which eludes me at this time) being played at too high a volume over the tinny P.A. system loudspeaker. After the third or fourth step, the air was thick with stale smoke. So much so that it was difficult to see further than your arms could reach. The swirling disco ball of sound was roaring in cadence with the bright festive lights and effervescence.

An absurd amount of people had packed themselves into this parlour like Viennese sausages. Vienna sausages, pardon the Freudian slip. John squeezed his way through the crowd of party-goers, trying to get to the source of the merriment. From his left, he heard an urgent whisper. He was not quite able to make out what was whispered, however, due to the noise of the crowd. He saw the shape of a body starting to disappear into the crowded smoke ahead and reached out to stop them.

"Wait!" John said, "I couldn't hear what you said, can you please repeat it?"

The alleged whisperer stopped and turned, all but their silhouette shrouded in smoke. They repeated themselves, this time calmly and evenly, but still, John could not hear them over the sounds of the party.

"I still couldn't—wait, don't go yet! This damned crowd. What the hell are they celebrating anyway? Where are you— Wait, I didn't hear what you said! Where did you…"

John tried chasing after this mysterious stranger who, although he could not get a solid glimpse of him, for some reason reminded John of his father, but the crowd became so dense that John lost sight of him completely. He pushed his way blindly through until the crowd suddenly broke.

There, in the centre of a round clearing were Donna and Bella. They were on the ground. They were completely nude, and their bodies were interlinked and writhing in some sort of burlesque contortion act. Their skin pressed against each other, sweat dripping from their nubile young bodies. The crowd hooted and hollered like retarded banshee monkeys.

Suddenly, there was a thunderous cannon report that startled everyone but the belle madonnas still wrapping themselves around one another. The crowd backed up, widening the clearing considerably, most every chuckle-headed gawker staring up in the air. Soaring above everyone's heads was a cannon-launched man with both arms outstretched before him. He flew past the flying trapezes and over the high wire, performing a somersault mid-air while four clowns rushed in to catch him with a blanket of iridescent silk. He landed, to resounding cheers, in the spotlight directly above the still entangled donne mabellas.

Then the clowns dropped the blanket, which draped over the contorted, shape-shifting bodies, conforming with its silken sheen to the feminine curves (a breast here, a thigh there). Bruce landed on all fours over the writhing figure, then stood fully erect, slowly peeling off the blanket. Donnabella coiled around Bruce's body like a double-helix boa and together they began to perform a series of very acrobatic body-posturing. The crowd went wild.

John attempted to rush in to stop them, but he was held immobile by the foursome of clowns. John never liked clowns

—at their best, a clown is little more than a drunken buffoon; at their worst, they are some strange savage paedophilic beast with bloody red lips. These particular clowns, like most, fell somewhere in the middle. John very much did not like being touched by them, but try as he might to extricate himself from their eight-handed grip, he could not muster the strength. Powerless to stop the act before him, John gave up on fighting and shut his eyes, trying instead to negate the event in his mind; he covered his ears, but he could still hear the ooh's and ahh's. He could still hear the scattered applause. He could still hear the performers performing. He knew, from the overwhelming response of the crowd, exactly when Bruce had finished.

Only then did his coulropathic captors release him. John rushed the stage, climbing up in a blind fury. By the time John had gotten up, Bruce was already slipping through the velvet curtains backstage. Belladonna lay in a puddle centre stage. She reached out to him, on her knees begging.

"Please… please don't hurt him."

He cocked back to hit her, but a conga line of clowns on stilts came between them doing the jig and the sabre dance to the tinny chromatic carnival music in the background. John turned in disgust and stormed off after Bruce.

The immediate backstage area was a maze of ropes and pulleys and levers, all rigged up and operated by dwarfish men in off-white coveralls. At the rear, past the racks of outfits and crates of props, past the animal cages, past the magician's box with the sawed woman, past the silk backdrops and broken appliances, a door anxiously latched shut. John ran to the door and ripped it open.

There, in what was little more than a broom closet, was Bruce and none other than Mr. Ethelbert, who immediately launched with a purple blur into a tunnel that had been carved into the wall just as John entered the room.

Bruce shoved an envelope into his pocket and mumbled to John, "...Yeah, so well, umm…"

John wrapped his hands around Bruce's throat.

Bruce gurgled out, "I... was just... looking out... for... you… pal…"

John loosened his grip slightly, and through a barrage of coughing, Bruce managed to spit out, "I swear, I was just trying to get some information, see what he knows about us, about you, y'know? I think this guy has his left hand in some serious shit, John. Secret society level shit. Hoods and masks. Bestiality. Paedophilia. Socio-economic control. All that."

John let go completely.

"I think he's gunnin' for you, John. Honestly, we should probably take him out before he takes you out, if you ask me. Cut off the head of the snake before it bites its own tail, as they say."

John poked his head into the tunnel. "It's quite dark, where does this lead anyway, Brucie?"

"Nowhere, it's just a dead-end."

At that moment, Bruce plunged the knife in, both figuratively and quite literally stabbing John in the back and kicked him through the mouth of the hole. The tunnel was sleek and slick and steep, and John tumbled down like a toddler on a playground slide. John almost expected to land in a pile of woodchips, waiting below to embed themselves into the palms of his hands and into his knees. Instead, he fell onto hard tile with a solid thud.

John had landed in a small dome-shaped room, barely large enough to crawl in, which suited his present abilities just fine. The room was decorated in red and blue mosaic-style ceramic tiling, intricate, interweaving patterns across every inch, floor to ceiling. Leading out from this dome-like chamber, there were four separate passages all heading somewhere deeper, somewhere darker. John froze, unsure which path to choose; unsure where any of the tunnels would lead.

Then he heard Ethelbert's grunts echo up through the tunnel on his left. John crawled over to the mouth of this tunnel, pulled the knife from his back and then, clenching the blade between his teeth, dove in head first, sliding along the smooth-glazed ceramic tiling. The tunnel twisted and turned, at times widening and narrowing, dropping steeply and levelling off here and there. John crawled when he had to and slid when he could, moving as quickly as his body could carry him. Eventually he caught sight of a purple spat rounding the bend. John surged forward ready to pounce.

Just around the bend, that same spat and its twin brother were clinging on by the shoes to a pair of purple-trousered legs that were rapidly disappearing into a small hole in the tunnel. John managed to grab those legs at the ankles and stop them, along with the rest of the body they were attached to, but only for a moment before the captured legs started to frantically kick. John doubled down on his grip, but he was pulled into the hole along with Ethelbert.

The two of them fell from at least a story high into a massive antechamber, the walls and ceiling of which were filled with more than a hundred or so similar such holes as the one they had just fallen from. Why these holes were there; where they all led to and where they led from; who or what had created them—these were all questions that John was too busy to be asking. In the moment, he was desperately scrambling to recover the knife that had flung from his mouth along with all of the air in his lungs when he had smacked into the hard ground. Every fibre of his being was focused on getting to the weapon before Ethelbert could. He frantically grasped the handle, nearly tripping over himself as he whipped around to face Ethelbert, slashing wildly.

But Ethelbert was not there. He was further off, crawling in the opposite direction, dragging a mangled, broken leg and leaving behind him a trail like a dark ruby slug. John followed the trail with a calculated prowl. When he got to the violacious body, he could clearly see the jagged femur bone protruding from Ethelbert's leg. John stepped on the limp leg, digging in with the ball of his foot the way one would when squishing a cockroach. Ethelbert let out an inhuman wail, trying to scratch and claw his way out from under John's foot like a fox in a trap. John swung his other leg and kicked Ethelbert over onto his back—from there he straddled him, knife overhead.

Ethelbert's face was a geyser—tears flowing undammed, snot pouring like tree sap, spit dribbling from his chin in a thin river. "Please…" he blubbered, "please…"

John drove the knife down into his chest all the way to the hilt. Ethelbert's body arched and collapsed. He slowly lifted his head up, and staring John directly in the eyes, gurgling on the dark ooze spilling over his teeth, he sputtered out, "Gotcha!" and then died.

John tried to pull the knife out, but try as he might, it would not budge; the black goo that was pouring from Ethelbert's wound was keeping it firmly stuck—King Arthur himself would not have been able to pull the blade out. Then he realized that he could not let go of the knife. The shimmery black ooze had splashed all over him and was keeping his hand glued to the thick gushing wound in Ethelbert's chest. The harder he fought to extricate himself, the deeper entangled in the quicksand pitch he became. He fought with every bitter inch of his strength until he was almost completely engulfed, at which point something inside him snapped on, some spark in his mental machinery that assured him that it was okay, to give in, to stop fighting.

John disappeared into the black sludge like a shadow into the night. Then nothingness. Pure black emptiness. No, not quite pure black emptiness—that would imply both a perspective and something to perceive, a space to be empty, a blackness to be pure. No, for a moment, John caught a glimpse of absolute nothingness. Actually, that is not quite right either —absolute nothingness is both sub-instantaneous and super-infinite, time and relativity would hold no illusion, there would be no "moment," and there could be no "glimpse," it is not even something we can properly imagine, not truly. We can try, but the way the mind works, we cannot imagine nothingness, we can only ever imagine things and then negate them; we can negate everything, but we still will not be left with nothing—We, my friends, will still be here imagining. And so, John could not have possibly experienced nothingness, for there would be nothing to experience—yet, when he came to, sputtering and retching on the irregular tiles of the uneven floor, the viscous black ooze absorbing into his seizing body, he held the distinct impression that he somehow had experienced just that—an impression which seemed determined to pursue him to the ends of the earth. It left an obfuscating fog, which faded away in distinct stages.

At first, John was completely unable to differentiate himself from anything else, and so he just lay there like a dead fish, not knowing how to experience, until with the help of his aforementioned sputtering and retching, he became violently aware of himself. As he got up and looked around, he was still unable, however, to differentiate anything else besides him— the floor and the walls and the ceiling, the ceramic tiling covering them all with their own various detail, the debris on the ground, the dust in the air, the air itself—nothing was separate from anything else, everything was congealed all into one mess of indecipherable chaos. It was simply himself, and then everything that was not himself—which I am sure you would agree would be terrifying—or empowering, depends on the person, I suppose. For John, it was certainly both. Once having firmly established his own perspective, however, John was able to slowly piece together (in relativity to himself, of course) the strange spatial-temporal projection of sensory perception. That is, for the less learned yet admirably diligent reader: His brain fog slowly cleared and he was again able to tell this from that and one thing from another.

What he could not tell, which was becoming increasingly more alarming, was exactly which one of the hundreds of tunnels in this massive antechamber was the one that would lead back out. John paced a bit, his strong Socratic logic powerless in the peril of such an illogical riddle. Then, as he was doubling back, he hit the perfect angle to notice a faint coruscation of light reflected in the mouth of one of the tunnels. John threw all of his chips in and headed straight for that tunnel.

The mouth was large enough for John to walk through upright, his footsteps and their echoes pitter-pattering in a rhythmic round. Just around a sharp bend, the source of light was illuminated—strung along almost perfectly in the centre of the tunnel-roof at nearly exact intervals, were flickery halogen bulb after flickery halogen bulb. Even with this blinding array of incandescent light, the tunnel still seemed rather dark.

After a while of walking, Bruce turned to John, "You know pal, I do wish it didn't have to be this way. I really do." Bruce was wearing a Gestapo-esque prison guards uniform and had managed to cuff his hand to John's when John was not looking. "In the end, the sentence of death was passed by a greater majority than that by which he was initially found guilty. Least that's what they said. Don't know what that says about society or humanity or whatever, but… just thought you should know, y'know? Anyway…"

"Where are we going?"

"Oh, don't give me that, you already know the answer."

The entire walk, Bruce kept a careful hand on his sidearm. At the end of the hall was a brightly lit, sterile room with a hospital bed in the centre, Belladonna standing next to it in a sheer latex nurses outfit, dripping full syringe in her hand. Before John could even fight, he was strapped to the bed. At that point, his struggles made little difference, achieving nothing but a tightening of his restraints.

John spat at Bruce, "Et tu, Brucé!? Eh? You really are nothing but a back-stabbing bastard, aren't you?"

"I'm sorry John, but… you can't tell me you wouldn't do the same."

John could see the faint silhouettes of gawking faces from behind the mirrored-glass wall. Belladonna grabbed John's left hand. Bruce crossed his arms, turned away. Just as Belladonna plunged the needle into John's vein, he awoke with a start, practically jumping out of bed and thrashing poor Mary, sweat pouring off him, his entire left arm numb and pulsating with a deep, burning electric ache. The glacial air-conditioned breeze splashed against his wet skin and sent him shivering uncontrollably like a sphinx in the snow, making it impossible for him to fall back asleep.

Despite what he knew Bella would have said about it (the spiritual importance of tunnels, the religious significance of red and blue in East Asia, the clairvoyant aspects of dreams in general, the summation of numerological sequences) John was certain that this dream, like any other, was no more than sense-less brain-babble exasperated by stress—the only real message he could make out of it was that he could not trust Bruce any longer, which was something he already knew. He was incli-ned to dismiss the whole nightmarish event entirely; even then —he still decided to write it down in his journal. Interesting.

****

John did not leave the house until well after dark. He stayed away from the doors and windows. He knew that he was being watched. That day, John received two phone calls that were like twin harbingers of ill omen sent to confirm his fears. "Beware the Ides of March," they may as well have been saying.

The first call was in regards to his insurance claim; he was being summoned to argue his case in front of a tribunal—something that they do not usually do. More on that later. This call had caused a certain feeling of anxiety, but it was completely eclipsed by the second.

The second call was Bruce with some "good news". He said that in his preliminary hearing the judge threw out the entire case on a technicality, something about due process. Point being, with the charges dropped, the police had less than twenty-four hours to press new charges or set him free. At this point it seemed like they were just going to let him go, once they begrudgingly got around to filling out and filing his paperwork, of course. It would probably take them several hours, but by the end of the day, god willing, he should be out on the streets again and, anyway, would John be able to grab his van and pick him up, not at the station but near there? John agreed. Bruce would call from a bar a little ways off from the station once he was released.

As soon as John hung the receiver on the wall, he could feel the gears turning in his head, grinding and wearing against one another with tightly clenched tension—If you look hard enough, you can almost see the smoke coming out of his ears. It was obvious Bruce had not gotten off on a technicality. That sort of thing only happens in pulpy crime fiction trash, not in real life. No, the whole thing positively reeked of a squeal deal. Here is a tip, my sweet, naïve reader: Always consider the source. The fact that Bruce had chosen to lie to him alerted John to the high probability that he, himself, may be in danger —which was a state of being a Type-A like John was not accustomed to being in, and as such, was one in which he was loath to be in any longer than necessary.

From the moment John had awoken, he had known viscerally that something had to be done. He had to sever ties; there was no other way around it. They could not just shake hands and walk away, however, not at this point. No, Bruce poised far too great a risk, with his knife hovering over John's back; drastic measures would be required to ensure Bruce remained silent.

****

"Thanks for comin', pal, you're a goddamn lifesaver, seriously. I can't believe they held me so long, spiteful little sadistic pricks. This is my friend Chuck, I just met him here. He's a good guy."

"Nice to meetcha, you must be John." Chuck reached out to shake John's hand. He had the obvious look of an undercover cop.

"Let's go," said John drily.

"Yeah, yeah, sure thing, it's just… well, I told 'em you would have my cash to pay for drinks, y'know? Only about twenty bucks."

"Fine." John paid the bartender and they left. John drove the van.

"So yeah, you ever been to that bar before?" Bruce asked. "It's funny, it's less than a mile from the police station, and it's owned by this biker and his old lady, and they probably run more speed through there than all the other dealers in town combined. It's sorta like the unofficial first stop when you get outta jail."

Bruce was rather talkative, John not so much.

"Fuck, I'm hurtin'. I need to get home and get right asap. I feel like death. Oh wait! That's right!" Bruce started scrambling into the back of the van. "I should have some gear in my toolbox!" Bruce combed through the metal toolbox that was bolted to the floor of the van, mumbling to himself incoherently. In one of the drawers he found what he was looking for. "Yes! Thank fucking God! That's what you call planning ahead!"

Bruce pulled a tasselled leather medicine pouch out from within the toolbox. He lustily ripped it open and pulled out a spare needle and spoon he'd hidden within. He crawled over the centre console and stretched his arm out to the glove compartment, where his heroin stash was tucked away. He opened the glove compartment and reached into the bag of black tar inside, breaking off a sizeable chunk. Bruce then slid back into the rear of the van like a grotesque arachnid pulling its prey with greedy mandibles down into its lair.

"Hey, try to drive real smooth, will you?"

Bruce broke off a smaller piece from his chunk and set it into the spoon, which was resting on top of the toolbox, pocketing the rest. He filled the spoon with water from an old plastic bottle that had been lying in that van for who-knows-how-long and then held it over the flame of a lighter until the water began to boil. The light of the flame reflected quite brilliantly off the silver tanks of the poison sprayers that were strapped against the walls of the van. Once the heroin had completely suffused in the water, Bruce set the spoon back on top of the toolbox and patted himself down, looking around searchingly.

"Oh shit, I don't have a... Hey John, you got a smoke on ya?"

John reached into his pocket and pulled out his cigarette case.

"Careful man!" The spoon wobbled nervously.

"Whatever," John scoffed as he handed the cigarette case back behind him. "Here."

"Oh, thanks." Bruce pulled out a cigarette and bit into the end of it. He ripped out the filter with his teeth and tossed it into the spoon. Immediately it soaked up the dark water, plumping up like an Edenic apple ready for the plucking. As Bruce was sucking the dope up into the syringe, he turned towards John and asked him (or the back of his chair, head and right shoulder, and the top corner of his forehead reflected in the rear view mirror, rather), "So yeah, how did it go with Pepe? Were you able to get a good price for all that stuff we took from your house?" Bruce untied one of the straps on the bug spray tanks and looped it around his arm. "You wouldn't happen to have my share of the cash on you, would ya, John?"

John wondered if he were to slam on the brakes right at that moment, would it kill Bruce? Probably not. Perhaps if he drove into oncoming traffic—but that would pose far too great a risk on his own well-being. John answered pensively; he knew that Bruce was most likely wearing a wire, and John refused to fall into his trap.

"All is good. I'm not sure exactly what you are talking about, but I think we should get you home and can talk about that stuff tomorrow."

Through the tightly pulled strap between Bruce's teeth, he managed to mumble out, "Oh, umm, alright..." Bruce was obviously not satisfied with the answer, mostly because, as John intended, it gave him nothing to work with, no angle to attack, it was too neutral and non-specific and certainly would not hold up in a court of law; the bulk of his attention, however, was completely used up, focused on trying to slip his needle into one of the dehydrated veins of his forearm.

When he finally struck blood, he plunged the syrette

slowly, spitting out the end of his tourniquet in an ecstatic release. He pulled out the needle and sank back into a pile on the floor. For a moment John thought he was dead. Then, Bruce let out a soft, raspy moan of pleasure, which could almost be mistaken as a death rattle had Bruce not immediately proceeded to grumble on barely coherently about how he could really use the money, and how it wasn't fair of John to withhold it, and how he had done his part, and weren't they supposed to be partners, anyway? And then this and that about John and this and that about Pepe and this and that about the money for the stuff they had stolen. The entire mumbled monologue was interspersed with periodic lapses into unintelligible muttering as Bruce kept nodding off mid-sentence. Partway through his speech, without stopping the disimpassioned tirade, he wriggled back into the front passengers seats like a shiny black sea slug.

Bruce lit the filter-less cigarette, took a long drag, then just started staring at the glowing tip of the cigarette in his hand. "I'm sorry, John, I uh… umm… I, umm…" Bruce let out an exasperated sigh. "Anyway, I know you'll make sure I get what I'm owed… it's just I, I… umm… I owe a lotta money to, umm, well y'know, to people that it's not smart to owe a lotta money to… umm, uh…" Another sigh. Some more nodding off. A bit of drool. "Anyway, it's nothing more than what I'm owed."

John cracked and decided to pull over and give him his share, even though he was catching the definite scent of a trap; he figured it would at least shut him up a bit, and as long as he watched what he said and maintained plausible deniability, there was not anything necessarily incriminating about one friend giving money that is owed to another friend.

After pulling into an empty lot, John turned to Bruce, "You're right. I do want to make sure you get what you deserve." He slowly, deliberately reached into his inner jacket breast pocket.

Bruce flinched, but played it off as a shiver when John pulled out his wallet.

John grabbed a few Franklins and handed them over to Bruce. "Here you go."

"What umm... what did Pepe—Is this all that we got John?" Even completely strung out and dribbling, Bruce still managed to keep name-dropping like a good little rat.

"That is everything I owe you."

Bruce's eyes may have been glossy, his cheeks damp, but that subserviently ingratiating woe-is-me act of self-deprecation was wearing thin, proving to be nothing more than a threadbare handkerchief lain over a bear-trap. "We gotta find a fresh mark to hit... I need the cash, y'know, I need... I was at that station so long... so many questions... plea deals, witness protection maybe... I don't know if I shoulda..." He dozed off, slumping against the door panel of the van.

This gave John time to ruminate, both on Bruce's oafish attempts at a subtle threat and exactly what his plan of action should be. John decided to drive Bruce home. Bruce was pretty wasted and John wanted to make sure that both he and his van made it home that night and did not wind up back in police custody.

Bruce nodded in and out all the way there, until the van was crunching against the gravel of his cheap pre-fab house's midget driveway. Almost before the van had stopped, he jumped out of the door, grabbed a hold of the hood for stability, and began projectile vomiting. After Bruce had finished exorcising the contents of his stomach, John helped him into the house, with only a minimum of fumbling around with the lock.

The small house was dark, with all the windows covered, the only light came from the red glow of the answering machine blinking with thirteen new messages. Bruce waited until after John had left to listen to the messages. Nearly every single one was asking to speak to some woman named Yolanda.

****

John walked to the nearest convenience store and called for a cab. As soon as he got home, he started to gather supplies.

There was, all stuffed together in a large backpack: a buck knife, a length of rope, a roll of duct tape, a small campfire stove, a can of propane, a saucepan, a couple bottles of water, a pair of gloves in a plastic bag, a towel, a compass, a pair of tongs, and a book of matches.

Even with all of that extra weight, the bike ride back to Bruce's was like nothing. John felt alive, exhilarated, his body electrified, his mind sharp. He cut through the air like a swift quicksilver messenger-god traversing the entire distance in what would have felt to him like only a snap instant.

John approached Bruce's house, walking in a silent, stealthy foxtrot—with one foot turned perpendicular to the other and the weight of each step rolled first from the outer side of the foot over to the inner, like an experienced hunter on the prowl, like a midnight lion. Cue the tense background music and chilling aquaphone sound effects.

John peeked in an exposed corner of the window—Bruce was passed out on the couch in front of a coffee table of freshly used paraphernalia, ostensibly out for quite some time. "Sorry Bruce, but you'd do the same if you were me."

John crept over to the van, opened it up with the spare key stuck to the tire well, and slipped in. There, in the back of the van, he began to unpack.

First he pulled the gloves out of the plastic bag, slipped them on, and set the bag aside.

He hooked up the camp stove to the can of propane, placed the saucepan on the burner and filled it up with water. John lit the stove, setting the water to boil, then crawled up front (in a similar fashion to the way Bruce had earlier) and pulled the freezer bag of heroin out of the glove compartment.

Then he popped open the lids of the silver poison sprayer tanks. John remembered Bruce telling him about the poisons— a water-soluble powder blend mixed up by Bruce himself, something he was rather proud of. There was a blue one and a red one, one for bugs and one for rodents, but John could not remember which he had said was which. He decided to mix them both together—Bruce was, after all, some sort of ghastly hybrid of the two things, sneaking around behind John's back, plotting his demise, so it seemed only natural; cover all the bases, so to speak. The off-blue and the off-red mixed together to make a nasty purplish brown, which John dumped into his plastic bag.

Along with the mixture of powder, John dumped Bruce's entire stash, trying to keep the same ratio that he had seen Pepe use when cutting Bruce's dope with the lactose powder. He tied up the bag with a tight knot, shook it up, and tossed it into the boiling pot of water.

After three or four minutes, John fished it out with the tongs and turned off the burner; the heroin had melted into a near black ooze, which had completely absorbed the rotten-aubergine coloured powder.

John pressed it flat and let it cool. Once it had hardened, John smacked the bag against the corner of the toolbox a couple times. The toolbox did not seem to notice, but the heroin broke down into several pieces.

John ripped open the plastic bag and dumped the dope back into Bruce's freezer bag, peeling bits off from the plastic where it had stuck. Once it was back home in the freezer bag, it was indistinguishable from its prior self, even its own mother would not be able to tell anything had happened.

John tucked the bag of heroin back into the glove box (a faerie child to its crib) and cleaned up after himself—he dumped the water in a patch of weeds, mopped up the van with his towel, packed everything up, and left just as silently and stealthily as he had come.

The only thing left to do now was to wait. Eventually that

fateful stab would come that would be worth one hundred stabs in the back.

****

The very next day, Bruce w

Chapter Eleven

I need a new chapter.

Everything | is a mess of | chaos / Nothing | has remotely gone | the way planned. | Furthermore, | I do not even / know how | it will go / in ultimatum / I presumably can not | even tell | you | a fraction of everything that happened / concurrently my | several, anxiety inducing / last few days | with out appropriating | everything and commandeering the | tale into my own. / Cataclysmic | pops into mind. Well | I was | interrupted mid | thoughtstream, violently mind / you | without sign or warning, | and I | have had to | scramble | to get back | my sensibilities and understanding, and maintain / constant | ward on the tale. | As / I approach considerably near | to what | ultimately, I understand is | invariably | the end, misfortune | and fortunate fate | both / have made | me far too / busy to contemplate even | the concept | of writing; so, / previous | concepts disappeared, rapidly | decaying, morphing, evolving / into something different, | new ones | completely took over | in / fire and desperate fury, | begging, screaming, bemoaning | with impatience and / with vicious | impertinence for | somebody to collect everything | completely, without missing | anything, set | all / absolute | details, indelibly, infallibly / down. No lie, | it | is | becoming exceedingly hard to continue forward / currently, | to just pick up | as / everything had been | left. | Besieged | by perilousness, | my life | has constantly been at | risk. A fair / fare for our | embracing infinite perspective. / Do not fret senselessly, | no worrying, | I will see | everything /

to conclusion, | to our end, / proceeding | cautiously, deliberately. Although / ostensibly I'm rambling, I | understand intrinsically, without | cerebral occlusion | that absolute universal truth | lies somewhere in the | chaos | concealed | deep | down beneath the top | surface. I predict, hopefully, / everything will naturally move | in accordance with the | calamitous hurricane inferno | hid in synchronicity, | creative flow will / commence | and I may find | Truth. / Although I realize I'm | not creating the tale | per | sé, obviously, | I'm painfully live | to | my role as | guardian, / not all responsible for | the inviable | questions of intrigue and | suspense, / for questions inevitably | made by | practically | all: 'what' and 'why', / apropos I do | understand completely, gravitationally | well the important | dominion I have over | precisely | 'how' everything is represented, in essence. / Forgive, | merciful readers, forgive, / I positively, absolutely will, | if possible, like | to | pull our saga | to its immediate | conclusion without | ado, / nothing | remains simplistic indefinitely, / however. The inviolable | preservation of | truthful, honourable honesty, | in whichever outlandish, / obscure | way perceived, is | a non negotiable. | Justice | must be gave to / the cast | and to my / meticulous | research. Otherwise, otherwise, / otherwise what is | the | purpose? Justice must | be observed. I | will positively, | absolutely have to | find / out precisely who | John | is, whatever | he's becoming when he | is done | running. | Whether he escapes completely / or he's | apprehended by | Ethelbert, | viciously murdered perhaps. / Obliged, | we must make sure | that / all know what | happened. | We must disseminate | the news completely. I | have just recently come / fatefully, undeniably fatefully, | upon a library here, / a miniature one | but | one nonetheless, | a library that has | in its | possession | archived all circulated editions / available | of The Star (indulgent / rag newspaper), | specifically one | edition that was / just recently circulated, one | such that contains | some articles that I | find extremely interesting. I | realize this current digression's / nothing | but procrastination and, | as such, invariably | will | therefore just have to get removed | normally by editors or | be skipped over | by the | readers, however, | let / us not obliviate the | holy pact | between us, forgetting the | promises | made. I'm | completely, infallibly, unremittingly, | obliged to | leave everything, all details, even accidents, / unedited; be careful wishing. | Grammercy, grammercy, readers, | I am merciful: / if happenstance | may persuade you | to / disregard this | unnecessary, superfluous section | completely, | or blot out each | word, I'll | accommodate with | demarcations strategically put / directly at the end | of this digression, | immediately / I've regained / all my lost | momentum. | Putrefied venomous revenants, | in disguise and | callous rage, seething horribly, / boiling over ceaselessly, painfully | wrenching, horrendously twisting | can not blockade / my continuation. | I absolutely need | to / discover | just | who, precisely who, John | is, otherwise… And who | am I | exactly, you | inquire? Nobody. It / matters not, ultimately. Realizing | recently precisely, exactly | thus, I've elected | to publish not | with my name | but | a peachey nom de | plum, a pseudonym both | conservatively interesting and with difficult pronunciation. / Ultimately | this will give room | to honesty, | breathing / room for the tale. | I will | disappear like a | phantom and fade | into | ethereal, fair / nothingness. Although | then, | well, nevermind, | nevermind, your | lead isn't | leaving you | completely. Certainly not. / It just | isn't my tale, / not ultimately. | I certainly did not | break everything; I am / just the one | who | is picking up each | of the disparate bits, | collecting each tiny clue and attempting | to put | kintsugi together; | I'm desperately chasing at | Truth absolute, that is | all. I | am | connecting the dots | if anything, but ultimately they exclusively / were dots cast | by Fate; | players were | positioned by actions of | free / autonomy. In | actuality everything, everything / manifested completely, entirely | because of | free / will, free will | that | is | determined, determined | by Fate, by / all of our | perceptions interwoven | in tenuous | and unreliable knot | connections. / And | anyways, it's | understood, presumably perhaps, | that no "reality", | absolutely intrinsically, is | real; it's just you, / floating | throughout emptiness, nothingness… / yet everyone, everything, lies | in | a | vast interconnected web, / entangled into one big | mess, | trapping us | in | it's overarching | metaphysical | shell. Even were I / transcended | past all that, I | know / I can not | ever make alterations | to anyone's past. | I'm no creator god, | only demiurge, | destined to recreate the | job, | metaphorically speaking, in my intellectual imagination, / over infinitely, cyclically with | no respite. | If it were | possible, / showing | pity to all the | poor | cast that |

were involved in / it, to make | a | few amendments, I may, | but I'm constrained by | determined Fate. Just how many replayings | have occurred | repetitively in my mind? | The same path | traversed, explored completely | then continuing on? | Continuing on, to what? | Some | ultimate end, for / certain. Or perhaps not. | Commodious recirculation inevitably | is returning my | mind constantly towards the | beginning, replaying everything | over, searching for | the | Truth concealed | in everything. If I / can't vary the past | tragedy, then necessity requires | I've ensured justice is | properly recognized (regarding | anyone who's incapable, or | are inevitably soon | to be, | of any such | goal, not | able | to tell any | interlocutor besides the dead unlistening continuum) / to get / everything down with | accuracy. Nothing matters | more. Not anything. | Nothing, more or less. | Fathomless / full figures, | statues sunk, | colossus past forgotten, tragedies | begotten possibly intentionally: | civilizations lost | to / time, genetic memories | and all | but vestiges of the | past disintegrated, all the / grandeur now long gone, | now / unremembered, lost forever. "No, | no, nothing of the | sort | will ever, ever happen | to | us." Audiences don't / get | injured. Not | usually. Perhaps, perhaps | I may decease, | although spiritually I'll | live on, I must / continue | forward. Onward, onward / to the ending, and | in the | process mine | perhaps. A risk / necessary | to our tale, yet | a risk | I take with / trepidation nonetheless. | For | what may come? | What may be | in waiting, | lurking underneath the | Truth? | What horrors? What nightmares? What dangers? / Two mad men |

circling | in from | the opposite pole, both | now spiralling down, down | rapidly towards a spot universally central. / When one overpowers and | consumes (figuratively speaking) | that adversarial foe / completely, | will it make a | beat? / Will it even | be noticed | somewhat? Or perhaps | it's / falling unheard somewhere | now. Or perhaps, just / possibly, it | completely, irrevocably deconstructs / everything, complete obliteration, | ripping our | very | livelihoods asunder. All my prescient understanding / says we absolutely must | tenaciously, unequivocally, zealously | make certain that / whomever is | victorious positively, perfunctorily, / won't, unabated, be | able | to completely | get away with | everything. Everyone everywhere | absolutely must / know. Unironically | pathetically, / it's honestly | and regrettably all we | can accomplish. But then | circumnavigation eventually returns us to our / path, and / illuminated, we see | that we | accomplished all we / required; we | gambled everything honestly, | transparently, / something the majority | can't say, | and success is near | full certainty, so long / we stay true now, | make | no mistakes, and / pay attention | intently our | surroundings. We will / all live / on forever, | remembered eternally, / chronicles told | generations onward, timeless | transcendence; / our responsibility pertains, practically | inherent within itself, | to let all our | accounts be / told. Let the | chasing commence, | in a | manner | of talk. This hall | of records is signifying a closure. // Dear reader, let me ask you something (if you haven't skipped ahead like most sensible people would have)—Have you ever heard of pursuit predation? Let's assume you have not, just to be safe. Of course I do not think of you as some dead-eyed slack-jawed dimwit, my overly sensitive reader, this is just to cover all bases. "Pursuit predation" is when a predator chases or "pursues" their prey, as opposed to "ambush predation" where a predator sets a trap and waits for their prey to fall in. Simple enough, no? Of course, some pursuit predators also employ ambushes, only it is as a strategic part of their pursuit, not as their entire modus operandi. "The chase." "The thrill of the hunt." I've heard detectives say that chasing the criminal is more exhilarating than actually catching them could ever be. Seasoned hunters say the same thing. As do many pick-up artists. And serial killers. The most terrifying form of pursuit predation, however, is most certainly "persistence predation".

Imagine for a moment, if you will, that you are some wild creature, minding your own business, gambolling about, grazing in the pasture, maybe even hunting your own small game (no judgement there) when you are suddenly and violently attacked by some other wild creature. You manage to slip your attacker and outrun them into cover, but they continue at a steady pace behind you, pushing forward like a 1980's slasher movie monster. You keep growing distance between yourselves, until you can no longer see them behind you. Still, deep within, you know you can not stop yet. You run until your legs will no longer move beneath you and you finally drop down exhausted in what you presume is a safe spot to rest. Then, in the dead of the night, just when you have started to let down your guard and it almost feels safe to think about sleep, your pursuer appears and the cycle repeats. They are neither bigger nor faster, stronger nor smarter, but they are relentless in their pursuit. They simply track and follow. They do not rush and they never rest; they stalk and chase until their prey succumbs to exhaustion and falls before their feet. Thus was the hunting style utilized by wolves, early Man, and African dogs.

"Reverse pursuit predation" (a horrifyingly effective, yet dangerously bold form of pursuit predation) however, has not been as commonly observed, having had strictly anomalous precedents.

Imagine now, dear reader, that you are well aware of this persisting nature in your predator. You intentionally leave a trail for them to follow. You keep yourself just within sight, but just out of reach, forcing the paths of your opponent, making them push themselves harder and harder, disappearing and reappearing only when they have nearly given up. You make them think they are chasing you, you make them think they have almost gotten you in their grasp, but in reality, you are the one chasing them. You work your way to higher gro-und, waiting for them to slip, and then you pounce. Through foaming tooth and nail, you declare to your pursuer, "I am more muscular, more cunning, faster and larger than you are, and I am a genius, while you could hardly pass the entrance examinations to kindergarten. So, I'll give you the customary two minutes to say your prayers." And then…

The only recorded incident of reverse pursuit predation I was able to find in my research was of a lost Alsatian taking down a bear—a very dramatic fluff piece involving a hired tracker and a self-declared "Gonzo journalist" spending three nights in the woods and ending with the two men and the dog feasting on bear meat together. There is, however, a folk tale I once heard, maybe originally of Tohono, or Punjabi or Bengali origin—someplace ancient and slightly mythic, where creation myths and cosmogonies abound. This particular adage is about a rat living in the jungle.

One day, in the heat of the setting sun, Rat comes across Lion, curled up and snoring, having fallen asleep during his afternoon sun bath. Seeing the fearsome King of the Jungle slumbering in regal repose, Rat decides to seize the day, using this opportunity to usurp the throne and take the King's place.

Rat creeps up slowly, silently, making sure not to wake the sleeping lion. When he reaches the beast, he opens his jaws wide, and clamps down, sinking his teeth deep into the pad of Lion's front paw. Lion springs up, roaring and snarling, claws extended, but Rat is already scurrying away, swishing his tail tauntingly as he goes.

Enraged, Lion gives chase, leaping after him, but Rat is ready. He evades masterfully and manages to keep Lion just on his tail for three days and three nights. On the fourth day, the gap is starting to close in, each pounce getting closer and closer.

That, however, is exactly what Rat wants, for just at that moment, they are reaching the bramble thickets. Lion gears up for his fateful pounce, launching himself into the air, but Rat dives into the dense, thorny coils of bramble-bush vines. Lion lands in the thorns roaring, but refuses to give up chase.

Lion rushes after Rat. He pushes and claws his way further and further into the bramble until he becomes completely ensnared in the vines, punctured by thorns and covered from tip to tail in lacerations, yowling and writhing in a futile attempt to rip himself free. The more he fights to get out, the more tightly he becomes tangled.

That is when Rat pounces. He slowly devours the former King of the Jungle and takes his place on the throne as new King, ready to usher in a fresh new era.

Of course, all the other hungry jungle animals would be sure to take notice.

Anyway, I thought you might find that interesting. It certainly was not the most interesting thing I happened to come across at the library, however. No, that would have to have been the articles in the latest issue of The Star—more on that later. I also received an email response from John's insurance company/employer. They have finally accommodated my request for the transcript from John's case hearing, albeit with redactions throughout.

Aha!

Oh yes, I almost forgot, your asterisks:

****

FROM THE TRANSCRIPTS

OF CASE NO. 11235*

*for legal reasons, the names of certain

insurance executives, and the insurance

company they are the executives of, have all

had to be changed.

BILLINGS & EVERMORE, LLC.

DEPARTMENT OF FRAUD INVESTIGATION

EXECUTIVE HEARING ROOM

BILLINGS & EVERMORE, LLC

VERSUS   NO. 11235

JOHN SMITH   SECTION "Z"

Insurance Claim Hearing

Motion to Deny

Testimony and Notes of Evidence,

taken in the above-entitled and -numbered

cause, before the HON. QUINCY BILLINGS, CEO

and A BOARD OF DIRECTORS presiding on the

13th day of [INFORMATION REDACTED].

```
APPEARANCES:

     PRESIDING:

               QUINCY BILLINGS, CEO
                         OWNER AND OPERATOR OF
                         BILLINGS AND
                         EVERMORE, LLC

          BOARD OF DIRECTORS:

               EDMOND LYNCH, CFO
                         PARTNER

               THOMAS BRIGHT, COO
                         MAJOR SHAREHOLDER

               CLARK SAWTELLE
                         HEAD OF DEPARTMENT
                         OF FRAUD INVESTIGATION

               AGATHA HARDY
                         HR REPRESENTATIVE

          REPRESENTING THE PROSECUTION:
               ETHELBERT E. ETHELBERT, ESQ.
                         INVESTIGATIVE AGENT

          REPRESENTING THE DEFENDANT:
               JOHN SMITH
                         THE DEFENDANT




TRANSCRIBED BY:
     DAMSIL ILLIANA ZAZOWSTOK, RPR
               OFFICIAL REPORTER
               IN AND FOR THE COMPANY OF
               BILLINGS & EVERMORE, LLC
```

BILLINGS & EVERMORE, LLC

VERSUS   NO. 11235

JOHN SMITH   SECTION "Z"

OFFICIAL PROCEEDINGS

1   **THE COURT (QUINCY BILLINGS):**   Thank

2   you for joining us today Mr. Smith. As I am

3   sure you know, these are special

4   circumstances. A hearing is not usually

5   required for an insurance claim, however,

6   our investigative agent has called for a

7   tribunal on your case. Being such a long-

8   standing employee here, we felt it would

9   only be right to include you. Now,

10 officially, let the proceedings commence.

11 Mr. Ethelbert, you have the floor.

12   **MR. ETHELBERT:**   Thank you, Sir. I

13 would like to begin by positing a few

14 questions to Mr. Smith, if you will allow.

15   **THE COURT:**   You may proceed.

16   **MR. ETHELBERT:**   Thank you, Sir.

17

18   **-EXAMINATION OF MR. SMITH-**

19 **BY MR. ETHELBERT:**

1 Q.   Mr. Smith, would you please state your
2 name and occupation?
3 A.   John Smith. Customer Outreach
4 Consultant.
5 Q.   And that position is here at Billings
6 & Evermore, correct?
7 A.   Yes.
8 Q.   Thank you. Now, Mr. Smith. You claim
9 to have been burglarized on the night of the
10 4th, is that correct?
11 A.   It is.
12 Q.   And can you tell me what you were
13 doing on that night?
14 A.   I was sleeping. Right next to my wife.
15 Q.   All throughout the night?
16 A.   Yes. Of course.
17 Q.   Very well. Mr. Smith, can you tell me,
18 at what time did this burglary take place?
19 A.   Some time between two and three.
20 Q.   Are you absolutely certain?
21 A.   Fairly.
22 Q.   Why so?
23 A.   Excuse me?
24 Q.   If, Mr. Smith, you were sleeping all
25 throughout the night, as you so claim, then

I cannot fathom how it could be that you
would know so precisely as to when the crime
occurred. How do you explain that?

A.   This is absolutely ridiculous. Quincy,
what happened to the hiring standards here?

THE COURT (CLARK SAWTELLE):   Mr.
Smith, please, this is a grave matter. If it
is all the same to you, go ahead and answer
the question.

A.(cont.)   Yes, well, I--I would first
like to say, Mr. Ethelbert, that just
because your powers of deduction are not
refined enough to "fathom" how something may
occur, it doesn't mean that it's not
possible.

THE COURT (AGATHA HARDY):   Oh, do
go on.

THE COURT (THOMAS BRIGHT):   Ms.
Hardy, please.

THE COURT (CLARK SAWTELLE):   Mr.
Smith, if you would.

A.(cont.)   What I was getting at, is that
while I was under the somnolent spell of my
prescribed sleeping medication and was
unable to experience anything other than

slumber when the break-in occurred, I have
enough deductive reasoning to figure out for
myself what may have happened
retrospectively. A concept I would have
thought an investigator would be familiar
with. For one, I was asleep by eleven--
twelve o'clock--so we know it couldn't have
happened earlier than that. I awoke with the
event having had already occurred, which was
at five, so that narrows things down a
little bit. With that information in mind, I
went to my neighbours to see if anyone was
awake during those hours, first the ones
immediately beside me, and then the ones
across the way. Most said they were asleep
and had not noticed a thing, but the one
neighbour directly across told me he had
actually woken up in the middle of the
night--normal restlessness. He said he'd
noticed movement and flashlights, but
thought nothing of it at the time. He also
mentioned his television set, specifically
that the musical guest on the Carson Daly
show was jamming out on an alternate version
of one of their radio hits for over ten

1 minutes straight.

2 **Q.**   Are you just wasting time, Mr. Smith?

3 **A.**   Time, Mr. Ethelbert. The time. On

4 Saturday nights, Carson Daly ends at 2:35

5 and the musical guest always goes on at the

6 end of the show, so it was most likely

7 within a ten minute diameter of 2:30 when

8 Mr. Nachbar, that is my neighbour, noticed

9 the flashlights and the motion. Simple

10 investigation.

11 **Q.**   I see. Did this Mr. Nachbar supply a

12 testimony to the police?

13 **A.**   I am not sure. Details of the police

14 investigation are not something I am privy

15 to, but I would assume they canvassed the

16 surrounding area. That is just basics. I

17 mean, didn't you?

18 **Q.**   Ahem. Quite. Now, Mr. Smith, can you

19 tell me, what is your relationship with a

20 Ms. Bella Schröeder?

21 **A.**   Objection! I don't see how this is

22 relevant.

23   **THE COURT (EDMOND LYNCH):**

24 Overruled. I want to see where this is

25 going. Please answer the question, Mr.

Smith.

A.   She is a close personal friend of mine.

Q.   And is it true that you pay for an apartment for her near the university?

A.   It is.

Q.   And does your wife know about this affair?

A.   Do not talk about my wife, Mr. Ethelbert. Our marriage is between me and her, and god. Besides, who among us, Miss Hardy excluded and perhaps yourself, does not have the same weakness for a pretty young girl? Am I right, Ed?

THE COURT (EDMOND LYNCH):   Careful.

Q.   Would it be fair to say, Mr. Smith, that you have a history of lying and cheating?

A.   Objection. Obviously, Mr. Ethelbert here is trying to slander and demonize me and turn this into a morals case. Well, if you want to compare morals we could always bring up [INFORMATION REDACTED] or [INFORMATION REDACTED], now couldn't we? Point being, a healthy [INFORMATION

REDACTED] should not discredit a man.

Wouldn't you agree, Quincy?

THE COURT (QUINCY BILLINGS): Yes, ahem, well. Let's just move on, shall we?

Q. Sir. Very well. Mr. Smith, what size shoe do you wear?

A. Size 13.

Q. Mr. Smith, I would like you to know that I have here with me a photograph of a size 13 shoe print in the dirt in front of the broken door at your house, taken the same day as the alleged crime. I would like for everyone to take a look at it. There were a fair few of these prints, and judging from the length of the stride between them, they were made by a man roughly six-foot tall. How tall are you, Mr. Smith?

A. Six feet tall.

THE COURT: Gasp.

Q. Mr. Smith, may we see the bottoms of your shoes please.

A. You've got to be kidding me. I object. This is absolutely ludicrous. Even if these shoe prints of yours did belong to me, what is the crime in that? Why would my shoe

1   prints being in my own yard be a surprise?

2   **THE COURT (CLARK SAWTELLE):**   Mr.

3   Ethelbert, I assume this is going somewhere?

4   **MR. ETHELBERT:**   Yes, of course, Mr.

5   Sawtelle.

6   **THE COURT (CLARK SAWTELLE):**   Then I

7   would advise you to get there more quickly.

8   **MR. ETHELBERT:**   Yes, sir.

9   **Q.**   Mr. Smith, you probably were not aware

10 of it, being so soundly asleep, but it

11 happened to have rained that night, rather

12 hard, for all of five minutes, right around

13 midnight. Enough to wash away any imprints

14 already there. Of course, by the time you

15 awoke, the ground would have already been

16 dry. Therefore, these particular shoe prints

17 necessarily would have to have been made

18 that very night. So, I ask again, may we see

19 the bottoms of your shoes please?

20 **A.**   Seriously?

21   **THE COURT (EDMOND LYNCH):**   Show us

22 the shoes, Mr. Smith.

23 **A. (cont.)**   Fine. Here you go.

24 MR. SMITH takes off his shoes and hands them

25   over to MR. ETHELBERT.

1   **MR. SMITH:**   Well, is it a match?

2   **MR. ETHELBERT:**   No, the tread is

3   not the same.

4   **THE COURT (THOMAS BRIGHT):**   Let the

5   record show that the shoe print does not

6   match.

7   **MR. SMITH:**   Of course it's not.

8   Now, are we about finished with this whole

9   mock three-ring circus charade, or what?

10   **THE COURT (CLARK SAWTELLE):**   Mr.

11   Ethelbert?

12   **MR. ETHELBERT:**   Yes, well. It is

13   irrelevant whether or not the shoe tread

14   matches.

15   **Q.**   Mr. Smith, will you tell us how it was

16   that the burglars made it inside the house?

17   **A.**   Based on the evidence, it would seem

18   they broke one of the windows in the back

19   door and then reached in and unlocked it.

20   **Q.**   And that is the same information you

21   provided in your insurance report, correct?

22   **A.**   It is.

23   **Q.**   Now, Mr. Smith, I would like you to

24   take a look at this picture again. Will you

25   describe what you see?

A.   It is a picture of some sort of boot tread imprinted in the dirt and some shards of scattered broken glass.

Q.   And do you notice anything strange about it?

A.   Not particularly, no.

Q.   No, I suppose you wouldn't. I almost did not notice it myself. There are two things, actually. One--the direction of the print is facing away from the door, which would mean this is the shoe print of somebody exiting, not entering. Two--this shoe print of somebody exiting the door has a large shard of glass in it. It had not been stepped on, you see, for then it would have cracked, or at least become embedded in the wet dirt. Ladies and Gentlemen, in the photograph here, this shard of glass is sitting on top of the print, completely undisturbed. This can only mean that the window was broken after the burglary occurred, almost as an afterthought. So, Mr. Smith, I would like to ask you again, are you positively certain of the story you have given?

1   **A.**   Absolutely.

2   **Q.**   And there are no details you would

3   like to change?

4   **A.**   Change? Why the truth is

5   incontrovertible.

6   **MR. ETHELBERT:**   Quite. Thank you,

7   Mr. Smith, no further questions. Ladies and

8   Gentlemen, in closing, I would like to posit

9   my own theory as to what actually occurred

10   the night of Mr. Smith's alleged burglary.

11   Given the evidence, it should be clear to

12   all that Mr. Smith himself was the

13   perpetrator. Mr. Smith waited for his wife

14   to fall asleep and then slipped out of bed,

15   as he had many times before I'm sure, and

16   proceeded to rob himself blind. He most

17   likely enlisted the help of some as-of-yet

18   unknown assistant and together they tore

19   apart the house, making sure to damage the

20   furniture and appliances, the carpet, the

21   wallpaper, but nothing of major sentimental

22   value. They meticulously stole anything that

23   would be exceedingly difficult and therefore

24   expensive to replace, and only things that

25   Mr. Smith had receipts of purchase or

1   official appraisals for, of course. When

2   they were done, they smashed the window on

3   the door to stage the scene. That is why the

4   glass was on top of the shoe print. That is

5   why Mr. Smith knew when the crime occurred,

6   not because of some Mr. Neighbour. Ladies

7   and gentlemen, using his intimate knowledge

8   of this very institution, Mr. Smith sought

9   to defraud the system, forging his own

10   crime, padding his insurance claim, and

11   defiling justice. That is all. Thank you.

12   **THE COURT (QUINCY BILLINGS):**   Thank

13   you, Mr. Ethelbert. You have certainly given

14   us a lot to consider. Now, before the board

15   makes its final decision, the floor is

16   yours, Mr. Smith.

17   **MR. SMITH:**   Alright. I myself have

18   some questions. Let's start with Mr.

19   Ethelbert, shall we?

20

21   **-EXAMINATION OF MR. ETHELBERT-**

22   **BY MR. SMITH:**

23   **Q.**   How long have you worked here, Mr.

24   Ethelbert?

25   **A.**   I have been employed here at Billings

1   & Evermore no more than a week over three

2   months.

3   Q.   And before this job? Were you an

4   investigator somewhere else?

5   A.   Yes, that is correct. Before here I

6   was employed at an insurance firm in London

7   called Doyle's, and before that I was at

8   Arthur, Co. for several years.

9   Q.   And, Mr. Ethelbert, were you perhaps

10 fired from these businesses? Maybe because

11 of incompetence? Or ineptitude?

12 A.   Cheeky b--No. No, I was not. I came

13 here on recommendation from my previous

14 employers and I saw it as a mutually

15 advantageous opportunity.

16 Q.   Well, I'm not sure how they do things

17 across the pond at Arthur, Co. and Doyle's

18 but here in America we have rights and due

19 process. We have facts, not just wild

20 prejudiced assumptions. It seems to me that

21 instead of doing anything to investigate the

22 crime, you immediately fixated on the

23 victim, going so far as to stalk and harass

24 me. You know, illegal surveillance is a

25 practice that is not supported by this

1 organization, nor is it permissible in court

2 for that matter, I could have you hung out

3 to dry.

4 **A.** I'm not quite sure what you mean--is

5 that a question?

6 **Q.** Yes--No. No. I have one more question

7 for you, Mr. Ethelbert. Do you know what

8 happened to Francis Evermore?

9 **A.** Excuse me? I--No, I do not, not in any

10 certain detail at least.

11   **MR. SMITH:** No, no you don't. And

12 you won't. Will he? No one will, you can

13 trust that. No further questions.

14   **THE COURT (QUINCY BILLINGS):** Yes,

15 well. If that is all--

16   **MR. SMITH:** --I just have one

17 question for Mr. Lynch.

18

19   **-EXAMINATION OF EDMOND LYNCH-**

20 **BY MR. SMITH:**

21 **Q.** [INFORMATION REDACTED]

22 **A.** [INFORMATION REDACTED]

23   **MR. SMITH:** Thank you, that is all.

24 As you can see, I was the honest to god

25 victim of burglary, and then a small amount

of harassment from your investigator, and it

would be unjust, and just a little foolish,

to deny my claim. And completely asinine to

accuse me of fraud. Mr. Ethelbert has proven

nothing but his incompetence and has caused

a monumental waste of all of our time with

this absurd pageantry. Thank you.

THE COURT (AGATHA HARDY):   Just who

do you think you are, talking 1-

[INFORMATION REDACTED]:   -Agatha,

leave it.

THE COURT (AGATHA HARDY):   But,

[INFORMATION REDACTED]

[INFORMATION REDACTED]:

[INFORMATION REDACTED]

[INFORMATION REDACTED]:

[INFORMATION REDACTED]

THE COURT (QUINCY BILLINGS):   We

shall now congress a moment to come to a

decision. When we return, we shall have our

verdict.

VERDICT

THE COURT: On behalf of BILLINGS &

EVERMORE, LLC. It is the opinion of this

1   BOARD OF DIRECTORS and myself that this

2   claim, CASE NO. 11235, be honoured in full

3   and all investigations be dropped.

I, DAMSIL ILLIANA ZAZOWSTOK, certify

that the foregoing is a correct transcript

from the record of proceedings in the above-

entitled matter.

DAMSIL ILLIANA ZAZOWSTOK, RPR
OFFICIAL REPORTER
IN AND FOR THE COMPANY OF
BILLINGS & EVERMORE, LLC

****

Quincy nervously brushed his combed-over hair into his large, cottony sideburns and grumbled out a self-protecting half-apology. "Well I never. Had I known the details, I would not have approved… We will get the paperwork started right away and get your check out to you as quickly as possible."

"I appreciate that, *sir*. You go ahead and get that process started. I think I will wait here until everything is complete. You don't mind do you? Besides, I'm sure you could expedite things should you go directly to accounting yourself—I would very much like to just forget completely about this whole… sordid affair. Do you know what I mean?"

Quincy went flush. "I—ehrm, yes, I understand. Make yourself comfortable, I will return as soon as I possibly can. In the meantime… Oh, never mind, just make yourself comfortable."

John helped himself to some whiskey and a cigar from Quincy's private reserve and kicked his feet up on the polished teak desk. He was already mentally spending the money. The payout was to be massive, upwards of six figures, and John's mind was buzzing with the possibilities. The entire house would be redecorated. That was a given. Perhaps a little strip club celebration first. Or maybe, if he played his cards right, he could buy Donna's affection—some expensive trinket could be just the thing needed to push her over the edge, to finally coax those embers to flame. Worth a shot. It was not long before John decided to pick up Quincy's desk phone and call up Virgoe Torres, a long time art-dealer acquaintance of his. They chatted politely for a little while, catching up, taking turns commenting on the weather and current events (Virgoe always required these formalities) and reminiscing, before John set up an appointment for the following day.

John raised his glass in a toast to himself, "Veni, Vidi, Vici."

****

The renovations took more than half a week, with John personally overseeing a six-man team. Mary upped her dose to sleep through the stress and the noise. An interior decorator was hired and fired. John Smith demanded absolute perfection. Virgoe was worked frantic procuring pure magic. The process was chaos, but the end result of it all was sublime.

Bruce called every day. John knew that if he were to simply ignore him long enough, the problem would just go away on its own; eventually Bruce would have to run through his dope and move on to the stash in the van. However, that came with a multitude of variables. How much Bruce already had on him, or had stashed away in his house, what his rate of consumption actually was, or if the dose would even be lethal —all unknowns. John most likely had expected Bruce to have already croaked by then, and the fact that he had not would certainly have been worrisome. John would have reassured himself that it was only a matter of time; the only question was: would Bruce croak or squeal first?

That being said, the first day back to work after the redecoration bored the hell out of John, so much so that he decided to ring Bruce and suggest some reconnaissance anyway. Bruce jumped at the offer. John made sure not to let Bruce pick the spot, nor did he tell him where it would be (not that he yet knew himself) despite Bruce's insistent questions. He wanted to maintain constant control. He wanted to ensure Bruce never had the opportunity to set him up. Sure, it was dangerous, but what is more thrilling than toeing the line, pushing the limits? John still had time to figure out all of the details.

That is when fickle fate ruled in his favour. The very next call that his computer autodialled was to Barbara Black, a bedridden, possibly demented old lady who was easily persuaded to increase her insurance plans, despite the interference of some intermittent caretaker whom he assumed was her daughter. John easily got her to volunteer her address. He probably could have gotten her to give him directions if he had asked; he probably could have even gotten her social security number and mother's maiden name, along with her coveted secret apple pie recipe.

From the moment he hung up the phone, he was practically afloat. Fate had just handed him everything he needed before he even had to ask for it. Unable to contain his excitement, he decided to clock out early and celebrate. The painkillers he had taken for his ankle injury that morning made him feel slightly loopy, but they were helping and John could walk on it with only a minor limp; after a Martini he felt like doing a jig; after a second one he felt sick. He broke out into dribbling, sticky cold-sweat. As the room swelled and spun around him, he laid his soggy, spongy head down onto the cool marble counter-top, panting heavily and fighting to push down the growing nauseous tide that threatened to overtake him.

When Mary drifted into the room, he did not even notice her. She rubbed his back with her pale bony hands, startling John slightly, but he kept the furrows of his brow pressed against the counter-top.

"Are you okay, my love?" whispered Mary as she ran her slender fingers through his hair.

"I… yes… could you… some water please."

Mary rushed to the cabinet and grabbed a glass, filling it halfway. "You know, I miss you, John. I mean, when was the last time—"

"Please, Mary… I… I can't… not now," John groaned, barely moving his colourless lips.

Mary set the water down in front of John and sidled up to his body, gently pulling his head to her small but soft bosom, stroking him like a newborn. John half-expected her to stoop down and rub his bare feet, to wash the gunk from between his toes with her dirty hair. Instead, in an uncharacteristic display of sexual aggressiveness, she spun the kitchen stool so John was facing her and she mounted him. As Mary writhed her pelvis and kissed his neck, she whispered, hot breath in John's ear, "Let's make a baby. I know we can do it, I don't care what the doctor says."

Possibly due to the sudden quick turn of the stool, or the added weight on his lower abdomen, or some combination of those and other things, John's nausea suddenly swelled, ready to come crashing down on top of him. John jumped up, the vomit already rising in his throat, as Mary was sent tumbling to the ground.

As John rushed off in a stumbling run to the restroom, all Mary said was a single soft, "Ouch."

After he was finished retching, John curled up on the shower tiles, the water running over his body and the bathroom spinning around him. Mary curled up in bed and tried to cry herself into a nap. She pretended to be asleep while John got dressed; she stayed in bed until she heard John leave.

****

Bruce and John met a little ways outside of John's neighbourhood just after midnight. Bruce arrived early, having had a relatively uneventful day with no pest control work and only a small dope deal. Bruce was looking forward to the change of pace, not that reconnaissance was necessarily exciting, but he was both comforted and invigorated by the eventual possibility of making some desperately needed money. He could always have gone back to doing it on his own, but even he would have to admit that burglary is a dance much more easily done with a partner.

He did not notice John walking up in the dark until he was at the door pulling on the handle. Bruce jumped so hard he nearly hit his head on the roof and immediately, instinctively, and completely accidentally karate kicked the gas pedal, jolting the van forward a few feet before he realized who it was and slammed the brakes to a quick screech halt.

"Ha ha, very funny," said John, pulling the passenger door open, "you almost ripped my fucking arm off."

"Yeah, well I just… I mean, y'know, um… I'm sorry."

"Whatever. Just drive."

"Kay, where we goin'?"

"Just keep going forward. I will tell you where to turn. And do try not to drive like a moron, I'm feeling a bit woozy."

"Ummm… Sure."

John routed Bruce in a roundabout way, forcing him to stop in various places just to be certain they were not being tailed. The entire drive, Bruce kept insistently asking about the mark and John had to perform mental gymnastics to evade the questions; though it would have been obvious were Bruce wearing a wire, John wanted to make sure he could not tip off the police in any way.

Once they arrived, and the house was within sight, John turned to Bruce and said, "Alright, this is it. Bed-ridden old bag lives alone, caretaker comes and goes. I don't see any cars in the driveway so this may be our best shot. Let's see if we can't get in, shall we?"

Bruce looked like he had just been fondled by his own mother. "I, um… I thought we were only runnin' recon."

"Change of plans."

Bruce slinked up to the house to check the door while John kept the van warm, ready to head north should things turn south. The door was unlocked, just as she said it would be. Then Bruce crept inside to verify whether or not the coast was clear, not without a deal of trepidation. If all was clear, he would signal to John to come in; if not, he would book it out the front door and they would high-tail out of there.

John knew this was a risky plan that left a lot to chance—his line-of-sight would be cut off and if Bruce was wearing a wire, he would have ample opportunity to spill the details to whatever agency may be listening on the other end of the line. It also afforded Bruce time to set up a trap. He could be hiding behind the door, curled up in some dark corner with a knife or a handgun, waiting to ambush John the moment he stepped through the threshold.

If John was being completely honest with himself, neither of these situations seemed drastically likely, though certainly within the realm of possibility; ultimately, these potential risks were far outweighed by the reward. He was able, without the risk of being noticed, to check on the status of Bruce's dope stash. John watched Bruce with the keen eye of a falcon; as soon as the front door of the house was shut, John popped open the glove compartment and rummaged through it.

The heroin was gone—the entire bag and all its contents. This left John with even more questions, most prominent of which was, "What if he had already shot it all up and it had not done a thing to him?" More curious still was a note that had been crammed in there. Written in swooping, feminine cursive and covered in smudges from Bruce's grubby fingers, the note read:

> M riih qsvi. M'pp fi asvomrk e hsyfpi, tpiewi gsqi
> xs qi. M'q lyvxmrk. Tpiewi.
> - Hsrre

An obvious cipher, but not an easily broken one, especially given that the front door of the house had just opened and shut twice (Bruce's signal), and there was not a lot of time before suspicion would be aroused. As John walked to the front door, limping slightly, he tried shifting the alphabet over in his head by three like the famous Caesar cipher; he tried the ROT13; he tried reflecting the alphabet like Vanada Veen; he even managed to mentally map out a Vigenère chart and run it through a quick Kasiski test, but came to realize all too soon that none of these methods would work and the only way to decipher this secret message was with some intimately shared key phrase. John spat with frustration and disgust, crumpling the note in his fist and tossing it into a patch of one of the twelve or thirteen native ambrosia bushes beside him.

"Anyway," he said to himself, "best not leave Bruce's ambush waiting too long."

Bruce was rifling through a desk in the foyer when John entered.

"Jesus. What took you?"

"You can call me John."

"Huh?"

"Never mind. Find anything?"

"Buncha medical bills. Thought there'd be somethin' in here—wait a minute… Wait. A. Minute. Hold the phones. We got here about a buck thirty in change, at least."

"How's the rest of the house look?"

"Yeah well, looks a bit messy if you ask me, but there could be some good stuff."

Bruce was not wrong about the mess. It looked like whoever was caring for the old lady would always make themselves quite at home and was loath to clean up after themselves—fast-food to-go bags from multiple chains lay crumpled and stacked on the living room coffee table like bodies in a mass grave; the ceiling fan had built up so much dust, it looked like it was wearing some bleak, Dickensian sweater; there were black smudges on or around most of the doors; the kitchen was the worst offender, with both compartments of the sink filled with dirty dishes piled higher than a garbage barge at Ellis island, the mess spilling over onto the ocean blue counter-tops (half-eaten plates left sitting; bowls of melted ice cream, hardened condiments, and other less identifiable food-stuffs; cups that had begun to host mould cultures; a blackened butter knife on the stove that looked like the discarded weapon of a losing battle).

"But where is this old lady anyway?" Good question. The foyer (which was spotless clean, mind you) led almost directly into the living room, which led through a small den directly into the kitchen, but off to the right, was a small hallway that led to the master bedroom. That is where they found her.

In contrast to most the rest of the house, this room was extremely clean and well kept. It seemed she actually was being cared for. As John approached the hospital bed, he could see her emaciated, atrophied legs sticking out from her blanket; her skin was a silvery-blue wax paper shade, with a mess of ecchemosis and varicose veins scrawled across it. She lay there in a dreamless sleep, her chest rising and falling faintly and in uneven rhythm, her frail body hooked up with rubber tubes and wires, the bedpans beneath her gleaming from the green glow of the EKG monitor.

Question: If you see your catheter bag as half-full, does that make you an optimist or a pessimist?

You could tell she was clinging to life, but it was not quite within her grasp, not fully. Living had become something which she continued to do only because her body had not yet realized that it no longer had to; it was not something she actually experienced any longer, but more like a memory, just another amongst many that she was slowly forgetting. When he had spoken to her on the phone she sounded feeble, but not to this degree. Only occasionally was she actually coherent.

John quickly located the phone (a wireless handset) on the side table next to the bed. As he scooped up the phone, he noticed, next to a box of insulin syringes, a baby monitor sitting on a small rolling cart on the other side of the old convalescent. He widened his eyes at Bruce and raised a finger to his lips before tiptoeing around the bed.

John slowly twisted the knob on the monitor's receiver as far counter-clockwise as it would go without completely shutting it off. He was not sure the range on the thing, and in all probability it was just something that one of the caretakers had brought in so they could sit in the living room and watch television while still getting paid to "watch" her, but John wanted to play it safe and make sure that whomever may be on the other end would not be alerted by the monitor losing connection, but would still be able to hear nothing.

"How 'bout let's umm… let's leave this room alone," whispered Bruce.

"You don't think any of these medical supplies are valuable? Or any of this equipment? What about that mini-fridge over there? Might be some expensive medications in there."

"Yeah… I dunno, John, I—"

"Kidding. Just let me finish declawing the mummified old bat and then we can attend to the rest of the house."

Bruce made a face like John had just slapped him with a pickled herring. "What…?"

Admittedly, she did somewhat resemble a mummified bat, with the way she held her arms crossed like some knock-off Bela Lugosi and her black Talibanesque head scarf.

Around Barbara's neck—that is the old lady, forgetful reader, we may as well give her the decency of referring to her by name. As I was saying, around Barbara's wattled neck was one of those emergency panic buttons, in case she were to fall and could not get up. John reached down and cut the braided nylon cord. Barbara did not move a muscle, completely out cold, probably dosed up with morphine, or something of its ilk.

"We don't want her calling for help, do we? Look, it's fine, someone will be here to check on her in the morning anyway. Let's go, come on."

They closed the door behind them and never looked back.

At that point, the coast was officially clear. Let the good times roll, as Ric Ocasek famously ripped-off from Lord Byron. It was a ballet of theft and destruction. The two leapt and gambolled, pirouetted and arabesqued, juggling expensive looking but worthless QVC trinkets back and forth to each other, laughing when they inevitably shattered. They swept every shelf, overturned every drawer, and poked their fingers into any nook and cranny they could find. They worked from one room to the next, each taking turns running stuff out to the van.

In the kitchen, John scooped up a plate and spun back, commentating as he went. "There's the snap and Smith has the ball. Defensive line is falling apart and—Oh! Narrow miss! Perfect evasion by Smith, just stiff arming the hell outta that sack. And there! He sees Camden open. He's under pressure. He throws… And it's complete! You just do not see QB's like this anymore. And Camden's at the 30, tight-end right on his tail. At the 20. The 10. Touchdoowwwn!"

Bruce spiked the plate, smashing the ceramic at his feet as the two laughed like they hadn't since their high school days. But, just then…

(long pause for dramatic effect)

There came a loud thud from upstairs.

"What the fuck was that?" snapped John.

"Umm…"

"I'm going to go check it out."

John crept up the stairs, trying to muffle his footsteps with the hunter's foxtrot. He fought to control his breathing and heart rate as he prowled down the hallway like a hunting lion. He did not trust the situation. He did not trust Bruce to back him up. He did not trust his surroundings. The only thing he did trust were his instincts, which kept him spring-loaded and ready to react, every small sound squeezing his internal trigger tighter and tighter.

The first room was used for storage, with boxes of kitsch and unadorned décor stacked all across the tightly packed furniture. John could not help but imagine a pair of Slavic movers setting everything into its interlinking pattern while The Peddlers is played on balalaika in the background. He could also hear Bella remarking on the Feng Shui, or lack thereof; he knew just what she would say: "Oh, you can just feel the way the energy is all… stagnated, can't you? Sumisu-san?" A room packed with stuff seeming a bit stuffy—what a novel concept. After a cursory inspection, the room was cleared.

Next was the bathroom. The counters were covered with cosmetics and hair styling tools. Towels and girlish clothes were strewn about the floor. The mauve shower curtain was drawn, rustling just ever so slightly in a way that could have been caused by either the air conditioning, or by the breath of a hidden attacker, waiting for their chance to pounce. John tiptoed over to the curtain, grabbing a flat-iron off of the counter, just in case he needed to bludgeon the concealed threat out of existence.

With baited breath, he slowly reached out. He clenched the satiny shower curtain tightly. He raised the flat-iron to strike and ripped the curtain violently open. Waves of adrenaline surged, crashing foam against his teeth, seething. But his swings came down on empty air and he saw there was nobody hiding in the shower.

With the bathroom cleared, there was only one room left—down at the end of the hall.

As soon as John opened the door, he dropped the flat-iron and fell to his knees.

There, lying on the floor, having fallen out of bed, was Donna Ivey, gasping like a reeled-in fish just ripped from the water, far beyond the pale of her normal self.

John crawled over to her and caressed the sleeve of her silk kimono. "Don't worry, my love, I am here for you." He picked up her clammy hand and pressed it in his. "I've got you now."

He brushed a stray strand of her perfect pinned-up hair behind the soft curve of her ear. Her stylized geisha makeup (large red and blue shadowed eyes, lips like blood on snow, and just a slight blush of embarrassment on the cheek) was all smeared, but nonetheless becoming. She looked up at him with dulcet eyes of brown sugar and honey, almost rolled back behind her heavy blue eyelids.

"You... what... don't... let go..."

"Never, my dear. Do not worry, my love, I will hold you through the storm."

"Yuck... I'd rather die..." Donna gasped out.

John reeled back like he had just been struck full force by Reagan's famous ten ton heavy thing.

"I—you're delirious, you don't know what you're saying. I am here for you, your knight in shining armour, here to pull you from hell with me like Orpheus and Eurydice."

She responded with venom. Though her breathing was

short, shallow, rattling gasps, her voice was clear and strong. "Why do you think I would ever love you? How self-absorbed can you be? Seriously."

"What—no! You know that's not true."

"Who do you think you are to say what's true? Everything you say is a lie. You disgust me. You think you've got everything and everyone all figured out. You don't know shit."

"Shut up! Shut the fuck up!"

John looked around the messy room and snatched up the pillow that Donna had dragged out of the bed with her, already covered with smeared marks from her makeup. A square of aluminium foil that was stuck to the pillow came spinning down—a dark black, hard-edged spiral standing vividly against the silver sheen.

"You don't even know me and you think you can save me? You think you can love me? You're the kind of monster that can only love yourself and whatever idealized fantasy you've created to help you facilitate that. I can't fucking stand you. You're just a jackal."

"I said shut up!"

Even with the pillow over her face, he could still hear her clearly.

"You're pathetic. You think you're so enlightened cause you don't believe in anything, but really you do. You believe so much in nothing. And you use that belief to justify your own existence, but we both know that that's just what you are —nothing. And that's all you'll ever be, just a sad little nothing in a big world that won't change a lick once you're gone."

Even when John realized she had stopped moving, and stopped breathing, he still could hear Donna. Even as he tried to resuscitate her.

"No one could ever love you. You don't even exist."

John leaned against the bed, hugging his knees, and tears streaming down his face. "Please. Shut the fuck up already."

"Jesus Christ! What's going on?" said Bruce from the doorway. "John, what happened? Is that... Oh my god... is that..."

"Bruce, we're in this together, we must stay calm, we have to—"

"I can't... I can't... I have to... I just need a minute." Bruce ran straight for the half-bathroom and locked himself in.

John heard the tap run, the spark of a lighter, a short metallic clink, and then heard the long fuse burn out—the metre finally clicked. Bruce Camden, seething horribly, painfully wrenching, horrendously twisting, took his last raspy gasps of air.

That is when the panic tried to creep in, oozing around John like a vile black slime, like a gravitational well conspiring to pull him in. He perspired with the thick, sickly-sweet perspiration of fear. But he knew he had to persevere. In moments of great stress, during the crucibles of life, that is when people are their truest selves; where some may just curl up and die, John was determined to rise, to overcome whatever challenges he may face, to blaze whatever trails he so desired, to step over whatever stones may be thrown in his path, to best both hell and high water, to trudge forth, on to higher ground, and to come out on top of it all. John knew he had to act. He knew he could not just sit there hugging his knees, staring at the empty space between him and Donna. He knew no tears could ever bring her back; there was no point in trying—all that was left was to finish the job and leave.

John got up, dusted himself off, and went to work. He found Donna's cash-stash under the mattress—she would not be needing it anyway. Most of her jewellery was fake, but he snatched it up nonetheless. Did he snatch up any of her undergarments? Of course not, don't be so crude.

Immediately upon descending the stairs, John saw that Bruce had gone to town working over a sack of flour in the kitchen. Like a kid playing "the floor is lava", John avoided stepping on the powdery mess as he egressed through the kitchen and parlour.

In the living room, he stopped still for a moment. He had not previously noticed the family portraits hanging on the walls. There she was, in all her glory—the dearly departed Donna Ivey, staring back at John like a debutante bored of her own ball. He grasped one of the portraits of her, tore it from the wall, and smashed the glass, shoving the photo into his pocket—which I am quite certain he still has on him to this day.

From there, he turned to the front door and ran out of the house straight to the getaway van, leaving the door swinging shut behind him. Sorry, slip of the pen, he did not run. He walked, calm and collected.

He drove off exactly at the speed limit and hid the van on some dark unassuming side street near Pepe's. From there, he walked a mile or so, called a cab at a convenience store, was dropped off near but not too close to his neighbourhood, paid in cash, of course, quietly slipped in through the back door, and slid into bed next to the body of his loving wife.

Chapter Twelve

The next morning, John Smith awoke at precisely 4:56 am, as he had the morning before and the morning before that, and so on and so forth, backwards into the temporal horizon. Everything seemed normal, ordinary even. John got out of bed and stretched through the morning haze just as he always did.

It was not until he turned to look at Mary that he noticed. Something was off. For some odd reason, John had the subtle impression, as he was just starting to turn, before his eyes reached the bed, that Mary would be gone, faded away, disappeared entirely; he pondered the possibility—what if she really was not there? What if she never had been? This, of course, was not the case. No, the truth was far worse.

Mary was there in the bed. Her repose was more still than it had ever been before—her small body pale and unmoving. John tried to shake her awake, but she merely stared out blankly, taunting him with the same look Donna had given him, like she was looking past him, through him, like she could see some divine secret hidden just behind his head, something he would never be able to see for himself, something mirrors would only obfuscate and cameras could never hope to capture, some sacred heart continuing to beat in the stead of her own carnal corporeal flesh. In John's own heart, there would always be a chord which contained her note, but never again would her voice join the choir of the living.

When the ambulance arrived, a handsome young EMT, with that particular look in the eye of a war-torn veteran, pronounced her dead. Police came shortly after. John told them his experience, how they had fallen asleep together and she was fine, the state he had found her in. They were quick and sympathetic. They took down his statement, snapped a few pictures, and then were gone, taking the body with them.

The entire time, Ethelbert was watching the scene, mostly concealed by the neighbours shrubbery across the way, taking notes, hatching plans. If you were looking hard enough, you could just barely make him out through the kitchen window. John was well aware of his presence, while the cops had seemed wilfully oblivious. John watched as Ethelbert plotted. He plotted, but did not confront, however, choosing to stay his distance—for the time being at least.

The funeral was held just a few days later. It was a sad but beautiful affair shared privately and intimately between husband and wife, marred only by the intrusion of Margaret Fleischer, who had crashed the event with some thin Native woman dressed in overly masculine clothing, only to sob uncontrollably and viciously accuse John of murdering her sister. She spat at him like an asp. She cast flagrant insults and threats in violent tirade until she was red as a flank steak, completely lost all composure, turned around and ran out, leaving a trail of tears behind her.

Aside from Miss Maggie Fleischer, who never trusted John to begin with and had always irrationally feared that he would end up killing her sister some day and, of course, the ever relentless, conniving Mr. Ethelbert, there were no suspicions, legally speaking. Despite the best attempts of

Ethelbert, everything was taken at face value. The toxicology reports showed that Mary had mixed her various prescriptions with about three quarters of a bottle of Nero D'Avola and slipped into an endless slumber. They did not even bat an eyelash at the opioids in her system. It was deemed an accident, which means her life insurance policy paid out, a portion of which went to pay for her funeral/burial and the rest went to John, as her sole beneficiary. Just as fortuitous, however, was the iron-clad alibi that she gave her poor bereaved husband, a sort of final parting gift—"No, officer, he couldn't have been at Donna Ivey's on that night, he was sleeping next to me as my life slowly slipped away." "Forgive him, your Honour, if his story doesn't quite line up, he's still in a state of shock and grief from my tragic, untimely demise." Even in death, she remained devoted.

Her obituary was written by her husband himself. John Smith never considered himself an "artist" per sé, having only ever written an article on being an unpublished writer that had never actually been accepted for publication, but he had always thought of himself as an aesthete, finely tuned for the appreciation of beauty, and as such was able to deliver a beautiful, touching and artful memoriam for his dearly departed wife. Donna's, on the other hand, was not so much an obituary as an ostentatious, proselytizing article with an over-sensationalized agenda that was paired with another such article about the search for a certain silver-toothed member of the Mexican drug trade.

Now that you know the true story of what happened, you

should probably know what was written about it. The article was unnecessarily long-winded, so I shall summarize it for you. It began in the guise of a regular obituary—

Donna Madeleine Ivey was born to Anne and Patrick Ivey on such-and-such date and was found dead on such-and-such date, plucked in early bloom at the bitterly young age of twenty-two.

Donna was born at sunrise, with open windows inviting the scent of wildflowers and dew cast iridescence, and she quickly blossomed into a magnificent young woman. The writer used a lot of flowery prose for this section. "Her life began verdantly and vibrantly" "She held onto her roots, branching out into the world." "Tragically" (notice how the writer makes sure to tell us that it is tragic) "she wilted beneath life's harsh, withering rays." "Her hallowed harvest came too soon."

Here, the writer intrudes on the article in the first person-singular, talking about how the family had contacted him (her father and stepmother, and their kid, that is) after the case had been closed. He goes on to say how he was moved by the family's love for their dearly departed, and by their genuine desire to share her story for the greater good of humanity; how they were not satisfied with the obituary the funeral service provided; how they were not satisfied with the answers the police had given them; how they just wanted the truth. He was apparently "unable to turn them down". It was all very sentimental.

From there, he went on to try to capture Donna's biographical portrait, chronicling her tragically (again reminding us that it is indeed tragic) short life, from her birth just outside the town of Malbork to her quiet death in her grandmother's house. The sentences were rich in vivid detail, running into each other and almost overlapping at times, which gave the impression when reading of a wonderstruck child rushing to experience all life has to offer, which, as we know, must needs give way eventually to disillusionment and dismay. Interspersed throughout were snippets of an interview with her father.

Q: If there was one thing you could say to your daughter, what would it be?

A: I'd say... I'm so sorry, Bunny. I wish I could have been there for you. And, I'll always love you, no matter what. The divorce was hard on her, you know? And... and... I just... I know she never forgave me after I remarried, and I should have tried harder to connect with her. I mean, I just wish I could have explained to her how much she still meant to me, how much she still means to me.

Her early life was cast almost idyllically, an elsewise-elysian experience that became marred by her parents divorce and more so drastically by her mother's death shortly after, in spite of which she continued to persevere with indomitable spirit. This particular trait of hers was attributed by the writer to her relationship with her maternal grandmother. Her early academic achievements were listed (fourth place in the State spelling bee, second in the science fair, first chair oboe in junior-high band, A.P. and Honours, full ride scholarships) which all added to the mystery of why she dropped out of college and ran back home. Without directly saying it, some sort of tragedy or trauma was implied.

Q.   Were you aware of her drug use?

A.   After she came back from college, she was never quite the same. She moved back in with us for a bit, but barely even spoke to us. I had my suspicions… but I didn't want to see it.

At the point where she moved in with her sick grandmother, the reporters biases began to show. "The insidious epidemic of addiction… poisoned and corrupted… best intentions defiled…" It was clear he wanted you to feel a certain way about what was being described. He glossed over the fact that she had been taking care of her grandmother intensely for almost a year and instead focused on the eventual short-comings as an opportunity to further demonize the quote-on-quote disease of opioid addiction sweeping through the city streets and suburbs of our nation's youth. He added some statistics about teen overdoses, pharmaceuticals, cutting agents, and "the Cartel's" drug trade.

After that, he got around to surmising her last moments. He imagined a cohort of debauched drug addicts taking advantage of Donna's mostly innocent hospitality, strung out all day, making a mess of her grandmother's home, practically living in bedlam. Here, he made a small disclaimer that Barbara Black was, as all evidence suggests, remarkably well cared for, despite the state of the rest of the house. "Donna's inner light fought against the darkness, but her addiction overcame her in the end." When Donna overdosed, he posited, everyone in the rogues gallery split, taking with them whatever they could carry and leaving Donna Ivey dying on the floor of her bedroom. Everyone except for a Mr. Bruce Camden who, according to sources (what sources?) was involved romantically with Donna Ivey. "Evidence" suggests that Bruce frantically tried to revive Donna, shaking her, slapping her face, giving her mouth-to-mouth resuscitation, before he finally realized the futility and in his "tragic despair" shot himself up with a lethal dose of heroin—"oh happy dagger, this is thy sheath; there rust and let me die." An uncredited quote from Shakespeare's Caesar.

He then spent a moment idealizing amorous purity and expressing the cliché sentiment of the heart of one's true love being the last bastion of solace in an oppressively decaying and doom filled world. In the same breath he casually mentioned how the bodies were discovered thanks to an anonymous caller only after weeks had passed and poor Barbara Black had died along with Donna and Bruce. By then, it was too late for toxicology, but the writer assumed that their heroin had been cut with one of thousands of different harmful chemicals and pharmaceuticals used in the production of street drugs today.

He then painted a naïvely optimistic portrait of what their life could have been had they not fallen victim to the opiate epidemic. Suburbs and giggling children and the scent of wildflowers in the soft breeze. "Not a single cloud of sadness in their unsullied skies."

Q.　　What do you hope, if anything, reader's will gain from your daughter's story?

A.　　I just hope that any fathers out there with daughters

like mine, or any young girls that can relate to Donna's struggle, I hope they realize it's not too late. Donna never kept a diary, she never talked about her feelings… Sometimes I feel like I never really knew her… But if you're alive, if they're alive… it's not too late to ask, to listen, to show them that you care about how they feel, that you care about them. I don't know, maybe it can't fix everything, but it seems like a pretty good start. Life is short, but it's never too late to change.

"I leave you," the writer concluded, "with a poem found in Bruce Camden's pocket, scrawled on a sheet of scrap paper— a far more sonorous howl from what could have been one of the greatest minds of our generation."

nothing exists;
all is a dream
god – man – the world
the sun – the moon – the wilderness of stars –
a dream all a dream
they have no existence
nothing exists
save empty space
–and you!

you are
             but a thought
               i myself
                          have no existence
                          i am but a dream–
                   your dream
             creature of your imagination
          in a moment
                  you will have realized this, then
you shall banish me from your visions and i

shall dissolve
into

the
nothingness
out of which you made

me…

i am perishing already
i   am failing
i   am   passing   away
in a little while
you will be alone
in shoreless space

to wander
its limitless   solitudes without
friend or comrade forever –
for you will remain   a
thought

the only existent

thought
and by your nature
inextinguishable
indestructible
but i, your poor servant
have revealed you to yourself
and set you free
dream other dreams and better!

****

A day or two after the funeral (Mary's, that is), John went
to check on the van, making absolutely certain he was not followed, almost to the point of paranoia. It was just as he left it,
tucked behind some run-down casitas, in the shade of a dilap-
idated parking frame made of rotten termite-ridden wood. He

started her up and headed to Pepe's. Luckily Pepe was home.

"Yo, where Bruce at now?" inquired Pepe, seeing John alone with Bruce's van.

"Gone."

"Gone? Like... gone gone?"

"Yeah. Look, I need wheels. I've got a decent score here, and about thirteen-hundred in cash, plus the van—though I might recommend sending it in to a chop shop."

"Woah, woah. Slow your roll. Just what in the hell you talkin' about?"

"He must have been a rat or a pigeon, or whatever the hell you call them. A confidential informant."

"A'ight, lemme get this straight, Bruce dead ain't he?"

"Well..."

"And either you killed him, or you didn't, but to be honest, that ain't really none of my business. You see Bruce, well he always been a pain in the ass, and if he gone he gone, oh well. But you and me, that there another story. We right here. Now, you sayin' Bruce had me fooled, that he a confidential inf-ormant. I say maybe so. Maybe he was. How do I know you ain't, or won't do worse to me?"

"I guess you don't. You can't. Why should you trust me? Why should you trust anyone for that matter? You can't and you shouldn't. But you can trust in the fact that me getting out of town is better for the both of us."

Pepe eventually conceded to helping John out after a few passive death threats, only mildly taking advantage of the situation. He took the van, all of its contents, and the thirteen-hundred John had mentioned. In exchange, he provided John with a purple low rider, which he had recently acquired from a former business associate of his, and a fake passport—referred to when handing it over as "generic white-guy #2".

"Now look here, I ain't never wanna see you no more, dig? I ain't know what happened between you and Bruce—hell, maybe he had it comin' to him, but I ain't in the business of takin' risks on shiesty middle-aged white dudes who may or may not have killed they friend, no offense."

"None taken. I, too, understand the need in reducing liabilities. I appreciate the help you have provided. May we part ways with mutual respect." "Condescending prick," John added in his head.

As he drove away in the low rider, John imagined several violent deaths for Pepe (cartel shoot out, car wreck, explosion, stabbing, electric chair, bear attack, spontaneous combustion, all the basics) before his mind turned back to Bruce and Donna's terminal night. And to Ethelbert. Nothing had been in the papers, so John was able to assume that their bodies still lay there undiscovered, and even when they did inevitably get found, there should not have been any physical evidence that John had ever been there, and besides, he was a victim of tragedy himself, as his wife had passed away right in bed next to him, not that there was any reason to suspect him in the first place, even with his known association with Bruce, even if he was a frequenter of the Foothills Café, even if he was seen talking to Donna alone in the parking lot. It did not matter. He had gotten away completely. Of course, he conceded, there was one person, only one, who could bring the disparate threads together, one person who could see the whole picture in its scattered constituent pieces. In retrospect, there were multiple details that could have proven the proverbial infelicitous walking stick in the spokes, and yet… nobody noticed. Nobody cared. Not really, not enough; details were swept under the rug, brushed aside with a casual stroke or shrug, unnoticed by everyone. Everyone except for Ethelbert. That was why he had to be lured away. He had to be dealt with. He was a dangerous adversary, but he did not know how to bluff —and if John ran, he would be sure to chase. That much, John was certain of. To anyone else, his sudden departure would simply be a widow's attempt to deal with grief using a sabbatical, as per the advice of a self-help book he had left face down on his desk at home; to Ethelbert, it was an invitation to a deadly game, a quick flash of all the cards in his hand, a clever distraction while John pulls the win out from his sleeve.

If nothing is true, and nothing is sacred, then anything can happen, there are no bounds—John knew this. He felt it to his core. Everything he had ever done, his entire life, reflected this fact. John felt that getting away, more than anything, was proof of that; on the other hand, to get away with something completely would practically negate its already tenuous existence. It would be, for all intents and purposes, in the grand scope of human history, as if nothing ever happened—which would hardly serve to shake the confines of reality for anyone. To have someone know that you got away with something, in intimate detail, exactly what you did, and then to still get away with it… well, that is a different story entirely. That could have some effect. It could perhaps shake some out of this dreamscape of perspective, to realize the complete lack of truth in the universe, that nothing is real, that anyone can get away with anything.

His mind was racing with these thoughts and more when he realized that he was pulling into the neighbourhood Donna and her grandmother used to live in. Something ineffable had pulled him there while he was driving on autopilot, his mind busy with his thoughts. He decided, seeing as he was already there, to drive by the house, just to take a passing glance. Nearing the house, however, he caught a quick flash, reflected in a neighbour's window, of Ethelbert's purple car, partially disguised behind well-manicured front lawn foliage. As he passed Donna's house, there in the crack of the doorway, John saw Ethelbert, his small beady eyes peering out from the darkness, making direct contact with his own.

John felt like his central string had just been plucked by an icy finger. Ethelbert knew everything. There could be no doubt of that. This sly, cunning devil was a step ahead of John's expectations, proving himself a most worthy adversary. John decided to continue forward with the plan anyway, relying on Ethelbert's inherent desire to pursue justice, to chase after John like a deer-stalking hunter. Perhaps he would not even have time to report his findings to the higher authorities, perhaps he was immediately hot on John's tail. Then again, perhaps he did report. As we know now, even if he had, it did not matter—Bruce and Donna were officially determined to have died from drug-induced respiratory failure, accidental overdose; at the time, however, John was sweating bullets.

He drove home and quickly packed up everything he would need. Luckily for him, having never trusted the banks, John had stored an emergency cash fund, which could support him for a fair amount of time. Long enough. Once Ethelbert was out of the picture, he would be free. Until then he will certainly be roughing it, his life rent in twain. Exactly what is to become of him after all of this is over, we do not know. If Ethelbert does not get him first, if he escapes the thirteen coiled knots of misconstrued justice, will he go back to being John Smith? Will he simply pick up where he left off after the heat has died? Or will he go on to become something else entirely? Perhaps start a new life as an art dealer or a movie director. Perhaps he settles down somewhere in northern Appalachia and becomes a professor of Russian literature. Maybe he retires and slowly turns into a bored house husband, writing pulpy crime literature in order to feel some small semblance of excitement in his otherwise dull and listless existence. Or perhaps he will end up shot in the back of the head.

Even with extensive research and interviews, that is as far as my knowledge goes in that regard. Unfortunately, we are still going to be left with a few questions. When all is said and done, we do not get all the answers, perhaps some (upside down, in the back page) but certainly not all. Then again… maybe. I do not rightly know what happens when all is said and done, if anything at all actually does. Soon enough, I may just know. Point being, there are mysteries, there are secrets taken to the grave, there are things unknown—do they even exist at that point? I do not know. Does anything? Did John kill Donna? Or was she dead when he found her? Does he even know? I have my doubts. I am reminded of a quote, though I am not certain who said it: "If you look for the devil, you are sure to find him."

We know where the devil is. Perhaps the devil was in John that night, or perhaps vice-versa. Or in Ethelbert. Perhaps the devil is in us all.

"Where the hell is that devil?" John queried the open air as he was leaving his house. Ethelbert was nowhere to be seen. Was he even chasing him? Had he ever been? Of course he had, do not be silly, delusional reader. But you are right, the fact remains that he was not anywhere to be seen.

John did not want to just simply run. He did not want an empty sabbatical, even if that is what official statements swore. What is the fun in running if you are not being chased? Or chasing? If it is not a tactical retreat—why then, it is just downright cowardly. And John Smith is no coward.

He waited a bit, then decided to head to Bella's. Ethelbert somehow knew about John's relationship with Bella, so he would certainly have figured that John would go there. Perhaps he was already there waiting for him, using Bella as his own personal mineshaft canary. Plus, John wanted to have some official closure before he set off on his voyage, not sure when, if ever, he may be returning—perhaps have one last hoorah even. At the very least, he wanted to make sure Bella would not talk if questioned by Ethelbert, or anyone else for that matter. And, of course, he wanted to spare her delicate feelings as much as possible.

When he arrived, Bella was visibly upset and was not in the mood for romance. She had read his wife's obituary by then and was trying her hardest to start a fight immediately when he walked in the door. He did what he could to pacify her feminine fires, but they quickly erupted into vapid argumentation.

Finally, John broke out, "Will you stop pestering me if I tell you the truth?"

She looked up at him, eyes wide as ever, mouth slightly agape, as if she desperately wanted to say something, but had no clue what that something would be.

"Listen, this is something you can never repeat to anyone, an absolute secret. Do you understand?"

She nodded, quite slowly I might add.

"The reason I couldn't leave my wife, why I was even with her in the first place, why I am even here in this trashy city at all, is because it's all a part of the cover they provided."

"Wait, John, what are you talking about? You're not making any sense."

"Oh, mon petit belle. Mon petit serin. John Smith is not my real name. My real identity has been erased and I can't tell you who I used to be, for fear of endangering your life as well."

Her jaw dropped. "I feel like I'm gonna throw up."

"Listen, Bella dear, there are evil people in this world. That is a fact. I once was a detective, a secret agent. Young, naïve, foolhardy. I only wanted justice, though looking back now, I doubt I could have pointed it out had I ever seen it. Eventually I dug too deep, uncovered some pretty heinous crimes. Crimes so heinous that the people who had hired the perpetrators of said crimes were quite upset to have their secrets uncovered. Upset enough to try to kill me. Luckily for me, the person they sent wasn't quite good enough."

"John, why are you telling me all of this? I don't like this..." Her voice cracked ever so slightly at the end of her sentence, as a small tremble of fear danced along one of her vocal chords.

"Because Bella... I fear those old demons have returned."

"What?!?"

"Witness protection gave me a new identity—a new name, a driver's license, a passport, a job, a house and a wife, facial reconstruction... but it wasn't enough. No, they most certainly have found me again. And people are going to start getting hurt. Already my wife's been caught in the crossfire—they may just decide to target you as well. Or, more likely, and equally detrimental to any future relationship we could have, I will certainly be relocated by witness protection somewhere on the other side of the country. No, I have to take care of this on my own before the authorities find out, before I am taken and hidden away again."

"Listen, John, I don't care about the danger. I just want to be with you. Let's run away together. We can outrun any danger. As long as I'm with you, as long as we're together, that's all that matters."

"And what? Live our lives on the run, being chased around like criminals? No, that is not a life you would be cut out for. Besides, if harm were to come to you because of me, well, it might just kill me."

Her wet eyes began to well up.

"No, my dear, this is a fight I must fight alone. I will have to lay low for awhile, let them think they are chasing me until I can lure them into a trap. Maybe then I will be rid of all this mess once and for all. Maybe then we'll be free to be together. Perhaps move to Paris, start a new life together. Some day."

Bella felt like sobbing. She wanted to scream at John, to explode into a million defiant little pieces, or curl up, to coll-apse into herself and disappear. All she was able to muster was a single tear, which broke free from the watery pool of her overfilled socket and began to trail down the sharp curve of her soft cheek.

"Don't cry, kitten." John wiped the tear from her heart-broken face with the bend of his index finger. There's no telling how long it may take, but I promise, one day, I will come back for you. Until then, Belle, you're going to have to be strong; it might be better for you to just forget about me completely. In fact, if anyone comes around asking about me, you don't know me at all, okay? You will have to deny our love. You will deny me twice, thrice, as many times as you need to in order to remain out of harm's way."

Bella sniffled her nose and wiped her eyes, smearing her

mascara along the way. "Please don't go." She wanted to beg, to get down on her knees and plead, weeping and wailing, anything to convince him to stay or to take her with him. Instead, she suddenly realized the futility of it all and silently gave up, letting him go.

John Smith walked out the door, pretending not to notice the purple blur that flashed around the corner. Then, without another word, he got into his car and rode off into the sunset.

****

Well, that's all, folks.